Where *the* River Runs

**Center Point
Large Print**

**This Large Print Book carries the
Seal of Approval of N.A.V.H.**

Where *the* River Runs

PATTI CALLAHAN HENRY

CENTER POINT PUBLISHING
THORNDIKE, MAINE

This Center Point Large Print edition
is published in the year 2005 by arrangement with
New American Library, a division of Penguin Group (USA) Inc.

Copyright © 2005 by Patti Callahan Henry.

The text of this Large Print edition is unabridged. In other
aspects, this book may vary from the original edition. Printed in
Thailand. Set in 16-point Times New Roman type.

ISBN 1-58547-663-3

Library of Congress Cataloging-in-Publication Data

Henry, Patti Callahan.
   Where the river runs / Patti Callahan Henry.--Center Point large print ed.
    p. cm.
   ISBN 1-58547-663-3 (lib. bdg. : alk. paper)
    1. Married women--Fiction. 2. Fires--Casualties--Fiction. 3. South Carolina--Fiction.
  4. Secrecy--Fiction. 5. Large type books. 6. Psychological fiction. I. Title.

PS3608.E578W47 2005b
813'.6--dc22

                       2005010002

There is a Gullah saying,
"When you are here, you are home."
With deep love, this book is dedicated to home:
my husband, Pat Henry,
and our children, Meagan, Thomas and Rusk.

Where *the* River Runs

ACKNOWLEDGMENTS

This book is a collaborative effort of many who possess both dedication and admiration for the art of story and the written word. Although words are the tools, heartfelt gratitude is the emotion for all those listed below.

I must thank my agent, Kimberly Whalen, whose unflinching belief in my work has been an inspiration. I am grateful to New American Library and all those involved in publishing my work: Kara Welsh, Claire Zion and Leslie Gelbman. My editor Ellen Edwards' sharp sense of story and dedication to accuracy have been invaluable. I can never find enough ways to thank Carolyn Birbiglia and her amazing PR skills, which have allowed us to get my stories into the reader's hands.

I am indebted to the booksellers who have supported my work. I am humbled by the support of Mary Rose-Taylor and the Margaret Mitchell House and Museum's Center for Southern Literature. Thank you to Amy; George and Sara at Chapter 11 for their indefatigable love of books; to Chris Stanley at Bay Street Trading Company in Beaufort, who believed in my story and offered me invaluable resources on the Gullah Culture; to Denise at Barnes and Noble in Norcross, for making sure they never ran out of my books; to Patti Morrison at Barnes and Noble in Charleston, for making me feel so comfortable that I wished I lived there; to John and Linda Stern at Port Royal books in Hilton Head, for an island signing. Appreciation is extended to Nancy Berland and her brilliant ideas.

My heart is overflowing with gratitude for the support of my beautiful friends, who not only encouraged my work, but also came to every signing and event possible. There is no way to list all of you here—but I love all of you. Special thanks go to Sandee Bartkowski, Susan Clark, Jennifer Cook, Vicky Day, Teri McIntyre, and Heidi Sprinkle, for shoring me up when I needed it the most. Innumerable hugs to Tara Mahoney; I could not have written a single page without you this summer—even if you did warp my children's taste in music. And to my long-time friends who have always known the real Patti, and are the inspiration for the fun-loving, young friendships in this novel: Beth Hamilton, Laura Kaye, Cate Sommer and Beth Fidler.

I'm beholden to my incredible family, not for what they *do,* but for who they *are:* to my parents, George and Bonnie Callahan, who believe in me more than I do. To my sisters, Barbi and Jeannie, and their husbands, Dan and Mike. To Gwen and Chuck Henry, who offer a place of respite in this crazy world. To Kirk and Anna Henry—I could not and would not have chosen any different in-laws. I love all of you.

I have been humbled by and grateful to all my readers who write me, email me, buy my books and pass them on.

PART I

"It was when I was happiest that I longed most. . . .
The sweetest thing in all my life has been the longing
. . . to find the place where all the beauty came from."
—C. S. LEWIS, *Till We Have Faces*

CHAPTER ONE

*"If you don't know where you are going,
you should know where you came from."*
—GULLAH PROVERB

A sweet, hollow nest below my heart tells me there is more as I stand at the dock's edge where the flowing river rounds the stand past my home to meet the sea. The wind caresses my face. Two dolphins, mother and baby, rise in synchrony; then their silver bodies disappear below the rolling surface of pewter water. I throw my arms wide, begging the world to bring to me everything I long for. It is my twelfth birthday. Mother and Daddy have given me a pink banana seat bicycle with tassels hanging off the handlebars. Yet this gift just doesn't seem like enough—sacred enough.

I turn from the river and jump on my bike. I am wearing my lime green party dress and I stand on the pedals, careful not to rip the tulle. I am eager for what

11

all the boys on the street already have—the freedom a
bike offers. I've learned to ride on my neighbor
Timmy's bike. I ride past my home on the long river
road that will end in a cul-de-sac. Mother is standing on
the porch yelling at me to come back right this instant
and change clothes before I run off on the horrid bike.
I push down harder on the pedals. Mother screams to
my daddy in the shrill cry of exasperation I often bring
to her, "Dewey, I told you we shouldn't have gotten her
a bike. She's wild enough already."

"Oh, Harriet, let the girl have some fun," Daddy says.

I never hear Mother's response; I am long gone,
rounding the bend of the dead-end street. I can't go too
far away, as we live on a street shaped like the curled
water moccasins running below our land and marsh—a
twist to the left, then the right, then the left again—one
long street following the curl of the river until it meets
the sea at the tip of the land. Even after I learned that
the expanse of blue river behind my house ran to the
sea, then across to Africa, I did not believe it. I don't
believe many things adults tell me. They have obviously stopped living life—always worried about things
like their hair, or their car, or what party they're invited
to.

I screech to a halt—a moving van with a dented black
ramp stuck out like a tongue from its open mouth fills
the end of my street in front of the Carmichaels' old
house. Large men, completely soaked in the heat of the
Lowcountry, unload boxes labeled "Danny's Room,"
"Living Room," "Library" in large black letters. I prop

12

my bike up with my legs on either side, my green tulle skirt puffing out like a dented balloon.

The door to the gray-silver shingled house stands open and another ramp leads to the front porch. A man, taller than most I know, appears in the doorway. He looks straight at me and waves, wipes his brow with a white handkerchief. I wave back. He holds up his finger in a hold-on motion and takes a step out onto the porch. "Daniel," he calls out.

A boy appears from behind a bush, jumps up onto the bottom step. "Yes, sir?"

"Looks like a friend has come to welcome you to the neighborhood."

The boy turns. His face is splattered with freckles. His eyes are so blue I see the color from where I stand. He wears tattered blue jean shorts and a Pink Floyd T-shirt. Oh, Mother would just die. I smile, wave.

The boy turns back to his father. "She's a girl."

The large man laughs, slaps the boy on the shoulder so hard he stumbles forward. "You're brilliant, son."

"Dad, I don't want—"

The man holds up his hand, motions for me to come up to the porch. I drop my bike and join them.

"Welcome to the neighborhood," I say, nervous in an unfamiliar way—like I've eaten too many raw oysters. "I'm Meridy McFadden and I live up the street and today is my twelfth birthday."

The man leans down, puts his hands on his knees. "Well, hello there. Happy birthday to you. You look like a little fairy. I'm Chris Garrett and this here is my son, Danny."

I stick out my hand toward Danny. "Nice to meet you. Where'd you come from?"

Danny grabs my hand, shakes it loosely, drops it and turns to his daddy.

"Answer her, son. Cat gotcha tongue?"

"Birmingham," Danny says.

"Alabama?" I stand on my tippy-toes—I think it makes my legs look longer and this boy looks down at me.

"Is there another one?" The boy named Danny turns away from me.

"Yep. There is. In England." I try to stand taller, but can't. I trip, stumble on the front porch.

Danny glances over his shoulder. "Do we look like we're from England?"

"Son." Mr. Garrett cuffs Danny on the ear. "That was rude."

"Sorry." Danny blushes and his freckles blunder into a red mass.

"Wanna go for a bike ride? I'll show you the whole street," I say.

"The whole street. Wow, that should take about five seconds," Danny says.

I feel like a puppy that has been kicked. I skip down the steps to the wilted summer grass—I won't show my embarrassment.

"Wait, little fairy." Mr. Garrett's voice follows me.

I turn. "Yes, sir."

"You're gonna have to forgive my son. He's a little

14

pissy about the move. He'd love to take a bike ride." Mr. Garrett points to a rusted blue Schwinn at the side of the porch. "Wouldn't you, son?"

"Dad, not with a girl . . . what if someone sees me?"

"Go on, son, and that's an order."

"Yes, sir." Danny slouches down the steps and grabs the bike, mounts it, then takes off down the driveway toward the road.

I jump on my bike and follow, calling after him, "Wait, wait. . . . You'll get lost. And it'll take more than five minutes—the street is two miles long."

We race up the street with nowhere else to go as Danny's house is at the very end of the road, surrounded on both sides by water. I catch up with him, come alongside him. "Hey, you don't know where you're going."

"Doesn't look real complicated to me," Danny says, stopping.

I jump off my bike. "It is. If you go too far that way"—I wave to the left—"you'll be seen by Mrs. Foster and then she'll come outside and you'll be obliged to have tea and cookies with her. You have to go on the other side of the tree line. And"—I point—"if you go too far on the right side there, Mad Mr. Mulligan will come out and start screaming at you about grenades coming and getting back under the foxhole. Mother says he thinks he's still in World War Two. I think he drinks too much whiskey. There's lotsa things you need to know about riding your bike here. You can't just go pell-mell up and down the street."

1 5

"Pell-mell? You sound like an old lady." Danny stands with his legs wide on either side of the bike.

"Yeah, well, then catch me." I jump back on my bike and pedal as hard as I can down the length of the road. Wind and marsh-sweet fragrance envelop me. The warmth of the sea-soaked air mixes with a sudden, piercing thought—Danny Garrett will fall in love with me. Why else would he show up on my birthday, on the day I received my first bike? Life is finally coming to me instead of me running after it.

The rush of his tires whirs behind me. I imagine I feel his breath, although I only hear it. He is trying to catch me—I won't let him.

My skirt flies out from the sides of the bike, my tangled blond hair flaps in my eyes, and I believe I am exactly what Mr. Garrett called me: a fairy. Then the tires make a terrible screeching sound. The ground rushes up at me and I soar through the air. My skirt catches in the chain of the bike and my face crashes onto the gray-sand dirt at the side of the road.

I roll on the ground and the bike flips over my head, bangs the side of my temple with a pain similar to the time Daddy used the spoon on my bottom when I'd told Mother to shut up. I curl into a ball and wait for the pain to pass, wait for Danny Garrett to be swallowed into the earth so he won't have to see me sprawled on the ground.

Laughter pours over me, but I won't open my eyes to see him. I want to fade away right there on my twelfth birthday before I am ever loved by the freckle-faced boy who is laughing at me.

Then the sound becomes familiar and I open one eye and look up at Timmy. "Meridy McFadden, what in the tarnation you doing?" Timmy Oliver, my next-door neighbor, childhood rival and best friend rolled into one, stands over me.

I jump up. "I'm fine . . . fine."

"Your mama is going to just kill you."

I look down at my party dress, smeared with dirt, rock and torn pieces of lime tulle. I groan.

Timmy's smile falls. "You okay?"

"Mother is going to kill me." I glance over at Danny; he is standing next to his bike, his mouth open. He looks so helpless and adorable, my heart opens wide.

"Timmy . . . that's Danny." I point at him. "He just moved in the old Carmichael house . . . today." I brush what dirt I can off my skirt.

Danny walks toward us, reaches his hand out and touches my temple. "You're bleeding. Should I go get your mama?"

"No, no, don't do that." I grab Danny's arm. "If I need something, I go see Timmy's mama. . . . This is Timmy."

Danny looks over at Timmy. "Hey."

"You just moved in?" Timmy motions with his hand toward the end of the road.

"Yep," Danny says.

They circle each other like dogs until Danny's face breaks open into the most stomach-butterfly-inducing grin I've ever seen. "You live on this street too?" he asks Timmy.

"I do. Welcome." Timmy nods.

I push my skirts to the side. "Hey, I found him first."

Timmy and Danny look at each other, double over in laughter, slap each other on the shoulders as if they've known each other for years.

"He's not a puppy, Meridy." Timmy picks up my bike.

I lift my chin. "Bet I can beat both of you to the dock."

"Since I don't know where the dock is, you probably can." Danny winks and my heart loses a beat.

"Let me grab ole Silver." Timmy disappears behind his house and emerges pedaling toward the dock at the far end of the road, playing cards flapping in his tires.

"No head starts," I scream after him, and stand hard on my pedals, suddenly hating my pink seat and pink pom-pom tassels. My older sister, Sissy, probably picked out the bike to humiliate me. I tuck my skirt up under the seat and lean forward over the handlebars. Danny is right behind me and I hope my hair is flying like a bird's wings and not a mass of tangles.

We all reach the dock's edge simultaneously and drop our bikes, each declaring ourself the winner.

I glance at both boys and then run to the start of the dock, screaming, "Only way to break the tie . . ."

"No way, Mare." Timmy runs up behind me, grabs my arm. "You can't jump in the river in that dress. You'll be double dead."

"No one can be double dead, dimwit. You just don't want to lose."

"Lose?" Danny steps between us. "Never." And he takes off running down the length of the dock.

I holler and run after him, but he reaches the end of the dock ten steps ahead of me—the fastest twelve-year-old boy I've ever seen. I catch up, stare at him.

Timmy comes up behind us. "My God, where'd you learn to run like that? I never seen anything like it."

"Nobody's won yet," I say, spread my arms, place my toes over the edge of the dock.

"Oh, I dare you," Danny says.

I close my eyes and jump out from the dock, arms splayed to the side as I imagine my party dress floating like the fairy wings Danny's father saw.

Both boys holler my name as the water envelops me. I stay under, like I always do for a moment or two, with the sweet caress of the sea wrapped around my body. The sea and I have a special relationship—it waits for me, hugs me, loves me. I speak to the water under the wave-filled top. *I found him. His name is Danny Garrett and he came here for me.* I always imagine the water reads my thoughts . . . knows what I want and need.

Betraying me, my lungs burn. I burst through the water and stare up at the boys looking down at me, my dress now a tulle bubble floating around me. "I won," I say.

Danny crinkles those blue eyes, turns his head toward Timmy. "She's crazy, ain't she?"

"We don't say *ain't* here in South Carolina." I wiggle my legs beneath me to stay afloat. "And I won."

The boys wink at each other and jump in after me. We wrestle in the water, the boys in their shorts and T-shirts and I in my party dress, and we bounce off the moss-covered floor of the river and laugh.

Danny grabs my arm and points. A few feet away a dolphin rises from the water, flips his tail and splashes us. A hush, the full quiet that comes of nature, falls over the three of us in the presence of the smooth animal. I reach out my hand and run it along the back side of the dolphin. Danny gasps and reaches out, and his hand comes next to mine on the mammal's back. The dolphin lifts his rounded nose and nods at us, dives back under the water and swims away. He has left a blessing.

When we pedal home, I know that whatever punishment Mother doles out won't touch my heart. My family stands on the porch when I ride up on my bike. Mother runs out, grabs me. "Oh, oh, my dear God, what happened to you, Meridy?"

"Nothing, Mother. Don't have one of your fits."

Danny and Timmy stand at the end of the driveway, glancing at each other, then up the driveway alternately. I wave at them to go on. Mother glances up, points her shaking finger at me. "You've been running around with those boys while I was so worried about you. Oh, I almost called the police."

Daddy steps up, wraps his arms around me. "You okay, precious?" He winks at me.

"I'm fine, Daddy."

Mother shrieks in that voice I dread—a high-pitched wail that means she'll be in bed for three days afterward and Doc will have to come visit and it will be all my fault.

"What are we going to do with her, Dewey? What? We just can't have a daughter . . ." Mother's words trail off; she slumps on the porch step and the tears start. It'll be days before they stop.

Danny appears at my side. "Sir." He looks up at Daddy. "It's all my fault. I'm new to town—moved down the street—and I asked your daughter to show me around and—"

"It's not his fault—" I interrupt.

"And I dared her to jump in the water, sir—not knowing she'd really do it."

"You've ruined your dress," Mother chokes through her tears. "You've ruined the dress from Mawmaw."

Sissy leans back in the wicker rocker on the front porch, a smirk on her face. "You are so, so embarrassing," she says, tosses her curls behind her shoulder. I stick my tongue out at her.

"Mommy, did you see that? Meridy stuck her tongue out at me. She is just so . . . gross." Sissy stands and walks back into the house, slams the screen door for emphasis.

Daddy wraps his arms around me and looks at Danny. "And who are you, son?"

"I'm Danny Garrett." He blushes, shuffles his feet in the stone walkway leading to the house.

"Well, Danny Garrett. Now you know—Meridy will

always take the dare. And it's not your fault."

Mother wails again. I pick up my dripping skirt and look up at Daddy. "It's really not his fault, Daddy, and I hated the dress anyway."

"Meridy, that is disrespectful." Daddy squeezes my shoulders.

"Please, sir, don't punish her," Danny says.

And right there on my twelfth birthday with my mother wailing like a dying animal, as I drip in my party dress from Mawmaw with my daddy's arms wrapped around me, Danny enters my heart without even asking.

I turn back to Danny and Timmy. Timmy is gone and I'm confused, turning left and right looking for him. Then Danny walks backward, becoming a smudged outline of a boy with wisps of trailing smoke at his edges. I reach for him; I am older now but not sure how much. Danny dissipates into the Lowcountry sage green edges of grass and marsh. I turn back to my family—scream, beg for help to get Timmy and Danny to return. But Mother and Daddy are gone too. I am alone. Utterly alone. I crumble in upon myself and know I deserve it.

I grabbed at the bedspread, awoke and curled into myself. The longing of youth returned with this dream, as it always had. It had been so long since I'd dreamed about Danny, and I waited for the feeling to pass, buried my head in the pillow for the few seconds before fully awakening and attempted to pin down the emotion still attached to the leftover impression of the dream. Outside the window the trees were still in the shapes of the night. The alarm clock blinked: three a.m.

I wasn't alone, although I felt it as surely as though the bed were empty. My husband, Beau, lay next to me, breathing the even, open-mouthed sleep I'd watched for twenty years now. He was adorable even in sleep.

I stood, careful not to disturb Beau so early since he'd been working late—into the hours I defined as morning. I stretched and tiptoed out of the bedroom. At the end of the hall, I stopped in front of my son's closed door. For the first time in years, I could open the door without knocking—B.J. wasn't there. The emptiness the dream brought to me widened, then deepened. I'd often thought that I wouldn't be like other mothers when I faced the proverbial empty nest, that I wouldn't go through the engulfing change and sorrow I'd observed in others.

B.J.'s door creaked as I opened it—a sound of intrusion. The room was shrouded in the predawn light falling through the open blinds. He'd been gone for only three weeks to Vanderbilt's baseball camp, and his room appeared as though he were still there. Except for the smooth plaid bed linens and the absence of uniforms, cleats, and baseball hats scattered across the floor, I could fool myself into believing he was home.

I shut the door and leaned my forehead against the doorframe; exhaustion beyond the lack of sleep covered me, as if my motor had been running on high

23

speed for the years I had raised, cared for and loved my son, and now that I wanted to stop, the momentum carried me forward.

The spiral staircase lay in shadow; I clicked on the foyer light and descended to the kitchen. I filled the coffeepot and grabbed the grinder. My elbow knocked Beau's briefcase; papers fell to the floor in an emblematic flurry of how busy his job had become in his quest for partnership in the law firm. I leaned down to pick up the files. Flowery, scribbled notes from the firm's new junior partner, who had been assigned to help with the overwhelming negligence case, filled the margins—her handwriting was as feminine as her clothes, her walk, her thin muscular legs carried on incessantly high heels. I shook my head. I ought to be thankful for her help— at least it freed Beau from some of the grueling tasks of the case.

So the dream had accomplished the goal it always had: to remind me to live my life responsibly or I would lose as much as I had lost back then, back when I took the dare, back when I thought all of life waited just for me.

CHAPTER TWO

"The heart doesn't mean everything the mouth says."
—GULLAH PROVERB

I could blame the remainder of the disintegrating day on my dearest friend, Cate. And sometimes I do. I'm not sure if her words and hints set off something that was already in motion or if she started the forward drive. Whichever is true, uneasiness settled over me like syrup—sweet, sticky and annoying.

She sat at a round table in the corner of Sylvia's Tea Room, a restaurant in the heart of the shopping district in Buckhead—perfect for eating, then making it to Neiman Marcus before any time was lost. I spotted Cate's brown curls as she read the menu I knew she'd memorized years ago.

I walked toward her, knocked on the edge of the table. "Cate."

She looked up at me and a smile spread across her face, but didn't light up her features in the manner I was accustomed to in previous years. Her blue eyes appeared faded, tired. "Hey, girlfriend, I didn't see you come in," she said, stood and hugged me.

We sat and I lifted the menu. "And you need to read this? Like you don't have it memorized?"

She laughed, tucked a curl behind her left ear in a familiar motion that tugged at my memories of better times—before her divorce, before all the changes in our lives. She'd been married to Beau's boss, Harland, and what was once the most convenient and perfect friendship had now become complicated and distant. I had almost forgotten the intensity with which I missed her until she said or did something I'd watched or known for the past twenty years—it was like looking at a photo of a forgotten vacation and allowing the nostalgia to wash over the memory.

She reached across the table, touched my arm. "How are you, Meridy?"

"I'm good—more importantly, how are you?"

She pressed her lips together so only a thin line of her classic red lipstick showed. "It's getting better, slowly," she said.

"I wish I could do something . . . more."

Cate shrugged. "Not much you can do unless you can snap Harland out of the insanity he's obviously come into. But then again—I wouldn't even want you to do that. I don't want him back now."

"You don't?" I pushed the menu away.

Cate looked sideways, nodded at the waiter walking toward us. After we'd ordered the gorgonzola and pecan salad—as usual—Cate asked for two glasses of white wine.

I held up my hand. "No way. I'll have to take a nap in an hour if I have a glass of wine in the middle of the day."

Cate looked up at the waiter. "Today she'll have a glass of white wine." And she turned back to me. "Today you will."

I held up my palms in surrender. "Okay, okay, but don't blame me if my head falls into the salad."

The waiter walked away and I looked at Cate. "You didn't answer my question. You don't want him back? Because I really think he'll wake up, realize he's lost his mind."

"It'd be a dollar short, day late. I just want to pull myself together now"

I nodded. "I miss you here so much. Any chance you'd come back to town when the . . . dust settles?"

Cate sighed, tucked her hair again. "Meridy, I don't think so. I have to . . . move on. Luckily I have the house in Wild Palms. I can't come back here and see him and his paralegal . . . of course I do mean his wife, running around town, living in my house. It's all too . . . lurid and I'll never be able to get on with my life while hanging on to . . ."—she spread her hands and made a sweeping gesture—"this life."

"Wow." I took a long sip of water.

"I have friends there. I'm painting again. The settlement is final."

I nodded. "Okay, so I'm selfish to want you back here."

Cate smiled. "Not selfish. You still live in the middle of all this chaos, all this fake . . . stuff. You just aren't able to see it from the other side."

I leaned back in my chair. The familiarity and comfort of our friendship shifted, wavered before me: miragelike. "Why do I feel like that was a vague insult?"

Cate's eyes filled. "Oh, oh. I didn't mean it that way.

Ever since the divorce I find myself saying things I wouldn't have said before. I didn't mean to insult you. You're my dearest friend. I adore you. It's just that I've been where you are."

The waiter appeared, placed our plates and wine before us. "You ladies need anything else?" We shook our heads.

"What do you mean, where I am?" I asked.

"It's all noise and chaos and busyness, and we forget to take the time to notice anything or talk about anything and the next thing you know your husband has a new Porsche and a new wife."

"Cate," I spoke softly, "that's not Beau."

She nodded. "It wasn't Harland either."

And I had nothing to say because she was right. If I'd had to bet on ten men in the law firm who'd have an affair and leave their wives, Harland would've been number nine. I took a deep breath. "So, tell me. How are Chandler and Becca?"

Cate smiled, and this time it did spread across her face. "Good. They have both decided to live with me, instead of Harland, for the summer before their sophomore and junior years at Georgia. I'd like to think it's all about me, but of course it's all about the beach."

Something familiar flashed in the corner of my eyesight. I glanced, winced. "Cate—you know how you don't want to live here so you won't bump into Harland?"

She followed my line of sight, groaned. "God, Meridy, just when I think I've come to a better place in

28

myself, I fall into this damn hole. Please don't let him see us."

I glanced over my shoulder, trying not to turn my head. Harland strode up to the hostess stand. Alexis held on to his arm and kept stride with him in quick, small steps in her pencil skirt and too-tall heels.

I rounded my shoulders. "Just keep talking about something else and they'll ignore us. . . ."

"What the hell are they doing here? Harland hates this place—says it's a women's lunching place."

I shrugged, then heard my name being called. My head snapped around at the familiar sound of my husband's voice. He waved, moved through the tables.

"Beau?" I stood.

He came to me. "Hey, darling, what a great surprise." He kissed me. "Nothing like running into you to make my *day*."

He reached down and hugged Cate. "So good to see you, Cate." She nodded, turned her fork in her hand. "You too, Beau."

"What are you doing here?" I asked.

He waved his hand toward the front of the restaurant, where Harland, Alexis and the new junior partner, Ashley, stood. "We've been working nonstop on this case and we had a breakthrough today, so we let the ladies pick where to eat lunch. Obviously a mistake. I voted for Chops. I lost." He held up his briefcase. "But we'll work through lunch."

"Oh . . ." I stared at the three of them at the front; Harland waved his hand in a "Hurry up" motion. Beau put his finger up, mouthed, "One minute."

"So," he said. "What kind of trouble are you two up to today?"

I glanced at Cate. "Eating, shopping . . ."

"I'm making her go with me to all the stores I miss the most," Cate said. "Then I'm going back to get the last few boxes of *my* family heirlooms from the house."

Beau glanced at me. "Oh . . . okay. Well, you have a great day." Then he swooped me into his arms, leaned me backward and kissed me. The patrons at the table next to us laughed. Two women clapped. He grinned.

I punched him in the shoulder. "Go back to work."

He sauntered past the tables and waved back over his shoulder. I sat. "God, I'm sorry that happened, Cate. I so wanted this to be our day, catch up, shop. I've been looking forward to it forever. Harland is such a—"

"Asshole." Cate finished the sentence for me, took a long swallow of her wine. "Such an incredible asshole." She covered her face, shook her head. "I'm fine. . . . Let's pretend this didn't happen."

I squeezed her arm. "Okay, do-over."

"No such thing," she said.

"Yes, there is. . . ."

"Meridy." She leaned forward. "Be careful. Watch. Listen. We get lulled into this life where it all just *looks* so damn good—but isn't. Like that big ole oak tree that used to be in our backyard. It was so gorgeous, at least until it fell through our roof and into the kitchen and we found out that the roots were rotted all the way through, under the ground where we couldn't see it."

"Are you trying to tell me something?"

"No, nothing like that. I guess I'm just trying to tell you how different it all looks from this side. Listen, Meridy, I know you've hinted to me that Beau doesn't know everything about your past. And I don't believe a woman should always have to tell every ugly thing she's ever done—a woman needs to have her secrets." She winked. "But I'm just telling you to watch and listen. The late nights, the not talking—it all adds up."

I nodded, then longed to tell her about my dream, about who I used to be before she knew me, before the designer clothes and the coiffed hair, before the husband, house and child. But instead I took a long sip of wine.

"I don't know how we get this way . . . so deadened to what is going on—but I do know I don't want to get there again," Cate said. "Remember when B.J. was part of that bus incident?"

I glanced over my shoulder. "That was years ago."

She nodded. "I know. And you never told Beau." She leaned forward. "Those are the things that rot the roots."

"I was just trying to keep the peace . . . just . . ."

"I know, girlfriend. So was I."

"I think I'm beginning to like this new you . . . the one who says whatever the hell she wants," I said.

"Ah, there you go. You cussed. I'm already a bad influence. Maybe I'll talk you into an outfit that doesn't match or even a second glass of wine."

"I'm not that bad, Cate."

31

"No, you're that good."

I lifted my wineglass and tilted it toward her. "To you."

"And you," she said.

The woman sitting across from me was my best friend, yet completely different. Almost as though she had removed shackles from her life—ones she'd thought she wanted.

But I was different and so was Beau. Weren't we?

After the full day with Cate, the last thing I wanted to do was go out to dinner with Harland, Alexis and two other couples. But it was Harland's fiftieth birthday party and we had committed to going. I shook the achy lonely feeling that had settled in my chest and leaned back against my granite kitchen counter with the phone tucked under my chin, stared out at an early-evening sky where a star cuddled up to the underside of the moon. As the night progressed, the star would move farther and farther away from the moon—or maybe it was the other way around, but in any case, the movement gave me a desolate feeling, like a deepening hole. I was preoccupied with the week's calendar and the party Beau and I were late for as Mother talked of her latest Ladies of Seaboro Society meeting.

"Mother, I've got to go now . . . ," I said, thinking more about which pair of shoes to wear with my linen suit than what she said.

"Okay, Meridy," Mother said. "If you're too busy for me . . ."

"That's not it. I'm just late. . . ."

"Oh, by the way . . ." Her voice pitched upward in the signal that she had some news of high import about Seaboro, where I was born and reared and which I had spent the last twenty-six years avoiding. "I forgot to tell you—the Seaboro Historical Society is trying to raise the money to *finally* renovate the Lighthouse Keeper's Cottage."

The memory of the Lighthouse Keeper's Cottage came like breath on my skin—so close I thought I could reach out and touch the weathered shingles. I shivered. "I thought they did that a long time ago," I said, quiet and still as if someone might find me if I moved.

"Well, when they relocated the foundation away from the sea after the fire all those years ago, there was this talk of rebuilding and renovating. Then the place just kind of . . . sat there. Now there's a new movement to renovate. It all started when the historical society tried to figure out how to draw more tourists here from Beaufort. That Lighthouse Keeper's Cottage is just full of so much interesting history. So now they are trying to raise money . . . well, not raise it, but obtain the funds from Tim Oliver. He'll finally have to pay his dues."

My numbness transformed to nausea. Mother hadn't mentioned the Keeper's Cottage since the fire twenty-six years ago.

"What? Why Tim?"

"Well." She spoke slowly, as if I were a small child who didn't comprehend her words. "They need a large amount of money and the city doesn't have it. The easiest thing to do is have Tim pay for what he did."

"God, Mother, you sound like Beau. Pay for what he did? There's no way Seaboro can make him donate that kind of money for an accident that long ago."

"Accident or not . . . someone has to pay and it was determined to be his fault all those years ago, Meridy. Just a little pressure from the town and—"

"Surely Seaboro can raise that kind of money." I wasn't even sure Mother heard me, my voice small and fading. "Tim didn't do anything to the cottage."

"I know you'd like to believe that about an old friend, but you know the truth and he did give the party." Her tone of voice filled the lines with haughty righteousness.

"The truth," I said. A gap—larger than the distance between past and present—opened before me.

"Meridy, are you there?" Mother's voice came from far away.

"Yes, I'm here." My body slithered down against the cabinet until I was sitting on the travertine floor. "I'll talk to you later, okay?" I pressed the END button and dropped the phone to the floor without saying good-bye to Mother—one of the deadlier sins.

Tim.

I had never, not even once in all these years, thought this shattered fragment of my past would return to me. I had spent too long building this life I dwelled in, this life in which I'd proved my worthiness.

Not now.

From across the space in time that Mother's words had awakened, I heard our old Gullah housekeeper's voice spilling one of her many proverbs. *"No matter how you try to cover up smoke, it must come out."*

The dream. The Keeper's Cottage.

Not now.

The doorbell rang and I jumped up from the floor, shook my head. I wasn't expecting anyone. Beau called out, "I've got it."

I moved toward the front door as Beau crossed the foyer, buttoning his baby blue oxford. He opened the door; Ashley stood on our front step. I came up next to Beau as she moved into our home. She didn't glance at me, but gazed up at Beau, held out a pile of folders. "Here are the files you forgot."

"Files?" I asked.

Beau didn't answer me. "Ashley, thank you so much. I really needed these. I'm glad you noticed them and called."

"You're welcome. Anytime. That's why I'm here—to take care of things." Her eyes flitted across the foyer to the living room on the left. "You have a beautiful home."

"Thank you," Beau said, wrapped his arm around me. "Meridy's the one with all the good taste."

Watch.

Listen.

I smiled. "Why do you need files tonight? We're going out. . . ." Beau squeezed me. "I have to read these before tomorrow morning. New info on the case."

He nodded at Ashley. "Thank you."

She hesitated before leaving, glanced at me, then

35

turned on her heels and walked down my front steps. I tapped the pile of papers in Beau's hand as I shut the door. "Couldn't you have stopped by the office and picked them up on the way to the club tonight?"

"I could've, but the last thing I wanted to do was go back there. I'm there too much as it is. Ashley said she drove this way going home." He tilted his head at me. "Is there a problem?"

"No, no problem at all. Just need to go get shoes on." I looked into his face. Beau had been and still was the most beautiful man I'd ever known. His black hair was a blank night sky, his eyes the dark blue of the deeper parts of the sea behind my childhood home in the Lowcountry. I'd once imagined—since I'd vowed never to swim in the ocean again—that Beau's eyes were the sea I could immerse myself in.

If he found out about the Keeper's Cottage, the knowledge would widen the space between moon and star, too far to draw them together again the next night. I grabbed some strappy sandals from my closet, then met Beau in the car and tried to swallow the fear rising in the back of my throat.

Beau stared out the windshield while driving us to the club. His mouth moved to the words of a song on the radio, but I could guess where his mind was—on the case he was prosecuting. Beau had been with the same law firm for twenty years now, and if this case went right, he'd be promoted to senior partner, on an equal footing with Harland. Beau had followed the perfect path—new hire to partner in less than five years.

I stared out the car window at the traffic on Peachtree Road, which was at a complete standstill, the cars like blood clots. But what I saw was Ashley standing at my front door, surveying my house and husband. I reached over and grabbed Beau's hand. These were the nights when I was the angriest at Harland Finnegan. I needed Cate, not Harland's substitute wife, to be at that dinner table tonight. I wanted a stabilizing force against the off-kilter feeling.

Beau's cell phone rang; he grabbed it from the cradle. "Beaumont Dresden."

I leaned my head on the windowpane as he mumbled agreements into the phone. I discerned it was another call from the press about the negligence case that had devoured every minute of his time the past year. I longed to grab the BlackBerry and throw it out the window. A part of me could not stand to hear one more word about the food poisoning that had cost the life of a small child.

"We will make them pay—they can't get away with this." Beau sighed after he spoke the words I'd heard him say a thousand times. "Once again, I'll repeat what I've said before. At first this negligence was probably an accident, a mistake. But then the company hid their mistake, covered up their incredible carelessness. They didn't tell the truth after the child got sick. This was their fatal error. The deceit is what will cost them the most. They must pay for the pain and suffering of my client. A child died."

And that was his job—the work of my husband,

whose sense of integrity was ingrained as deep as the furrows in his forehead from staring at legal documents into the wee hours of the morning. I'd heard it as many times as I'd ever heard anything in my life—if you caused pain and suffering, you paid.

Beau hung up and looked over at me as we pulled into the valet parking at the club. "You okay, honey?" He touched my leg.

I nodded. "Just fine, you?"

"You look . . . I don't know, like you don't really want to go tonight."

I forced the best smile I could from below the quivering in my chest. "I do want to go."

"I know you don't like Alexis . . . but can't you just . . . try? She's here to stay."

"Just because Harland traded Cate in for a new wife doesn't mean I'll trade her in for a new best friend." Then a hidden idea whispered across my mind, *Or maybe you'd like to trade me in for a new wife.* I closed my eyes and mind to the thought.

"Okay, then . . ."

"Sorry," I said, unsure what I was actually apologizing for. "I'm just a little tired."

"Talking to your mother would make me tired too."

This time my smile was real. "You got it." I glanced out the window. "How far away are you from closing this case?"

"It should go to trial in the next couple weeks."

The car pulled up to the curb, and I climbed out and nodded to the valet.

"Hello, Mrs. Dresden, you look beautiful tonight," he said.

"Thanks, Jack." I looked down at my outfit—an off-white Tahari suit and high-heeled sandals that matched the shade of the pearl buttons down the front of the jacket. I walked through the double front doors of the club; Beau came up behind me and grabbed my arm. For the first time I felt as though I was trespassing on a life meant for someone else.

Six people sat at a white linen-covered table waiting for us. Shouts of hello, backslapping and cheek kisses greeted us. I sat, placed the swan-formed napkin in my lap. I picked up the sterling silver and rolled it over and over in my hand as I stared out the window to the immaculate golf course spread like a carpet to the horizon.

Across from me sat Penni and Harvey. We'd known them since B.J. went to preschool with their oldest daughter, McKenzie. We'd plotted for our children to get married to each other, but McKenzie's experimentation in the world of Goth nixed that entire idea for B.J. Penni and Harvey had come to a place, as had most of the parents I knew, of complete apathy in the midst of the noise and chaos of their children's adolescence. Their opinion seemed to be that they'd given their children everything they could possibly want; now the kids had to figure it out for themselves.

Penni looked tired, as if the race she ran would never end. She was a fragile-appearing woman, but anyone who knew her well would never use the word *fragile* to describe her. Standing at only four eleven, she didn't command attention—but she garnered it nonetheless. Her beauty was that of the well-bred women whose mothers had warned them of the perils of the sun; her wavy brown hair fell to her shoulders in a bob of Jackie O. distinction. Harvey's hair had whitened with age, but he was a handsome, broad-built man with a gentle voice that belied his size. They had been our friends for at least fifteen years now—a companionship that I'd often thought was built only on the commonality in life's circumstances: children and job.

Betsy and Mike sat to my right, rigid and still. Their marriage—always tottering on the verge of collapse—was not holding up well under the strain of building their new "dream house" in Brookhaven. Betsy's lips were white with a bloodless grimace. Mike was already on his second glass of bourbon and the waiter hadn't taken our order yet.

Mike and Harvey both worked with Harland, and the underlying knowledge of Beau's probable promotion shimmered over the table in unspoken tension.

The couples were all talking, and no one, as yet, had turned to me. So I watched them with an odd fascination at my membership in their ranks. Mother's phone call became the reminder of how I didn't belong here, in this world, with these people. It was as if, at a very young age, they'd known their place in life and never once wavered from it. I had once had that confidence about where I belonged, but that had been shattered long ago.

My vague discontent morphed into agitation—something was amiss or off-balance, and I didn't know what. I had reasons and explanations for everything; I even had lists for everything. Then in the middle of Penni's complaints about the ladies' locker room running out of mints, I found a need to run away—a feeling no more or no less than that when I was eight years old and had packed my Barbie suitcase and made it as far as Mrs. Foster's house at the corner of our street.

"So, Beau, what are your plans for the summer?" Harland bellowed across the table, because that's what Harland did, bellowed. He'd played college football for Georgia and I imagined he always thought he was calling out plays to a huddle.

Alexis took his hand and made a shushing noise with her forefinger over her pursed lips.

Beau glanced at me. "We haven't really talked about it yet."

I offered a close-mouthed smile. No, we hadn't really talked about it, but we really hadn't talked about anything lately. B.J. had left early for Vanderbilt, to play baseball, and we shared only the case that ate Beau's time like a starving, clawing animal.

Beau continued. "I'll be working . . . I assume." He lifted his glass and nodded at Harland, then squeezed my hand and laughed.

"Well," Harland said, "I'm sure Meridy knows how to hold down the fort while you're working."

Alexis giggled, "Yes, I'm sure she does, perfectly."

Beau smiled at me. "Yep." He patted my knee. "She's

41

the one who keeps it all together."

I needed to get away from the table, from the inane talk and Alexis. I stood; all four men at the table stood. I nodded and turned to walk to the ladies' dressing room. The loneliness, which had been only a nagging feeling of emptiness the past few months, now covered me. I had once vowed never to feel this vacant ache again—but it nestled underneath my ribs, beckoned by the combination of a dream, lunch with Cate and Mother's mention of the Keeper's Cottage.

I pushed open the door to the ladies' room, plopped down on the couch that looked like it had been covered in a Lilly Pulitzer sundress. I put my head down, let it rest in the palms of my hands and stared at the striped pink-and-lime-green carpet. I knew how this feeling went—eventually the swinging sameness of my full days would numb the ache.

The squeak of door hinges startled me. I looked up—a smile already in place. Penni stood in the entranceway with a martini in one hand, her Prada purse dangling from the crook of her other arm. Her hair was pulled behind her neck so her face appeared as if it were poking out from behind a closed door—neck out, face eager.

"You okay, Mare?" she asked.

"Just perfect, Penni. Just perfect."

Penni sat down on the couch, offered her martini glass to me. "Want some? You look a little . . . tired."

I looked at the glass—an olive danced at the bottom.

"Meridy . . . hello . . . you there?" Penni poked my shoulder. Martini drops landed on her Chanel jacket.

"Aren't you . . . sick of all this?" I was stunned by my voice.

"Sick of what? Oh, that the ladies' locker room is never as nice as the men's? Ah, nah. I've gotten used to it. The men—they rule it all. We're just along for the ride." She laughed.

"Really?" I said.

"Yep. At least it's a fun ride. You know? What's the alternative, darling? Working at the Publix cash register, being an administrative assistant to some bald boss trying to feel you up? Please . . ." Penni shook her head. "Dare you to try." She giggled with her hand over her mouth.

Now you know Meridy will always takes the dare.

Betsy and Alexis walked in, laughing. Penni shot up from the couch. "What's so funny? What'd I miss?"

"Nothing, nothing." Betsy pushed her hair off her forehead. She claimed she had to wear bangs until her husband approved of Botox—permission must be granted.

"Nothing?" Alexis walked over to the mirror and pulled out her bright red lip liner. "Ms. Betsy received a nice pass from the landscape architect working on her new house."

"What do you mean?" Penni downed the last of her martini.

"Well," Betsy said, "I've been working with him for months now on our new house plans and last night— right in the middle of planning the front rock garden— he tells me that he can't sleep or eat because all he does is think about me. He's been dragging out this job just to be around me. . . ." Betsy stood taller, as if her designer's declarations were something to be immensely proud of.

"Oh, how sweet." Penni gazed up at the ceiling. "It's so nice when someone notices that we're more than someone's mom or wife or housekeeper."

"Sweet?" I stood up. "I think it's creepy. Did you tell Mike?"

"No way." Betsy crinkled her eyes. "He'd freak out, fire him."

"Well, shouldn't he?" I said.

Alexis finished her lip application and turned back to the conversation. "Please, Mare, don't be so perfect all the time. Nothing's going on with them. . . ."

"Perfect?" I felt the floor shift below me. *I'm faking it; I've always faked it.* The reasons for my unsteady emotions began to take shape, form and definition.

"Oh, you know we're always jealous of you," Alexis said. She came over and dropped her arm around my shoulder. I resisted the urge to push her away. "You do freaking everything right. Your jacket matches your shoes; your purse is one of a kind; your son has a scholarship to Vanderbilt for baseball; your husband is adorable."

I shook my head.

Betsy took a step forward. "And you're the most beautiful woman I know. What's not to be jealous of?" She kissed my cheek.

I stared at the women. Jealous? They didn't know I

44

hadn't picked up the dry cleaning today, that I'd for-gotten my mother's birthday last week, or that I was an impostor.

"Come on, girls." Betsy tossed her hair over her shoulder. "They'll come in after us if we don't go back out there."

"They probably don't even know we're gone," I said, and walked out the door.

I sat down at the table and the other women followed, all glancing at each other with that aren't-we-so-wor-ried look. How could they include Alexis in that look, as if by marrying Harland she now belonged? I patted Beau's knee and smiled.

The plans-for-the-summer conversation was still going on. "Well," Mike said, "Bets and I are headed to our house in Wild Palms. She'll stay with the kids all summer and I'll come and go."

"More go than come," Betsy murmured.

"Someone's gotta feed the family." Mike laughed, head back.

"We haven't decided about our summer yet." Penni looked at Harvey. "Have we?"

"Well, I was thinking we'd take it easy," Harvey said. "Maybe a couple trips to the mountain house. The kids only want to hang out with their friends now. They hate family vacations—like totally."

Harland leaned back in his chair, making the tapered legs groan. "I'm taking my baby on a cruise in the French Riviera. Anyone wanna come? That's why I brought the subject up—I organized it today and

45

wanted to see how many of y'all would be up for it."

Alexis leaned into Harland. "Doesn't it sound divine?"

"Just divine," Betsy said, and looked up at Mike. He looked away from her and Betsy's pained, drawn look made me cringe. Maybe Mike had someone else he'd prefer to spend the summer with.

We were all saved by the appearance of the waiter. The evening progressed as hundreds of evenings had before, with talk of kids and school and, of course, work. Near the end, Harland raised a wine-glass. "To *my* birthday, happy, happy birthday to me."

Everyone laughed a bit too loudly, and lifted their glasses. I took a very, very long swallow of Merlot.

After the good-byes, after everyone had told Harland to e-mail them the specifics about the French cruise, hugs and kisses were offered all around.

When only Alexis and I remained on the front stoop of the clubhouse waiting for Beau and Harland to return from the men's locker room, where they went to get some things from their lockers, Alexis placed her hand on my arm. "Meridy, I'd really love it if you and Beau came on the cruise with us. I just adore being around y'all." She winked. "And I bet Beau is adorable in his swim trunks."

Beau came up behind me, touched the small of my back. "You ready?" I nodded, climbed into the car without answering Alexis. I began to smell smoke— like the burned char of a leftover log from a camp-fire—surround me.

46

CHAPTER THREE

"No matter how you try to cover up smoke,
it must come out."
—GULLAH PROVERB

T he night arrived with blurred, scattered images flying across my consciousness, like birds whose wings I'd hear, but as soon as I turned to see them, they were gone. I awoke relieved at the sight of the sunrise behind my home. Today was a new day and I'd shake the unsteady feelings of yesterday. But the emotions lingered like the residual ache of the flu.

I stood in the kitchen, leaned against the back-door jamb and stared at the lush summer backyard. Atlanta was thick and moist, overgrown emerald and yellow in the heat of the season. Earth bore the deep hum of nature, and sometimes I imagined I heard the plants growing in a thick buzz. The landscape was not at all similar to where I grew up in Seaboro, where the hints of nature came from deeper places of the sea. There, in the Lowcountry, I heard the dolphins' squeal, the crunch of shell and sand, the whisper of unseen, primal life in the marsh.

Seaboro. Maybe it was time to go visit Mother this summer. B.J. was away at Vanderbilt. Beau was so pre-occupied with this case, I couldn't reach him with words or touch. Daddy was gone now—he'd died of a stroke five years ago while fishing off the dock behind our house, just the way I imagined he would've chosen to leave us.

It was Daddy who tied us to Seaboro, to the community and all it defined for the McFadden family. Daddy had possessed a combination of gentleness and strength I could attribute only to his firm grounding in knowing who he was, who he was meant to be, and living that way. The family house stood on the foundation of the family name more than on concrete and pilings. As expected, on their wedding day Mother and Daddy had received the McFadden family home, which overlooked the wide, undulating river. It was the house where Daddy was reared, where he was expected to raise his family—and he had. The family name was carved in plaques, signs and monuments all over Seaboro.

Mother wasn't from Seaboro, and my entire life I'd watched her efforts to prove she was worthy of its various clubs, luncheons, dinner parties and teas. Mother had come from "lesser means"—I'd heard it whispered in the quieter moments of the debutante balls—and acceptance in Seaboro was her heart's desire. The desperate craving for this belonging had never been transferred to me. I had somehow evaded the grasping need I had seen in my mother and older sister for the approval and cheek-kissing enclosure of Seaboro society. In childhood and high school I had longed only for the other attributes of the Sea Islands: the sea, the river, the wild call of the denser pieces of land—the sacred mystery of the thirty-five or so Sea Islands running like jewels on an unhooked necklace down the coast of South Carolina and Georgia.

The reasons I had left all of those revered places behind were too obscure and painful for me to have ever discussed them with Beau, beyond the normal need to get out from under childhood constraints and have one's own life.

Beau entered the kitchen, touched the back of my hair. I inhaled, closed my eyes.

"You're up early," he said.

I turned to him. "I didn't sleep well, thought I'd get the day started."

He dropped his briefcase on the counter. "What do you have on today?" He poured coffee into his mug—the green one with THE MASTERS etched on the side.

I pushed my hair out of my eyes. "I have a board meeting for Williams Prep."

"When are we done with that?"

"I think I have two more meetings, then freedom." I tried to smile.

"Well, have a good day, honey. I have a late meeting with Harland tonight—don't worry about dinner."

I nodded, picturing whom he'd be spending his day with—Harland, Alexis and, of course, Ashley. "Beau?"

He turned and looked at me, but in the off-glance way I'd noticed lately when he wasn't really paying attention. "Yes?" he said; then his gaze fell on the counter, on a pile of papers he'd forgotten to stuff in his briefcase. He picked up the stack Ashley had dropped by the night before.

I stepped toward him, touched his arm covered in a starched white shirt. "Are you okay? Are we okay?"

He dropped the papers into his briefcase, then squinted at me. "What? Of course." He kissed the top of my head. "See you tonight, honey."

The disconnection with Beau left me lost, wavering. I was once able to see how Beau really felt—see the softer places of him. But now I saw only a glaze of disinterest and preoccupation. I was lost, falling farther and farther into the dreams of smoke and an ancient fire.

By the time I got to the Williams Prep board meeting, I had used willpower to talk myself back to reality—I had experienced only a few melancholy moments. I wanted to blame the unsteady emotions on my conversation with Cate.

I pulled my aqua leather satchel with the initials MMD up to my chest as if I needed to protect myself from whatever emotion threatened the edges of my consciousness. I glanced at my Rolex: five minutes late. Ten people sat at the long mahogany table; taupe-on-beige striped wallpaper set the backdrop for the blank faces that stared at me as I rushed in. An air conditioner hummed in the background, and the wilted fern in the middle of the table dropped brown, curled leaves on the scratched top. Everything looked dead and pale.

"Sorry." I sat in the only vacant chair, dropped my satchel on the floor.

"As I was saying," the headmaster, Greg Henderson,

said, "we will be covering a different culture each year. Part of this decision stems from complaints from our Lower School parents that there isn't enough diversity in our school or our curriculum, but I also think it's a great idea. By the time our children leave Lower School, they will have had an in-depth exposure to five different cultures. The first year will be the Gullah culture."

I sat up straight. "What?"

Deidre Anderson turned to me. Her hair didn't move at all—how many aerosol cans had been sacrificed for her head? "If you'd been on time . . ."

Greg held up his hand. "We're talking about adding Culture Week in the Lower School—one week a year, one hour a day, a different culture each year."

"And," Deidre said, "we'll start with the Gullah culture. Doesn't that sound like fun? I've seen that kids' show—what's it called?" She glanced around the table.

"Gullah, Gullah Island?" I answered.

"Yes," Deidre said, bobbed her head.

Her Aqua Net odor washed over me, and irritation bubbled to the surface. She acted like Gullah was a cute little cartoon that elementary school kids would enjoy with *Scooby-Doo* and *SpongeBob*. But I knew of the Gullah culture through our old housekeeper in Seaboro, Tulu.

"Deidre." My voice was tight, an octave lower than usual. "Gullah is both a culture and a language. These are real people, not characters in a children's book. They've been in the Lowcountry, the Sea Islands, for over a hundred years." I stood up, my hands moving against my words. I watched myself in amazement—detached and aware. Why was I standing up, lecturing Deidre about the Sea Island culture? "Gullah is the longest-lasting African culture in the country—"

"Aren't we all worked up?" Deidre said. "If you know so much about it . . ."

"Why don't I write the curriculum?" I turned to Greg Henderson with a surety I hadn't felt in a long, long time. The sting of pluff mud filled my nose; the briny taste of marsh water ran against my lips. Maybe I hadn't woken up from my dream about Danny after all.

"Well . . ." Greg glanced around the table. "We weren't quite there yet, but . . ."

"What qualifications do you have?" asked Mr. Chamberlain, who was older than the city of Atlanta.

"I was born in the Lowcountry, raised there. . . . I had a Gullah housekeeper. Mother still lives there . . . at home. I have a business degree." My ears rang with a vibrating hum; I spoke against my will in a desperate attempt to accomplish something I didn't understand.

Deidre slapped her hand on the table. "Great idea for you, Meridy. With B.J. gone and an empty house, you'll have plenty of time."

Greg leaned forward. "Perfect. You can go home and get all the information. Well, that worked out just great. . . ."

Home.

Greg flipped a page of his notebook. "Then the next year will be the Celtic culture."

All faces turned and looked at me.

I sat down in my chair. "What?" I held up my hands. "Just wanted to see if you had anything to say about Ireland," Greg said.

The entire group at the table laughed. Blood rushed to my face; my hand flew to my throat. I smoothed my linen pants and cleared my throat.

Greg winked at me to let me know he was joking, then continued to tell us about the other Culture Weeks that would follow in the ensuing years. He discussed admissions, fundraising and all the subjects that normally constituted our board meetings and often interested me. The meeting seemed to last longer than usual, but Greg closed the meeting with, "Well, we've gotten out early today—we won't meet again until three weeks before school gets back in session. If I don't see all of you, have a beautiful summer."

A beautiful summer—the words echoed as some sort of warning.

I wiped a damp rag across my desk in the kitchen where a round coffee stain had settled from that morning—before I'd volunteered to write a curriculum, something I'd never done before. Why did I think I could do it?

I could get much of the information from the Internet or from history books. But the best source would be our old housekeeper, Tulu. I lifted the phone and dialed 411, received her number in Seaboro, South Carolina, and dialed before I gave any more thought to the ramifications of opening a door I'd locked long ago.

Tulu's cracked voice came over the lines just as I was about to give up on the incessantly ringing phone without an answering machine.

"Tulu?"

"Yes?"

I closed my eyes, tried to envision her carved mahogany face, her braids running down her back, her gentle eyes that had often found the softer places of my own heart when she looked directly at me.

"Hi . . . ," I said. "This is Meridy Dresden . . . McFadden."

"Oh, oh. My lil' one. I've done prayed all these years that someday I'd be hearing from you." A small sound came over the line that sounded like a stifled cry. "Where are you, child? Are you okay?"

"Yes, yes. I'm fine. I think a lot about you too, Tulu. I'm calling because, well . . ."

"Because you're coming home."

I laughed. "Yes, but the reason I'm coming home is to write a curriculum for our private school about the Gullah culture, and I was hoping you'd be able to . . . help me. Give me some information and such. I just wanted to make sure you were . . ."

A long laugh poured through the phone line. "Alive? You wanted to make sure I was still alive?"

"No . . . Mother tells me she sees you. No . . . not that. But that you'd be around for an interview. I'd really like to see you."

"Little one, I'll always be here for you. Always have been. You just forgot."

"Forgot?"

"Now you'll remember."

"Remember?" Tulu was still alive, but maybe she'd, as they said, gone off her rocker.

"Everything, little one. Maybe now you'll remember everything."

"About Gullah?"

"About you, Meridy. About you."

I coughed, and realized I'd had my eyes shut for the entire conversation. I opened them to see a framed photo of B.J. in his baseball uniform. Beau and B.J.— that was all I really needed to know about myself. "I just need some information on Gullah. . . . I'm probably coming at the end of the week. Can I call you when I get there?"

"Of course you can. But, most of all, you can just come on over. I rarely answer the phone, but this time I felt the whispers of a voice on my arms and I knew I must answer this call. But there's a thunderstorm comin' and you remember—we must be perfectly quiet during those storms—God is doing his work. I'll hang up now."

"Okay . . ." I remembered sitting on the front steps of my house, Danny and I huddled together until a storm passed because Tulu had warned us that God was doing his work.

"Good-bye, lil' one. I'll see you next week. I knew someday you'd be coming."

55

"Bye, Tulu."

Now you'll remember everything.

I sat at the polished kitchen table with Chinese takeout tucked in the warming drawer. I sipped a glass of Silver Oak Cabernet and waited for Beau to come home. I'd spent the day in the most unproductive, loopy manner—wandering from room to room in my house, touching things, feeling them, staring out at the backyard, then finally ordering kung pao for dinner.

The need to go back to Seaboro had grown exponentially since my phone call with Tulu, although I still didn't quite understand why. Williams Prep had handed me an excuse today.

The garage door's opening, then closing, hummed through the kitchen. Beau walked in, dropped his briefcase on the barstool and opened the refrigerator. I made a small noise in the back of my throat; he turned and looked at me.

"Oh, hey, honey. Didn't see you sitting there. What're you doing?"

"Waiting for you . . ." I stood, took another sip of wine.

"I told you I had a meeting with Harland tonight." He glanced at the set table. "Didn't you remember?"

"I forgot."

"Sorry." He came to me, kissed me. "Hope you didn't go to too much trouble."

"No, ordered in." I sat back down, patted the chair

next to me. "Sit down a sec." I poured him a glass of wine.

He sat and looked at me. "Something wrong?"

"No, I just wanted to tell you a little bit about my *day.* At the board meeting, I offered to write a curriculum for the Lower School."

"Okay." He took a sip of wine. "Good for you."

I explained the Culture Week, my volunteerism. "It'll mean I need to go to Seaboro for a little bit. I'll stay with Mother because it's the best way to do the research."

"Well, I guess this is a perfect time for you to be gone—I'm buried with work; B.J. is away." He grabbed my hand. "But you know I hate it when you're gone."

So it was a perfect time because they didn't need me right now. I felt a nervous pinch in my chest as I searched for words to tell, or at least start to tell, Beau about the Keeper's Cottage. "There is also this historic lighthouse—well, it's not really a lighthouse as much as a cottage that had a light on top of it—and now Seaboro is restoring it."

Beau tilted his head. "What does this have to do with the curriculum?"

"Nothing . . . it's just another reason why I want to visit home. Anyway, it burned down when I was a senior in high school, and well, I was there and—" I took a deep breath.

Beau stood up, ready to go. "Well, you can help out with that too, huh? That's just like you—getting involved in all kinds of projects to help others." He kissed the top of my head, stretched. "I've got to get out of this suit." My mouth dropped open without words.

The tenuous line of our connection disappeared in the still air of my unspoken words. An empty hiss filled the space Beau had just vacated. He didn't have time to listen to me tell him about what had happened at the Keeper's Cottage.

I closed my eyes and attempted to find my original love for Beau, the emotion that had once grabbed me by the heart, then the soul. In those days before I met Beau, I hadn't felt much beyond pale thrill, beyond thin joy. A few months after we started dating I knew I loved Beau. I awoke that morning after a date and became aware of the outline of the trees outside, the way the quilt felt heavy over my body—I was noticing touch and emotion. Since the fire, only small moments had carried this alertness to me: standing beside the ocean as the sun gilded its wave tips, river rapids that flowed over boulders as if nothing could stop the water from reaching the sea, the slant of a barn roof, or maybe freshly stacked hay along the road as if the earth had gift wrapped the bales. The awareness felt like butterfly wings against my ribs—and I understood I loved Beau.

I've often searched for these slight wings in other moments—sometimes I've found them; other times I haven't. I've thought that maybe this is what holds some couples together—finding that one moment, maybe two, where they feel those particular wings that allow them to know the promise of more between them.

I also thought I knew how his love for me had started: admiration. I would not dare tell him that the integrity and character he saw in me were part of a facade. He'd met me years after I'd left Seaboro, and his vision of me had been formed after all I'd once been as a child and adolescent had been neatly packed away.

I hadn't deliberately deceived Beau—I had just hidden all those pieces of the past that seemed irrelevant to who we were together. The thought of attempting to explain all of the past, all of who I once was to Beau, exhausted me. I wondered when I had stopped really trying to talk to him, when had he really stopped listening, and which one had come first.

I stood and reached for the phone to call Mother, let her know I was coming home. Beau moved in the back of the house; I felt his presence more than I heard it. After I spoke to Mother, I'd see if Beau was in the bedroom waiting for me. Sometimes, only sometimes, I could feel the wings if he held me and I knew he was really there.

Mother answered on the first ring as if she'd been standing next to the phone—waiting.

CHAPTER FOUR

"Death is one ditch you cannot jump."
—GULLAH PROVERB

Beau's hug still sat warm on my back and shoulders—his strong squeeze and instructions to have a good time and hurry home lingered in the car. I drove with the radio off, the windows rolled down on the stretch of I-16 that bore nothing but exit signs signaling Dairy Queen parfaits at the next stop. I passed sloping farms with white homes, silos and red barns. Although, as Mother often told me, farm life was much more romantic in imagination than in reality, the carpet of fertile fields, the cows and the patient machinery waiting to be put to use did look idyllic.

The rush of tires against pavement, the swish of cars passing, the thump of a bump or gradation in the road, made me feel more alive, more exposed, than if I'd closed myself up inside the Lexus.

Beau had been agreeable and even slightly cheerful about my trip and I wished I could attribute it to his understanding of my need to visit Seaboro. But I couldn't. Beau was too far down the rabbit hole of winning the negligence case, of earning the big promotion, to see or hear the feelings I could barely articulate. Beau's long hours; his preoccupation; the junior lawyer with her long legs and adoring gaze; my best friend divorced and moved on; B.J. gone. Each thought was a punch to my mind and I didn't want to dwell on any of them. Except B.J.—I longed to hear his voice.

I picked up the cell phone and dialed his number. His slow drawl came across the lines, warmed me.

"Hey, darlin'," I said.

"Hey, Mom. What's up?"

"Just driving . . . I'm headed to Grandmother's for a few days. You?"

"Is she all right?"

"Just fine. It's a long story. I'm just calling to check on you."

His words became garbled, drowned out by music and voices in the background.

"What?" I said.

"Sorry, Mom. There's a lot of people here. Can I call you back?"

"B.J., it's five o'clock in the afternoon. What kind of big party can be going on this early? Aren't you supposed to be at baseball practice?"

"Practice ends at four o'clock and this is Nashville—there's always a party." He laughed and his voice sounded different, larger.

"Be careful, honey."

"Always, Mom. Always."

"I love you, B.J."

"You too, Mom. Gotta go, 'kay?"

I hung up the phone and turned on the radio to drown out the empty space inside me that reached for my son so far away—a nagging fear that any youthful wildness he'd tamped down for us was now coming to the fore.

As I drew closer to Seaboro, the air grew moist and warm from the nearby sea. Then the bridge over Seaboro River, a large pewter swell like the back of a dolphin rising from the water, appeared before me. Soon I was on top of the bridge, the water blue and aqua, green and sage, in islands of color, like multihued clouds hovering beneath a plane. Live oaks—older than the founding documents of our country—bent over the banks and corners of the river as if they were worshipping the flowing water.

Cate's words about rotten roots and fake lives came to me. Had I merely covered up B.J.'s problems, allowing everyone to believe that nothing ever went wrong in our family? In the many times I'd concealed his youthful foolishness, maybe I'd been protecting my own.

I now wondered what would have happened if I hadn't hidden B.J.'s mistakes, if I hadn't placed my shield over him all those times. Maybe Beau's love would have been enough, but I'd been too fearful to find out because maybe, just maybe, it wouldn't have been enough and the family's equilibrium, which was meticulously balanced on the fulcrum of goodness, would collapse.

The culmination of B.J.'s mistakes had come when he'd said he was spending the night at his friend Tyler's house. I hadn't checked if this was true. He was sixteen, and the team had a late baseball game; he'd be riding the school's athletic bus across the county.

And as is the mother's curse of hearing everything, I heard the back door click open, then shut at five thirty in the morning. I opened my eyes and stared at the dark ceiling, heard the slow, even breaths that let me know Beau was asleep. He'd worked late and slept soundly. I walked into the hall just as B.J. opened his bedroom door.

"Mom." He held his hand on his doorknob. My name came as a statement. His clothes and hair were damp; drops of water fell onto the wool carpet.

"What happened?" I whispered.

In a quiet blur of fatigue, B.J. told me the story. He and Tyler had left the baseball game with the team, but after they'd arrived back at school, they'd decided to stop by a party given by a friend whose parents were out of town. In a stunt inspired by a dare from one of the football players, the few boys from the baseball team at the party hot-wired the athletic bus and drove it into the lake in front of the school.

As B.J. told me this story, I motioned for us to move into his room. By the time he'd finished, I'd sunk into his desk chair with my hands covering my face. "Where is the bus now?" I asked.

"In the lake." His voice quivered.

"No."

He nodded. "I'm dead, Mom. It was a dare from the football team after we'd lost the baseball game. I wasn't . . . thinking. We just took the dare and . . ." He sank onto his bed. "I'm so dead. The recruiter from Vanderbilt is coming to the game tomorrow and if I play badly or don't play at all because Coach finds out about this . . . I'll lose my chance to—"

I held up my hand. "Let's get some sleep, B.J. We'll figure it out later—just try to get some sleep." I stood, kissed him on the cheek and walked from his room. I curled back into my bed with numerous options floating above me and they all seemed to land on top of my culpability: I hadn't called to find out if he really spent the night at Tyler's or arrived safely after the game, I hadn't gone to the game because we'd had a dinner party, and more importantly—he'd taken the dare because he was *my* child. I groaned and rolled over; then knowing sleep wasn't returning, I rose and began the day.

Morning arrived full and chaotic—a doubleheader baseball game, a luncheon and a dinner party for a friend's anniversary. No moment, no impetus, remained to take this piece of our life and fit it into a puzzle where it did *not* belong.

That afternoon I sat with Beau in the bleachers and we held hands while B.J. pitched a no-hitter for the first time in the school's history. Beau ran onto the field, gave his son a high five and hugged him in front of the overflow crowd. The baseball recruiter from Vanderbilt met them on the field and I knew I'd made the right decision not to tell. Or had I?

Eventually the blame for the destroyed bus fell on a rival school we'd beaten in football too many years in a row. After that, B.J. seemed to try even harder to be good. God, what had I handed down to my son in the DNA of my wild nature, then in teaching him the art of covering up?

As I now crossed the river that divided not only the land, but also the separate pieces of my life, I remembered my longing to tell Beau about the incident, but I hadn't. Maybe I'd ignored longing so many times through the years until eventually I'd just stopped feeling it.

I wound the car through the streets of Seaboro in the early evening until I arrived in Mother's driveway. I stared up at my old bedroom; the curtains were drawn as if the room slept with blankets pulled up tight. I hadn't stayed in my childhood bedroom since the night before I left for Mawmaw and Grandpa's, three days after the fire that had destroyed the Keeper's Cottage on my high school graduation night.

Although I'd visited my childhood home at least once a year—alternating holidays with Beau's family—I'd never come without my husband and my son, and we'd always stayed in the guest suite. Every time I'd visited Mother, I'd had Beau to shelter me from both the memories and the old friends. I had run into Tim a few times through the years at the grocery store, a Seaboro Festival, or the five-and-dime, which still stood on the corner of Magnolia and Main, but I'd never talked to him—just nodded and smiled.

I climbed out of the car and stared at the porch. The steps up to the front door had been recently painted and not a single scuff mark marred the surface. After all, a visitor's first impression was the most important.

I stood at the front door, ran my hand over the doorknob and suppressed a laugh at the impulse to sneak in the back window rather than walk into the polished front hall, which would smell of lemon and moist wood.

The door swung open, bands of light fell onto the porch, and Mother stood in the doorway. She looked exactly as she had in the days when I'd ridden my bike up to the front porch, or jumped off the school bus at the end of the driveway. Her hair was now silver instead of blond, but the oak-filtered evening sunlight blurred the distinction. Her lips straight, her hands on her hips, she could have been frozen in time. But when I came close, I saw the slight stoop in her stance, the wrinkles set in the familiar facial expressions.

"You're late," she said.

"So good to see you too, Mother. The traffic was terrible between Atlanta and Macon with the construction."

"You should have called." Mother hugged me, but it was more a placement of her forearms around my shoulders than an embrace.

"Well"—I smiled—"I'm here."

"I bet you're famished. . . . Would you like something to eat or drink, dear?"

"I ate dinner on the road. But I'd love some hot tea."

Mother turned and walked down the hall and I swore I heard her mumble, "That would be 'yes, ma'am.'"

I was thirteen years old again, grounded for forgetting my manners, and following Mother down the hall with my tail between my legs.

No, I wouldn't let it happen that way. I leaned my

head far back and stared up the curved staircase. The ceiling twirled above me and I almost saw a pin-straight blond girl sitting on the top step, dreaming of floating down the stairs without touching the floorboard. The little girl who actually thought she could fly, until she broke her right arm trying to do so.

I closed my eyes and sighed, leaned against the banister. When was the last time I thought I could fly?

Mother came into the hall. "Are you coming, Meridy?"

"Mother?" I opened my eyes.

"Yes?" She walked closer, her eyebrows squeezed together.

"Do you remember when I broke my arm and I had that terrible cast? . . ."

"Of course I do. You scared me to death."

"I did?"

"What do you think? I heard this banging and whumping in the hall and I came out, biscuit dough all over myself, and there you are, all twisted at the bottom of the steps. You weren't even crying. . . . You had the silliest little grin."

"I was trying to fly. I thought I could go down the stairs without touching."

"You what?"

"I thought I could fly. . . . I sure don't feel like that anymore."

"Meridy, you couldn't fly then."

I looked directly at Mother. "But I thought I could."

"Are you okay?" Mother lifted her chin; her wrinkles

deepened as she furrowed her brow in worry.

"Fine," I said, sure that we weren't going to truthfully answer the question in the hallway with tea on the stove, my luggage in the car. There wasn't anything to answer anyway . . . except maybe why the past few days, I was remembering more of who I had been than who I had become.

I walked down the hall behind Mother, past the portraits of family members, past the pine trestle table handed down from Great-grandma, past the sword on the wall from Great-granduncle Haywood's last battle in the Civil War. So much behind me, so much contributing to who I was.

Late, muted sunlight spilled through the floor-to-ceiling kitchen windows, scattered on the pine table. I sat; Mother's prize peonies sprang from a Waterford vase in a wild mass of beauty. She placed a teacup next to my elbow and I lifted it, pinkie out, and took a sip. "Thanks, Mother. You want to sit on the back porch with me and have this tea? It looks like it's going to be a beautiful night."

"Oh, you go ahead. My sinuses are bothering me and the pollen is terrible right now."

I held up my hand. "That's okay, Mother. I'll stay in here with you. So, tell me, how is everything here?"

"Not much to tell." She placed her cup so gently in the saucer that there was no clink of china. "Mrs. Foster—you know, down the street?"

"Of course I know her. She's only lived down the street my entire life. She never gave candy away for

Halloween—only apples. Always." I scrunched up my nose.

"Have some respect," she said, her lips tight, her eyes narrowed. "She passed away last week."

I lifted my hand to my mouth. "I'm sorry, Mother. What happened?"

"She was alone in the house and must have had a heart attack. Her son hadn't come to visit her in days. By the time he stopped by, she'd been dead for almost a week and . . . you do not want to hear the details."

"That's terrible. I'm sorry you lost a friend."

Mother shrugged. "That's what happens at this age. . . ."

"Is Charlotte Hamlon still in the old house next to Mrs. Foster?"

Mother exhaled. "Oh, yes. She's still there."

"And probably still spying on the mischief in our neighborhood."

"I'm sure. . . ."

"Not much to spy on with me gone, huh?" I winked at Mother, leaned forward. "Can you tell me what's going on with the Keeper's Cottage and Tim? Have you seen him or talked to him since the historic society asked him for money?"

"I don't run into Tim Oliver at church or bingo or the Ladies of Seaboro Society meeting, Meridy, so I don't really see him, and you'd do best not to either."

"Why?"

"No need to go digging up bones."

"Thanks for the advice."

"Let the historical society take care of it."

"But there have to be other ways to get the money to renovate," I said.

"Why? Tim should pay."

"Our private school in Atlanta has raised money a hundred other ways than taking it from someone."

"The historical society is not taking money, Meridy." Her voice sounded exasperated, as in the days when I had been relentless in gaining permission to do something I'd already been denied ten times. She continued. "They are asking for it from the man who is responsible for the demise of the cottage."

"They could have a campaign or a festival or a raffle or anything else besides having Tim pay for it."

Mother leaned back in her chair. "Why are you so worried about Tim Oliver?"

"He's an old friend." I averted my eyes from Mother's glare. "And I'm good at this kind of thing— raising money, I mean. I've done it for the school many times."

"Oh?"

I leaned forward, an idea percolating so far down I wasn't yet sure what it was. "Our biggest fundraiser is our arts festival. We've raised . . ." I stood, the idea bubbling out like I was a soda can someone had shaken. "My God, Mother. Arts. Where is the arts more prevalent than here? Sweet baskets, painting, storytelling, poetry, photography, net crafting. The Lowcountry has more artists than oysters, I swear. What about that?" I started to pace the kitchen, my hands flying.

"Meridy Dresden, what are you all worked up about? Why do you care where the historical society gets the money? Is that why you're here?"

I stopped. "I'm here to write this Gullah curriculum, but how can you not care what they do to Tim? He doesn't deserve the kind of pressure I know this town can drop on someone. He's probably been ostracized—his parents, his poor wife."

"His wife left him a few years ago and . . ." Mother stopped, tilted her head. "Arts festival, huh?"

"Yes."

"Hmmm. I'll say something to Charlotte Hamlon at the society meeting tomorrow. She's also on the histor-ical-society board."

"Gee, what isn't that lady in charge of?" I rolled my eyes. The memory of Charlotte, the abrasive spinster of Seaboro, uninvitedly entered my mind. "This town still tolerates her?"

Mother actually laughed. "I don't think they have much choice." I laughed with Mother and it felt warm, like wine. I reached down and hugged her.

"It'll be nice having you here," she said, becoming stiff again. "I just don't know why you didn't bring Beau or B.J. It's not right for a lady to travel alone like this. . . . You can't just leave your husband at home."

"Beau's too busy to come and B.J. is off at baseball camp. It's actually the perfect time." I repeated my hus-band's words, but felt the ache of deceit. I kissed Mother on the forehead. "I'm going to unload my car."

"Well, I've prepared the guest suite for you. . . . Clean

71

linen sheets, and I've even had a TV with cable put in there."

"I think I'll stay in my own room this time."

She drew backward, almost as if I'd hit her or just lifted my hand to do so. "You haven't stayed in there since . . ."

"Danny died," I said.

Mother gasped and I didn't turn to look at her. We hadn't discussed Danny since the Keeper's Cottage fire; there seemed to be an unspoken agreement to never speak his name again—especially since my marriage.

I turned. "I want to stay there. I want to be in my own bedroom."

Mother recovered. "How long are you staying?" Her voice came softer, lower, as if she was embarrassed to ask.

"I haven't decided yet. I'll see how much information I can get from Tutu and go from there."

"You haven't told Beau how long you'll be gone?"

"He's so damn busy. . . . He's fine without me for a little while."

"Don't curse in my house." Mother stood up. "Do I sense trouble?" She wrinkled her nose as if she smelled it more than sensed it.

"No trouble here, Mother. No trouble at all."

It had been twenty-six years since I'd laid my head on my childhood bed, when I'd slept for three nights in a haze of pain and fear before Mother had shipped me off to Daddy's parents in the north Georgia mountains.

I lay down on top of the coverlet in my silk pajamas—the pink ones Beau had given me for my birthday last year—and rolled over, stared out the window across the room. The oak tree that had hidden my dreams and room in childhood was gone now. Mother had said it was struck by lightning and needed to be cut down. The view from my room now went farther. The stars sat in their firmament and if I stayed awake long enough, the moon would come over the house and into view.

The sleep I'd thought would come quickly eluded me. I didn't want to be who I used to be—that had brought death and heartache—and I didn't want to be who I was now—that carried loneliness and emptiness. So where did that leave me? Alone, once again, in the same bed— full circle.

I did have and love Beau. But when I searched for the emotion, I found only a blank slate—no anger, no resentment, no pain. Nothing really. I couldn't think about all that now.

I finally got up and walked to the window. Being in this room, surrounded by the paraphernalia of childhood, the smells of youth, I wondered if I could still make it down the roof to the trellis.

The window lifted with a squeak. Dust flew from the sill and wandered out the window to nature's night air. I leaned out the window and felt, more than saw, the roofline below me. My feet stepped out onto the shingled roof. I imitated a maneuver somehow remembered in my body until my feet caught hold of the trellis. Then my long-unpracticed foot slipped from the wood; I tumbled in a heap on the grass, rolled to my side.

A shrill cry met my landing. My head snapped up; Mother sat on the back porch, a hand over her mouth, her nightgown fluttering around her legs.

"It's just me, Mother. Just me." I stood up, straightened my silk pajama bottoms.

"Oh, my dear, Meridy, what are you doing?" Mother stood, walked to the back stairs.

"What are *you* doing?" I walked toward the stairs. "It's after midnight."

"I couldn't sleep. . . ." Mother stopped, placed her palm over her pursed lips as if she'd just revealed an intimate secret.

"Neither could I," I said, thinking maybe this was the first time in our entire lives that we'd shared the same restlessness.

"Please tell me you did not just jump out that window," Mother said.

"Well, I guess I could technically say I jumped off the roof, or really the trellis . . . not the window."

"Now, why would you do that?"

I shrugged my shoulders and climbed up the stairs, sat in a rocking chair and hoped, in the silence, to say something that would bring us together. But the only piece of mutual interest I found was my sister.

"How's Sissy?" I asked, rocked back in the chair.

"She's doing great. The twins love their new school. You know they started high school last year."

"Of course I know that." Maybe Sissy wasn't such a

good subject; maybe the tranquil night was our best bet at avoiding confrontation.

"Well, Sissy says she doesn't talk to you that much and—"

"I talk to her. . . ." But then I couldn't remember the last time.

"Well, she comes to visit at least every other weekend and brings the girls. Penn travels so much for work and she gets lonely. I know she wishes that they'd move here, but he seems determined to stay in Charleston—two hours away seems even longer when you want to see each other."

I wanted to say, *I'm five hours away and that doesn't seem to bother you.*

"I'm sure Sissy will figure out a way to get back here," I said instead.

"I hope so," Mother whispered.

Jealousy started to rise, then sank in the quiet night. There we sat in the dark, both unable to sleep, both McFadden women, and that was enough for tonight. Then my mother turned and whispered a question I'd dare not have thought.

"Are you leaving Beau?"

I stuttered, "No, of course not."

"Usually that is why women . . . go home alone."

"Not this time." I gripped my fist, curled my naked toes under the chair and braced myself for the coming lecture about irresponsibility and foolishness. But the lecture never came. Only the sounds of the Lowcountry behind the house filled the night until the soft change in

Mother's breathing told me she'd dozed off in her chair. I stared out to the dark backyard; I knew where each tree stood, where every bush and flower bed lay. I saw only the shapes and forms of nature, yet I sensed, as one does at night, that something waited for me out here, something that needed to be found, or maybe lost.

CHAPTER FIVE

"Old firewood is not hard to rekindle."
—GULLAH PROVERB

I dragged my toes through the sand and walked up and down the beach in the early morning. I'd lost track of time, unable to determine whether I'd been out here an hour or two or even three. I walked back and forth across the expanse of sand that stretched from our piece of land, which turned the corner to an oyster bed and then curled around the bend to Danny's house with the long, wide beach facing the sea. Danny's parents had moved—years ago—to a retirement community about forty minutes away. I had never seen or heard from them after the fire. In the suffocating log bedroom of my grandparents' summer home I'd wanted to call them, but I never blamed them for not contacting me.

Danny was an only child, and he was gone and I was alive. I had spent the summer in the mountains, which hid me from the mourning, the blame and the sorrow washing over Seaboro in my absence. I'd gone home for only a week, to pack my bags for college. By the time Christmas break rolled around I was sufficiently hollow and numb not to seek out my high school friends or Danny's family for comfort.

At the university, where other girls starved themselves to appear rail thin in the torn sweatshirts and leg warmers of the eighties, as they smoked cigarettes to suppress their appetite for food, so I suppressed the longings of my heart. I began the arduous journey of being a good girl. I remained on the honor list all four years; I was student body president and sorority vice president.

Beaumont Dresden entered my life on a day when my heart must have been mildly hungry without my knowledge. He had stood at a table under the Forum portico, signing students up for the Annual Fraternity Blood Drive. Even now I don't know if I was attracted to what appeared to be his absolute perfection.

I had known who Beaumont Dresden was; everyone had. He was born of the Atlanta Dresdens and was by far the most gorgeous dark-haired, blue-eyed boy on campus. A date with Beau was as prized as a 4.0 grade point average. He was a senior and I was a sophomore. He'd never gone steady with a girl for more than a few months. I had seen him, but not really noticed him any more than the scenery of the university until the morning I went to relieve him of the post at the blood drive volunteer table.

"Meridy McFadden, correct?" He held out his hand. I swore I actually felt my heart skip and I wasn't sure of the last time I'd felt my heart at all. I ignored the skip as best I could and nodded, took his hand.

"Yes. And you are?" As if I didn't know.

"Beaumont Dresden. Been wanting to meet you for a long time . . . Seems you are quite the busy girl."

"Meet me?"

A boy, blond and freckled, came up beside us. Beau nodded at him. "Hey, Mark," Then Beau looked at me. "This is Mark. Mark, this is Meridy McFadden." Beau's head nodded between us.

"Ah." Mark bowed. "Ice princess McFadden?"

A warm flush ran up my arms to my face.

Beau punched Mark in the arm, turned to me. "Forgive him. He is uncouth and barbaric." He laughed. "You're blushing. I knew it wasn't true because ice princesses don't blush."

He brought his hand toward my face and I backed up. He laughed. "You have food on your face."

"Oh . . ." I raised my hand, wiped my cheek. He reached across the space between us and ran his thumb along the opposite cheek, toward my lips. Something curled and asleep inside me awoke, stretched and left me loose and wordless.

"Ketchup maybe," he said, smiled at me.

I nodded, mumbled something about having just eaten french fries for lunch as it was all that looked edible in the cafeteria that day.

From that day forward a piece of my heart yearned for one more touch from Beau Dresden, as if his finger running along my face had fractured open my closed and padlocked desire for intimacy. I soon sought reasons to be around him, find the nearness of him. I fell in love with him before I ever admitted it to my heart or mind, much less to another human being, including him.

Beau had thawed a portion of my heart with his smile, his carefree attitude and his light touch. It had all seemed so right to me. And right was important. I'd dated him, then kissed him, and then met his family. He'd met my family; we'd inched a little farther along than kissing, but not too much. I would wait for the ring we never discussed, but which his mother had told me was hidden in the family safe in the library off the foyer in his Habersham Road family home.

We dated all through my last years at college. In my junior year, he left for law school in Atlanta. I stayed at college until my graduation day when Beau knelt before me under the portico of the Forum building where we'd met, and offered me a three-carat diamond ring and the Dresden name.

Everyone had said we were the perfect couple, came from the same kind of family. I heard what the girls said behind my back, in the corners of the sorority halls. "Wasn't Beau Dresden just breaking hearts everywhere when he fell in love with prissy little Meridy McFadden?"

Now I bent down and picked up a white shell as pure as the dress I'd worn twenty years ago when I'd said "I do" to Beau, allowing him to believe, if only by silence, that he was marrying a girl who'd never loved anyone but him. I placed the shell in the sweetgrass basket I carried in the crook of my arm.

I sat down, carved my initials in the damp-crusted sand above the waterline where the tide receded. I tilted my head and lifted my palm against the sun. A wave crashed below my toes and splashed my face; I licked my lips and lost myself in the sound of the sea. A pressure that could have been a hand if I wasn't alone lit upon my shoulder. I brushed it away. Startled, I jumped up to face a man with brown curls, a grinning face, sun-settled wrinkles lying in the places where his laugh lived. I dropped my basket of shells. He stood in a pair of torn khaki shorts and a faded blue T-shirt.

"Meridy McFadden . . . do I look that bad?"

I tilted my head—his chin, his laugh, his curls. "Timmy!" I yelped, threw my arms around his shoulders and hugged him before my more mature self told me not to.

"I thought I told you never to call me Timmy again." He pulled me back from him. "Now, didn't I?"

"Timmy." I touched his chin, his curls.

He threw back his head and laughed. "I thought it was you out here. I've been watching you for a couple hours now—pacing back and forth, back and forth, picking up and throwing away shells. . . . What are you doing, crazy girl?"

I smiled and it felt good. "Nothing, absolutely nothing."

Tim leaned over and picked up my basket, handed it

to me. "I wasn't sure it was you until you sat, leaned across your legs . . . Then I knew."

"Where were you?"

Tim pointed. "Right there . . . the small cedar shake house." I lifted my hand and shaded my eyes. "New house?"

"New to you, I guess. It's mine, been there for five years or so now."

"How come I never knew that?"

"Maybe because when you come to visit your mom, you never leave your property."

I looked back toward Mother's house four hundred yards away, not visible from the bend. "No, I guess I haven't." I looked back at Tim. "Oh, how are you?"

"I'm good for an old man. I can't tell you how glad I am to see you." He grinned again and my heart swelled as if the sea had given me back some piece of it full of wave and water.

"I'm so glad to see you too. And if you're an old man, I'm an old woman, and I'll have none of that. Forty-three is not old." I lifted my basket up to my elbow, let it dangle. I had missed the past twenty-six years of this man's life, this man whom I had once fiercely loved as an ally in my war against the world of expectation and responsibility. Goofy Tim with his bowlegged walk and his mass of untamed curls and his wide grin: my friend. "Tell me everything, Tim. Everything I've missed in your life . . . how have you been? I'm so sorry I haven't kept in touch, haven't . . . ." A bittersweet sorrow flashed through my gut as I remembered who we were.

"I haven't been the epitome of communication either, Meridy. No need for apologies." He pulled at my hand and motioned to start walking.

"Okay, where do I start?" Tim asked. "When was the last time we saw each other?" Tim asked.

"I think I saw you at the Christmas tree lighting two or three years ago on the square. . . .

He laughed. "Okay, when was the last time we talked?"

I stopped, put my hand over my face to say it. "That night."

"No . . . that can't be right." He stopped, turned.

"Yes, it is right. I know it is."

He walked, flip-flops flapping against the sand. "Usually I see you go within a day or two of when you arrive. . . . Each time I see a Fulton County license plate at your mother's house, I think you might have come for a real visit."

"I'm sorry . . . Tim."

"No *sorrys*. How long are you staying this time?"

I turned to the thin stretch of aqua horizon melting between sea and sky. "I don't know. . . ."

Tim turned toward the sand dunes and a boardwalk. "Remember this?" He pointed at a wild area of sea oats, maritime shrubs, palmettos, and pines.

"No." I rubbed my forehead. I'd walked farther up the beach than I had since before I'd moved away.

"This is where we used to hide when your mother was hollerin' for you to come home, ringing that damn dinner bell off the back veranda, remember?"

Blood rushed from my fingers in a prickle of recognition. "Our forest, our hideout . . . Mrs. Foster's land."

"Yep." Tim stopped at the boardwalk. "Now it belongs to the city—it's a preserve and bird sanctuary. Our path—the one we cut with the clippers we stole from your gardener—is now marked with little signs and posts telling what plant you're looking at: Here's a loblolly pine, a live oak."

"Borrowed, we borrowed the clippers—not stole them."

"Come on." He headed up the boardwalk.

I paused, ran my fingers along the basket rim. My throat constricted in one motion. I hadn't entered these woods in twenty-six years—these wilder places of youth and nature.

Tim stopped to wait for me. "I'll show you what they've done, catch you up on the gossip of Seaboro proper. . . ." He squinted his eyes, moved toward me. "What's wrong, Meridy?"

"I don't know. . . . I really don't know. I've become a poor excuse for a Lowcountry girl. . . ."

"Not true . . . come on."

Maybe because he expected me to follow him, I did. My breath caught in the small places below my throat and fluttered. I stopped at the edge of the boardwalk.

Tim smiled at me. "I come here every day to check on an osprey nest. It's in a dead oak tree I'm afraid won't stand much longer—and there are three babies. . . . It's only a little bit ahead. Tell me all about you first. How are you, really?"

"Good, I'm really good. We live in Atlanta. My husband is a lawyer; his name is Beau. . . . So is my son's." I laughed. "It's a good life.

"Good, then." Tim slowed. "Real good."

I wanted to laugh with him at my own absurdity, but the laughter caught on the back of my tongue.

"I know it must be hard for you to come here, Meridy . . . but I have missed you."

"You too, Tim."

"So what's brought you here?"

I told him of how I had volunteered to write the curriculum. "And, Tim . . . Mother told me what the historical society is doing to you."

"Oh . . ."

"I want to help."

He pressed his lips together. "I absolutely do not need any help."

"I know you don't. But I want to—really I want to. I have a couple ideas I ran by Mother. They can't just come after you and demand money twenty-six years later. I know how people talk around here and—"

Tim laughed. "And when have you known me to care what other people say? Now, my family is another matter. My parents are sick about it. But you don't need to go worrying about it."

"Ah, don't worry my pretty little head?"

"I didn't say you had a pretty head." He dodged me as I pulled my hand back to punch his shoulder. He laughed so loud a flock of sparrows flew from the oak branches above us, the sound echoing across the

84

thick brush, as well as my heart.

"I want to help," I said.

"Why?"

"Maybe to make up for something, for Danny, for you." I struggled with words to explain. "To try and be . . . as good as I can." The minute the words left my mouth they sounded ridiculous.

"Good?" This time he did laugh. "Since when have you tried to be good?"

"Not funny, Timothy Oliver."

"You know I wouldn't say anything to hurt you. . . . I'm just a tad too crass sometimes. It just doesn't sound like something Meridy McFadden would've said."

A love of childlike proportion—the largest kind of love there is—washed over me. "I've become everything we hated, haven't I? I've turned into Mrs. Foster in her pearls at breakfast complaining about the noise of the young ones who have no manners." I looked at Tim. "I'm everything we hated. . . ."

"God, I hope not." He laughed. "There is no way you're everything we hated."

"Okay, then maybe I'm just losing it."

"Great . . . I haven't seen you in twenty-six years and I finally get to talk to you and you're officially losing it. Just my luck."

Laughter rose up from a place low and vibrating. I threw my head back and let it come. "God, I'm so melodramatic. Leave me here in the forest and forget you ever saw me. I'll stop by in a couple days and you can meet the real Meridy, who, by the way, wants to

85

help you out of this mess."

"Oh, this is the real Meridy. And I don't need help. It's not that big a deal. I can handle it. Come on, I'll talk about me."

"Can we go back out to the beach?"

"This path winds back around to the beach. I have to check on the osprey babies. You don't like it back here anymore?"

I looked left and right. "I feel . . . stuck in here. I don't know why." I touched a net of moss, pulled a strand loose. "Where was our hideout?"

"About a hundred yards back . . . nearer to the property line."

"So what's happened to you? You've stayed all these years . . . here?"

"Why would I leave?" He waved his hand in the air. "In a nutshell, I married a girl I met who was here on vacation and we built a house on a side portion of Dad's land. Then he had a heart attack years ago—now he's disabled. It wiped out all the family money . . . what there was of it. So I stayed to help. Then I got divorced and now I build houses. . . ."

"Oh, Tim, I'm so sorry. Mother did tell me about your divorce."

"Ah, she hated it here, and I wouldn't leave. I think what finally happened is that the way she felt about this place turned into the way she felt about me: stifling, hot, bug-filled and slow. She just hated everything here—the marsh, the smell of the shrimp boats coming into harbor, the extreme tides, the unreliable weather, you know . . . and there's no way I could leave this place even if Mom and Dad didn't need me."

I lifted my hand to my mouth. "That's it."

"What?"

"I've let how I feel about Danny dying—scared—change the way I feel about this place."

Tim touched my arm, pressed his lips together and whispered, "You miss him."

"I don't know . . . I really don't think that much about it." I stared up at the moss-outlined sky. I needed to change the subject. "Can I ask you why y'all never had kids?"

"She kept saying she wanted to think about it and then it just never happened. I think she knew she'd eventually leave me. I've heard she has a couple kids in Chicago—married her high school boyfriend who she'd broken up with to run off with me. Sordid, I know."

"It's not sordid. It's sad."

"Not anymore. It always works out for the best. But I do love kids . . . maybe because I am one."

I laughed. "Good point."

He raised his eyebrows at me. "You could've argued the point."

I smiled and the eddy of uneasiness about being in the forest subsided as I strolled through the woods with an old friend, checking on an osprey nest and talking.

As we rounded the curve of pine straw and emerged back onto the beach, I hugged Tim. "It was so good to see you."

"There's something I'd love to show you if you're staying a little while."

"I am. What is it?"

"A surprise."

"Okay . . ." I glanced off at the ocean; the sun had slid farther up into the sky. The morning had passed into afternoon and I felt more content than . . . I had in a long time. "When?"

"Today's Saturday. How's Monday morning? I'll meet you at the public dock on the river at about . . . let's say ten a.m.?"

"I'd love that, thanks." He walked with me until I rounded the curve of beach and spotted the pillars of my family's back porch. I kissed his cheek good-bye.

As I meandered back down the beach toward home, my contentment faded like watercolors. Guilt rose in the back of my throat. When was the last time I'd laughed and talked with Beau like I just had? The betraying thought slithered across my mind before I could grab its slimy tail and yank it away. I stopped, dug my toes in the sand. *When?* whispered the thought.

Ah. I kicked the sand. *I can answer that. When he surprised me by taking me to Mexico for our fifteenth anniversary.*

Beau had pretended to forget the entire event. I'd hinted, prodded, asked if we had plans for the weekend, but he'd changed the subject, walked out of the room. My feelings had been bruised. But all along he'd planned a trip. Cate had come over and packed my suitcase with all my favorite things and picked up B.J. to stay with her and Harland.

When I returned from a meeting there was a limousine waiting in the driveway. Beau stood in the front yard waiting and wearing the most raucous palm tree shirt and bathing suit. He held cold margaritas in his hands—one for me, one for him. I'd laughed until tears rolled down my face. We'd climbed into the limo—he hadn't even allowed me to go into the house and make a single arrangement, as he'd taken care of everything.

We'd flown on a private chartered jet, something he often did for work, but I'd never done. When we landed in Mexico I followed Beau, content that he had arranged every detail. A car met us at the airport and drove us along the Mexican roads as dust flew in circles and children ran after the car trying to sell us trinkets, jewelry and Mexican dolls. We pulled up to a long, thin metal building that looked more like trailers backed one up to the other than the Motel Cabana it claimed to be on its flashing sign missing the letter E.

Beau leaned up to the driver. "This is not our hotel. We're staying at the Cabana Resort."

The driver turned around. *"No hablo ingles."* Then he opened the driver's-side door and walked back to his trunk, yanked our luggage out, dropped all of it on the parched grass.

Beau jumped out of the car, attempted to communicate in sign language of large arm swaying and exaggerated body movements. I climbed out of the car to watch this scene in a blur of margarita and pounding Mexican sun. When I began to giggle, then laugh, Beau's absurd attempts to tell our driver where we wanted to go increased.

The car drove off, leaving a trail of dust as Beau attempted to use a dead cell phone. Then we stood in the parking lot of the Motel Cabana with our Louis Vuitton luggage, our beach bags and riotous laughter between us that sent us both to sitting on the ground next to our paraphernalia, holding each other and wiping away tears of frustration and hilarity.

This memory, on the beach in Seaboro, brought a smile, then a laugh. Warmth spread over the memory, over my mind. I sat on the same wicker chairs I had with Mother the night before, and the screen behind me creaked in a song of childhood.

"Your husband called. . . ." Mother's voice came from behind me. I craned about in the chair. "Hello, Mother. I'll call him back."

"Are you going to tell him you spent the morning with that wild Tim Oliver?"

"Please, Mother." I closed my eyes. She must've seen me round the corner with him.

She shut the door behind her, but I heard her through the screen: "There's lemonade and cucumber sandwiches in the kitchen if you'd like some."

Like some? I'd love some. Then I'd call Beau, try and find a way to tell him how I felt. The warmth and the love I carried for him still existed, but I wondered if he still felt any of it for me. And how would he feel about the Meridy who'd once lived here, run wild in these woods, rivers and sea? The Meridy I wasn't sure I'd ever shown him.

CHAPTER SIX

"Bad children may not be thrown into the fire."
—GULLAH PROVERB

The floor-length silk curtains moved in a slow dance across the heart-of-pine boards in my bedroom. The soft hush of the tide outside my window whispered into the predawn light. I'd opened the window before bed last night and must have fallen asleep before remembering to close it.

I'd ended up spending the afternoon and evening of the previous day wandering the house, opening drawers, trying to unearth something, I wasn't sure what. I'd tried to call Beau, but no one had answered the home phone.

Eventually I'd fallen asleep to the frogs' lullaby and the sweet wind outside my window while flipping through my seventh-grade diary. I read that I'd once wanted new waders for fishing, I'd hated my reading teacher, and I'd wished popular Weatherly Jones would invite me to her thirteenth birthday party at the country club. The smaller pieces of my childhood rose like stray filaments to the magnet of my adult self.

I rose from the bed, stretched, walked over to the desk and yanked the file folder labeled "Gullah Curriculum" from my canvas bag. I flipped through the questions I intended to ask Tulu today—what was most important to teach the children about the culture?

The file folder tucked under my arm, I attempted to sneak down to the kitchen without waking Mother; I stepped on the right side of the third tread where the left side creaked, moved to the left on the seventh tread and smiled as I reached the foyer landing. I could still do the entire set of stairs without a single groan. I moved toward the kitchen; the aroma of coffee met me at the door.

Mother sat at the kitchen table, staring off into the distance. "Mother? What are you doing up so early?"

She startled; her white hair fell to her shoulders for the first time I'd seen in years. "Sorry . . . did I wake you?" she asked.

"No, not at all. I left the window open and the dawn woke me. So much better than a screaming alarm clock. You okay?"

"Yes . . . just like my coffee early."

As if the blood we shared now flowed together, I sensed the emptiness that filled this house with Daddy gone. I reached for Mother and hugged her; although she didn't hug me back, I felt a softening. "It must get lonely here, Mother."

"No, I'm just fine. I'm used to it."

I didn't know why I'd never thought about her being alone in this huge house without Daddy. Maybe it was because of all her friends and activities. I'd never applied the word *lonely* to her. *Involved, cantankerous, nosy* . . .

I grabbed a coffee mug from the kitchen cabinet. "Have you ever thought about moving into a smaller place?"

"Never. This house has been in the McFadden family for five generations. I would never give it up. I'm sure Sissy will take care of it after I'm gone. Are you implying I can't take care of the house?"

I laughed. "No, Mother. I am just thinking of you. . . ."

"Hmph." She lifted her coffee cup. "I'm going to get ready for the day. I have a garden-club meeting and a luncheon at the club with the Ladies of Seaboro Society. Would you like to stop by and say hello?"

The Ladies of Seaboro Society was an invitation-only organization and represented Seaboro's embodiment of acceptance. Mother held her membership as proof of pedigree.

"I'm going to visit Tulu today . . . but thanks for the invitation."

"Did you know her husband passed last year?"

"No . . . you never told me."

"Well, I guess I forgot." Mother stood and started to walk out of the kitchen. "Have you called *your* husband?"

"Are you implying I can't take care of my family?" I said, although I smiled.

She walked out of the kitchen and the sound of the slammed bedroom door upstairs was my signal that I'd crossed some "appropriate" line drawn years ago.

Tulu's shack appeared to be composed of earth and dirt as it slanted to the left, winking at me. The front porch hung loose from the right corner and a dog barked from under the wooden front steps. The corner of Seaboro where Tulu lived was only ten minutes away from my house, but a world away in style and prosperity—if one defined prosperity by money. The rich marsh and river running behind the homes on her street were the same as those behind my home. I looked at the mailbox—212—it was the right house. In all my childhood I'd never visited Tulu, loving her only on the safe ground of McFadden land.

The doorbell sounded strangled, as if someone had put a hand over its mouth before it finished. The door opened and Tulu stood before me: the same and yet completely different—as if she'd grown older at twice the rate I had. Her gray-splashed hair sprang out in a hundred directions in braids woven of such intricate patterns her head looked like a sweetgrass basket unraveling.

Tulu threw her arms open. "Oh, lil' one. You've finally come to my door."

I reached for, then hugged, Tulu. Because she was tall and large boned, it shocked me that she felt as fragile as butterfly wings under my arms. I realized I had never had any idea how old she was. "I hope it's okay to come see you—I'm at Mother's and—"

"Aha, but bad children may not be thrown into the

94

fire—your family must always let you come home."

"How are you, Tulu? How are your children?" I was suddenly ashamed that I didn't remember Tulu's children's names. Had I always been so selfish that I only remembered what Tulu did *for* me?

We entered the cramped living room, and the smells of mildew and Lysol washed over me. Nothing looked dirty, yet everything appeared worn down, cracked, faded.

"My children? They're all wonderful. Spread all over the place. I don't get to see them as much as I'd like—but they're out building their place in this wide world."

"Do they come very often?"

"No, and it is hard for an old woman to travel, ahya? But I do talk to them all the time, and all their children. They bought me some fancy cell phone so that they can reach me whenever they want. . . ." She rolled her eyes. "Guess they got tired of me forgettin' to pay the phone bill. Then they'd have to send Sheriff to check on me. Seaboro was about to start charging me for visits." I followed Tulu to the kitchen table. She plopped down on a ladder-back chair that was missing three of its rungs up the back of the seat. "Here, sit, sit." She patted her hand on a chair next to hers.

These women from my childhood—Mother and Tulu—seemed so lonely. Was that what awaited me?

I touched Tulu's arm. "Mother told me about your husband passing. I'm sorry."

"Did she tell you how she almost fainted at the funeral?" Tulu laughed, a rich deep sound.

95

"No. Please tell."

"Well, we have a tradition at Gullah funerals; we do pass the youngest baby back and forth over the grave so that the leaving spirit doesn't come back to bother the child. I thought your mother was gonna leave us right there, on the spot, next to my husband's grave. She began to sway and sweat—'mist,' she'd say—with strangled sounds I'd never done heard from her."

"Oh, I wish I could've seen that." I laughed and hugged Tulu.

"Now, what brings you to me?" Tulu leaned across the table, pushed a jelly jar glass toward me. "Would you like sweet or unsweetened tea?"

"Sweet," I said. "I'm here for the Gullah curriculum I told you about on the phone. Our son just graduated from high school. . . . Anyway, I thought you could help me. So"—I took a deep breath—"I'm here to write it and . . ."

"Figure out what you want."

"No, I just need to do some research."

"You can't lie to me." Tulu stood, holding her hand to her back. "You can't be telling me stories. I'll be the one to tell the stories around here." She opened a cupboard and reached in, pulled down a box and placed it on the table in front of me. "This is yours."

"Mine?" I touched the wooden box, ran my fingers along a dolphin etched in the top of the pine. "I don't . . . remember this." I looked up at Tulu.

"You threw it away the morning you swam like you were headed to Tybee Island after that terrible fire. I

96

found it in the trash behind the house—knew you needed to keep it, that someday you would come back for it."

A knifelike pain shot through my forehead. The box. Dear God, how could I have forgotten about the box? Tim had made it for me. It was filled with scraps of paper that Danny and I had written our dreams on. I placed a hand over my eyes. "Tulu, I forgot about the box."

"That, right here, is your problem, lil' one. You've forgotten about it. . . ." Tulu lifted the box in the air and then placed it squarely on my lap. "I knew you'd come back here one day, come to see me. I didn't know what would bring you, but I knew it wouldn't be for the reasons you thought. You're not here to write a curriculum. . . . You're here to remember who you are."

"No . . ."

"I'm afraid so, my dear. But if you'd like to say it's the curriculum you're seekin,' then we'll start talking about it now."

"Now. Yes, now would be good." I shoved the box to the side of the table as if a serpent resided under the bottlenose dolphin.

"I knew you wasn't swimming into that sea to kill yourself, Meridy."

I leaned across the table. "How did you know that?"

"Your spirit, little one. Your spirit—it shone brighter, longer and more shimmery than any one young soul I'd ever met."

"That's not what Mother would have said." I fingered the file folder in front of me, needing to talk about the history of the Gullah, but also needing to discover what shimmery soul Tulu could possibly be talking about.

"You do what we all do—you only remember what you want, what serves your idea of who you are. And our mothers' voices speak the loudest in our head. But you were a wild child, full of life and longing. I saw you going through life with your arms wide open. Laughter be pouring from your mouth. Love be swelling everywhere. Then I saw all that wither. . . . I knew it would come back one day."

I closed my eyes and tried to find the girl who was full of all Tulu had seen in her. But I couldn't get past the fear and smoke that came after.

I opened my eyes, pulled a pen from my bag, lifted my iced tea and drank the entire glass in one long swallow as if it were whiskey. "Tell me a little bit about the Gullah culture, Tulu. Where did it come from? And why? I'll divide this into five days with a different subject each day." I held out the paper I'd written the outline on.

Day One: History and Proverbs
Day Two: Stories/Songs/Parables
Day Three: Folk Medicine
Day Four: Sweetgrass Baskets
Day Five: Burial Customs and Names

"Yes." Tulu nodded. "This is good. I'll start with the history—because it is what makes us who we are. As we say, *'If you don't know where you are going, you should know where you came from.'*" She winked and lifted her chin.

"Okay, Tulu. I know your tricks by now. We are talking about this curriculum, not me."

"Ah." She rolled her eyes. "No tricks here—you're just hearing what you need to be hearing."

"The history, Tulu. The history, please." I lifted my pen.

Tulu took a deep breath, settled back in her chair. "The Gullah culture is still alive here. It is not just a history in the past. It is all over these here islands. I am a *binyah*—meaning I come from here, a descendant of the West Africans brought here to the Lowcountry to work as slaves. Sixth generation." She nodded as if she saw the other five generations at the side door of her shack. "Visitors and newcomers are *cumyahs*. Our culture grew out of the West African culture. We farmed, worked the rice and cotton fields before we were freed and offered a chance to purchase the land. The way we've stayed here has let us keep our culture longer than any slave descendants in America. Everyone thinks it is just the language, but it is so much more than the Gullah language—it is the struggle, spirituality, perseverance and tradition. We keep our traditions— whether it is the sweetgrass baskets, casting the net for seafood, our stories, or music."

"Yes." I leaned forward. "More . . ."

"The language is a combination of all the languages brought from different communities on the rice coast of West Africa. To communicate, the slaves combined similar words and phrases from their own languages with the English to form the Gullah language."

As Tulu told me the history of her African culture for the next hour, the information added little to what I'd already read on the Internet or in history books, but her melodic voice with its authentic Gullah clip made what she was saying come alive and fed my hunger for her stories and songs.

"Lil' one, that is all for today. You can find a list of proverbs anywhere. I can tell you my favorites, though. . . ."

"I bet I remember some." I smiled.

"Come back when you are ready for more."

"I'm ready now."

"No, you're not. You have other things you need to attend to for a little while and I'm . . . tired."

"Oh." I stood. "I'm so sorry. I've exhausted you." I glanced around the kitchen. Plywood shelves were lined with canned foods and exquisite sweetgrass baskets filled with vegetables, mail, sewing and other paraphernalia. I walked over, touched a basket. "These are amazing, Tulu. Did you make them?"

"Aye." She nodded.

"These are worth a lot of money to the *cumyahs,* ya know?"

She laughed. "I don't make them for money. They keep my soul satisfied and my hands useful." She walked over, picked up an empty basket. "Here, this one is for you."

The basket was larger than the others, woven in an

intricate pattern. The design, I remembered, was called a "fanner"—a flat basket with a small slanting rim that was used to separate the chaff from the rice.

"I can't take your most beautiful fanner, Tulu."

"Oh, *yes,* you can. You go on now and get started on your own journey."

I held the basket, stretched, lifted my papers from the table. "Thank you so much. I'll come back for more. At least I have an outline now. . . . I can begin to write and then we can go over each subject."

Tulu grinned. "You can find out any of this at the Penn Center in Beaufort."

"Not as good as finding it out from you."

"Use me. Then . . . use me as a reason to stay."

I waved my hand. "I don't need a reason. . . . I'm . . ."

Tulu reached over and hugged me. "I have one more piece of Gullah history for you today, little one."

"What's that?"

"In our culture, when you're seeking the sacred, you know you've come out on the other side when someone gives you something in a dream."

"I'll use that in the section on stories, songs and parables." I bit my lower lip.

"It's not a story or a parable."

"I'm just seeking some history." I smiled, hugged her again. "And you're giving me information. Guess I'm all set." I took in the broken house, the crippled chairs, and then Tulu reached under her chair and handed me the pine box.

I shook my head. "I don't need that."

Tulu placed it on the kitchen table and abruptly walked toward the front door. I picked up the box without looking directly at it and followed her outside. I hugged her good-bye and went to my car, where I dumped my papers in the trunk.

The car ride home wound down dirt roads leading from Tulu's neighborhood, through oak-shaded lanes of leaning shanties, over the bridge crossing the creek to my home ten minutes away. I drove by Lowcountry arts and crafts stores and sweetgrass basket stands, then past the stone and brick entry signs leading to River Oaks—my strip of land.

Once the carved wooden box was shoved beneath my bed, and my files were stowed on the desk, I went downstairs to call Beau. The answering machine with my voice answered. "You've reached the Dresden home. We're not here; leave a message." Beau wouldn't even check these messages—I was always the one to check the home machine. Home was my domain; anything important for him would go to the office and Elaine, his assistant. It was Sunday and no one would answer at his office. Instead of leaving a message, I pressed the pound button to enter my code. There was a voice mailbox full of reminders: the book club, Carol's surgery—friends were organizing dinners for the family—Beth's birthday luncheon.

I hung up and stretched my neck. I was shirking my duties. Although I'd once cut high school classes for the thrill of watching an incoming storm raising the waves to record heights, I was a different woman now.

The need to talk to my son filled me: I dialed B.J.'s number only to receive his voice mail also. Voice mail everywhere—I wanted a human.

I ran up the stairs I had once thought I could fly down and changed into a sundress, slipped on the sandals with the tiny shells that matched the trim on the dress. I'd stop by Mother's luncheon, maybe find more common ground between us. I clipped my hair into a barrette at the base of my neck just like Mother preferred.

I wound my way among the tables until I found the neat knot of Mother's hair. The women sat around a table in the Seaboro Tearoom—once a farmhouse saved by the diligent efforts of the Ladies of Seaboro Society. According to them, tearing down old buildings for further development was the eighth deadly sin.

Ten faces turned and looked up at me as I touched her shoulder. "Hello, Mother. I finished my work early and thought I'd stop by."

She looked at me. "Well, hello there, darling. I thought you weren't coming—and you're twenty minutes late and there are no more seats." Her face appeared slanted as if half of it wanted to welcome me and the other half disapproved. All of sudden I remembered once showing up at a tenth-birthday party in shorts and my favorite striped T-shirt, only to find all the other girls had worn taffeta party dresses—no one had told me it was a dress-up tea party. The same sinking realization of my own inadequacy came now.

"I'm sorry." My voice was tinny and hollow. "Thought I'd . . ."

A woman stood, laughed. "Meridy Dresden, you sit right here while I go get the hostess for another chair. We haven't even ordered food yet. It is so good to see you." She walked around the table, hugged me.

Who was she? I smiled at her. "Thank you."

"You don't remember me, do you?" She lifted her eyebrows—eager.

I smiled. "I know you. . . . I just forget how."

"LuAnn Martin, Danny's aunt." She threw her arms wide-open.

I glanced around the table; all the women stared at me with their mouths open like they wanted to say something but couldn't. Danny's aunt—how humiliating that I hadn't remembered. Somehow years of Southern etiquette reared a beautiful, polite head, and I hugged Mrs. Martin.

I looked at Mother, her face blanched and closed, and I once again understood the disgrace I had brought to the McFadden family name. "Thanks, LuAnn . . . Mrs. Martin . . . I just wanted to stop by and say hello to Mother on my way to . . . Y'all go ahead and have a nice luncheon."

"No, dear, we insist that you stay." Mrs. Martin grabbed my hand.

Insisting was a nonnegotiable act of obligation. I smiled.

"Meridy," said a woman whose hair was more lavender than the white it was meant to be, "do you remember when you took cotillion and lost your white gloves six weeks in a row?" The woman laughed. "I bet you don't even remember that." It was Mrs. Hodge, the cotillion, dance and etiquette teacher.

"Want to know a secret?" I asked, winking. "I didn't lose them—I hid them every week, hoping you wouldn't give me another pair. I will now officially apologize."

Laughter poured across the table. I sat on a chair Mrs. Martin had the hostess bring for me.

"You don't think I knew that, my dear? You were quite the adorable handful. I'm so glad to see you with such a nice life."

"Well, thank you, Mrs. Hodge. Yes, a nice life."

Conversation around the table turned to censored books in the library, to gossip about Seaboro names I didn't recognize, until Charlotte Hamlon spoke of Tim. She was a pinched-faced woman, her face and mouth tight in an expression of disapproval she'd probably made her entire life. Red lipstick had bled into the lines around her mouth.

"Well, I heard through the grapevine that Tim Oliver has agreed to pay the historical society the full amount for the renovation," Charlotte said.

You are the grapevine, I wanted to say but didn't.

Mrs. Martin lifted her sweet tea. "You sure about that, Charlotte?"

"Oh, yes. I'm sure. I do believe the final straw was when we asked his mother to take just a small sabbatical from the society meetings." Charlotte held her

105

thumb and forefinger a millimeter apart to show her sarcasm for the length of the sabbatical.

I gasped. "You what?"

Charlotte turned to me and squinted her eyes as if she had never seen me show up. "Did you say something, dear?"

I blushed, held both palms in the air.

"Well," Charlotte continued, "we can probably get started on the renovations as soon as next month, if this is the case."

Tim's face, smiling and open as he walked through the maritime forest, came to me. I spoke before I knew what I was saying. "I have a better idea for raising money for the Keeper's Cottage."

Mother's hand fell on my knee, squeezed. I firmly slid her hand off my leg and continued. "Our private school at home always raises lots of money with an arts festival. Where are there more arts than here?" I glanced around the table. Forks were poised in midair, mouths were open, but no one spoke. Maybe no one ever crossed Charlotte Hamlon—but this was Tim we were talking about.

I continued in a stream of flowing words I didn't stop. "Anyway, even today when I was driving through Seaboro County, I saw stands and shops selling original artwork. Y'all are constantly trying to get the outside world to notice the merits, of which there are many, of Seaboro. Gathering artists from here to Savannah to Hilton Head to Charleston would bring that attention. Don't you think bringing the arts here makes so much sense?"

Charlotte took a long swallow of her tea. "Dear, that just wouldn't work at all. Not one little bit. We could never raise the amount of money we need at a festival."

Everyone avoided my eyes and the talk shifted, awkward and stilted, to Mrs. Foster's house and, oh, yes, how her son's wild children had tipped the casket when they ran through the church parlor.

I nibbled on my pecan chicken salad and listened to Mother: a woman who smiled and talked and offered warmth and support to everyone at the table—except me.

CHAPTER SEVEN

"It's impossible to get straight wood from crooked timber."
—GULLAH PROVERB

Sunlight fractured into arrows off the stern of the metal sloop. In the past few days I'd become accustomed to the quiet that was never really silent—the cry of a loon, the song of the marsh frog, the whisper of the tide rising or falling. I leaned into the filled silence. I didn't even care where Tim took me as we rode over the waves. It had been so long, so damn long, since I'd been out on the water.

I sat on the back bench of the boat, my face lifted to the sun. Tim piloted the boat in the front—looking back at me every few minutes. I was so content to be on the water. In the past years when we'd come to visit Mother, the boys had gone sailing, fishing, swimming, while I visited with the relatives, cooked the meals and cleaned up, shopped and read books to quell the reminders of the past that rose and fell outside the windows of my home.

This was the trip Tim had promised me the first day I'd come to Seaboro. I'd arrived an hour early, dangling my legs over the dock. For two days in a row, I'd worn a pair of khaki shorts and a tie-dyed T-shirt with the words PEACE, LOVE AND CRABS, which I'd found in the dresser in my room. It was probably left by one of Sissy's twin daughters, who spent the night with Grandma when Sissy and her husband, Penn, were away. I laughed to think of what Annie and Amanda would say if they saw me now.

Tim turned at the sound of my laughter and lifted his eyebrows, then raised his hat in a salute. He throttled the boat forward and the wind settled as he steered into a slip in an unfamiliar marina. I stood and walked to the bow, motions I thought I'd long forgotten came to me easily as I jumped to the dock, dropped the side buoys and tied the ropes around the cleats.

"Where are we going?" From the dock, I looked down at Tim as he grabbed a bag from below the seats.

"We're going to an island where you need an escort. It's owned by a heritage trust and this company will take us out." Tim pointed at a boat with the words LOWRY LOWCOUNTRY scrawled across the side in black letters.

I tilted my head. "Island? Why?"

Tim jumped from the boat, put his arm around my shoulder. "I'm taking you out to the island where they found Danny that day . . . three days later."

A numb rush began at my temples and pushed forward and upward through my head; a thin veil of confusion covered my thoughts. "No" was all I managed to mutter.

"Yes." He squeezed my shoulders.

I pushed him away, stumbled backward on the dock. He grabbed me, steadied me before I fell into the river.

"This was not nice, Tim. You should have told me. . . ."

"You wouldn't have come."

"Maybe I would have come; maybe I wouldn't." I kicked at the cleats, and pain shot through my toe to my ankle. Skipping backward, I hollered at Tim, "You should have told me where we were going. Take me home." I waved my arms frantically in the air. "Forget it. I'll take myself home." I lurched forward, stomped up the dock toward the boathouse and street.

Laughter rolled across the waves still bouncing against the dock. I twirled around, my big toe throbbing.

"It is not funny, Timothy Oliver."

"Oh, yes, it is." He ran toward me, grabbed me by the shoulders and spun me in a circle. "Here is the Meridy McFadden I once knew." He kissed my cheek. "When did she show up?"

Blood rushed into the numb places of my mind. Tears

replaced my anger. "I'm sorry, I'm horrid. I'm sorry, I know you're trying to . . . what are you trying to do?" I wiped away my tears, laughed.

"Letting you say good-bye to someone you loved. I know *they* didn't let you do that, Meridy. I know you never saw him again or saw where they found him. It's time."

I bowed my head. "I shouldn't have said those . . . things to you." I looked out to the sea. "I have no idea what is wrong with me . . . at all."

"Nothing's wrong with you." Tim shaded his eyes with his hands, looked up toward the boathouse. "Here comes our ride."

A man in a faded red T-shirt that looked softened by the sun and sea walked toward us. Brown curls flashed with streaks of sun. His steps were long and when he reached us, his face broke into a grin. "Hey, I'm Revvy." He thrust out his hand. "At your service."

Tim shook his hand. "Hi, I'm Tim Oliver. . . . This is Meridy Dresden. Thanks for taking us out to Oystertip. Did your partner tell you why?" Tim glanced at me.

"Sure." Revvy nodded, tipped his baseball cap.

I stared at the man who was about to take us across the sound to what I thought of as Danny's final resting place. For me, Danny didn't rest in the Seaboro grave-yard, but in the sea he loved. We jumped onto Revvy's boat. Tim and I sat at the bow as it cut through the sound to open sea. This was the memorial service I'd never attended, the funeral I'd missed when my parents had sequestered me in the house and then shipped me off to Daddy's parents.

The day they'd sent me away, I had curled in the backseat of Daddy's Volvo with my pink-and-white-striped suitcase and my favorite pillow, laden with the sorrow now transformed into a boulder inside my heart. Daddy had played an eight-track tape of Simon and Garfunkel as the scenery changed from shaded oaks and sun-dappled dusty roads to harsh black pavement aimed straight through carpets of south Georgia farms. Cotton fields spread beside us like overblown popcorn bowls. The roads rose and dipped with my stomach. Graveyards of discarded tractors, slanted road signs selling jalapeño jelly, silver corn and homemade peach jam replaced the wooden announcements to buy fresh shrimp and Vidalia onions.

When Sissy was born, Mawmaw and Grandpa had retired to a north Georgia mountain community and they'd given the Seaboro house to Mother and Daddy. Sissy's birth was marked by the inheritance of the grand home; my birth was marked by exhaustion. It was only right that now I was being sent away—it didn't matter anyhow. Nothing really mattered.

Every once in a while Daddy looked back at me and grimaced, as if he had stomach pains but couldn't stop the car. I stopped looking back at him; it only caused waves of sorrow, and I'd promised myself that feeling was something I'd never do again. I buried my head in the pillow until the car stopped. I wanted to hear the pure sound of silence in my heart that let me know it felt no more.

"Pumpkin, we're here. Wake up."

"I'm not asleep." I grabbed my suitcase, spilled out of the car in the dazed state I'd become accustomed to the past few days. I stopped, listened. No tide, no wind—just the odd silence of the forest.

I hugged Mawmaw and Granddad and politely thanked them for allowing me to come and stay. I knew this was for my own good. It had been explained to me in various ways: The Lighthouse Keeper's Cottage was the town's historic landmark, and when the graduation party's bonfire had destroyed the cottage, charges were pressed against any teenager involved in the fire or trespassing. Mother and Daddy had told the police chief, coincidentally a second cousin, that I had not seen the gas thrown on the bonfire—which was determined to be the cause of the fire—and I hadn't. Friends had also told the police the same thing: Meridy McFadden had been nowhere around; they didn't know where she'd been. Mother and Daddy had never asked where I was or what I knew. So paralyzed in my armor of grief, fear and isolation from the outside world where blame throwing existed, I had been completely unable to tell the truth. If they'd only asked, I might have told, but they didn't and the family name was left untarnished.

Mother and Daddy had also explained to me that the best way for me to get over the devastation and grief was to escape, focus on preparing for university and resting. Avoidance and Repression, the family motto.

This memory brought a profound sense of loneliness. I reached my hand across the seat to Tim and he leaned toward me. "Whatcha thinking?"

"Remember when Mother and Daddy made me . . . leave?"

"Of course." His words filtered into the wind and were carried back toward Revvy.

"What?" Revvy cupped his hands around his mouth and hollered toward us.

"Nothing," Tim mouthed, shook his head and leaned closer to me. "I remember. You never really came back."

"No, I didn't . . . but I'm here now."

Tim squeezed my shoulders, pointed to a growing curve of tree and a thin stretch of beach. "That's Oystertip."

I nodded and tried very hard, unsuccessfully, not to envision Danny's body washing from the Lighthouse Keeper's Cottage, carried by the waves and wind to the shore of a barrier island.

The boat slid into a dock at the tip of the island. Tim jumped off and helped Revvy tie up the boat.

"You coming?" Tim held out his hand.

"I don't know. . . ." I glanced back to the mainland, toward safety. What was I thinking, coming out here? This was insane. My hair was probably a mess from the wind and I was sure I looked like an idiot in a teenager's T-shirt. My legs were way too big to be wearing shorts—I should've worn capris. Yet I knew where I was taking my mind—to the land of preoccupation with looks, perfection, clothing and image—a place far from nature and sea, death and chaos.

I held up my hand to allow Tim to pull me to the dock. Revvy walked toward a small building at the end of the dock. "Come on, follow me, y'all. I'll take you to the other side of the island in the Gator."

He drove us in what looked like an oversized golf cart, along paths through nature-cluttered acres of land. He explained that the island was a nature refuge. He offered us the names of the nearly extinct plants we passed, animals that scurried into bushes and trees. His explanations and labels didn't diminish the wildness of everything surrounding us. God, Danny would have loved it here.

Revvy stopped the cart, pointed to a strip of beach seen in pieces through the palmetto bushes. "I think you told me you needed to go to this area."

"Is this the northern tip?" Tim asked.

"Yep." Revvy jumped from the Gator. "Now, on barrier islands the sand washes from the north end to the south end, but this is where your friend would have . . . been found."

"Washed up," I said, and jumped to the gray-brown soil soft enough to take me under, swallow me in the unspoiled unruliness of nature. I sucked in my breath and my heartbeat rose higher in my chest. Earth and sky and sea all met in the place where Danny came to rest.

I turned away from Tim and Revvy and walked toward the beach. No path led to the sea and I pushed away thorns grabbing my legs, yanked holly branches from snagging my hair.

"Always look down for water moccasins. Be careful." Revvy's voice came muffled through the trees.

"She grew up here. . . ." Tim's voice called back as he came up behind me; branches snapped under his weight.

I burst through to blue, so much blue, nothing but blue sea and sky. The land ended abruptly in cobbled mounds of oyster shells and broken clam halves. I stumbled backward to avoid the waves licking the empty shells. Tim ran into my back, his chin bumping the top of my head. "Slow down. . . ." He laughed. "You're gonna end up swimming back to Seaboro."

"This is where . . . they found him?" I swept my hand across the expanse of blue as if it were the only shade of color left on the earth.

"Yes," I saw Tim say more than I heard him.

I squatted, touched a shell, understanding that Danny's body had drifted here twenty-six years ago. It could not have touched this shell, this place, but underneath the shells and sand lay the same earth. I looked up at Tim—now he was eighteen and had just lost his best friend.

"Oh, Tim." I held up my hand.

He pulled me up to stand. "You know I lost my two best friends that day," he said.

I wrapped my arms around him. "I never thought of that. . . . I was so absorbed with all I had lost, I never thought of all you'd lost. I'm a selfish woman who was once a selfish girl. God, Tim, I'm so sorry. I never called or wrote or visited."

"Neither did I, Meridy. Neither did I. It was all just . . . too much."

"How did you stay here?" I stared into his face. "You've built a life. You've . . . done fine."

"I didn't leave and I believe it's easier that way. I see the seasons change, the land change, lives change. It's all stayed the same for you—it's all still here and it's probably like it all happened yesterday."

"Tim." I took a deep breath, sat on a log. "I need to tell you something."

He sat down next to me. "What is it?"

"This'll take a while." I looked at him.

"Got nothing but time." He threw a shell toward the waves.

I glanced out toward the endless blue and told Tim Oliver the story I had never told a living soul, never uttered a word about until now. It was time, and the story came out fully formed as I unlocked the door to the sequestered dwelling of hidden words and deeds.

PART II

"How many of us dare to open ourselves to that truth
which would make us free?"

—MADELEINE L'ENGLE, *Walking on Water*

CHAPTER EIGHT

"A burned child dreads fire."
—GULLAH PROVERB

High school graduation had tasted like the freedom of a dive into the river off the dock behind Danny's house. We'd waited so long—since we were twelve years old—to taste this freedom, to drink of it, immerse ourselves in it. Free. Free from my mother's cold stares when my grade point average was three points below Sissy's. Free from lectures about my irresponsibility for drag-racing Danny's Camaro on the dirt road behind the old moonshine still. Free from expectations I could never meet and didn't want to anyway.

The graduation ceremony had ended as hundreds of thousands of graduations had ended before and since. Hats flew in the air; my friends all swore they'd change the world, that they'd be different and better than those before us. I knew where I was going and why. Danny and I would be married, have babies that swam in the sea before they walked, and live a life of beauty and freedom.

Danny dropped me off at home for my family celebratory tea before the graduation party on the beach at the old Lighthouse Keeper's Cottage. This tea was a compromise Mother would never have made years before. Lately, though, she appeared too exhausted to argue with me about much—as if I'd finally worn her down after eighteen years of behavior inappropriate for a McFadden lady.

I kissed Danny good-bye in the car, my graduation hat in my lap, his blue-and-green tassel dangling from the rearview mirror.

"I'll pick you up at seven thirty for Tim's party," he said.

"You better come in and say hello to Mawmaw and Granddad."

"Can I do that when I pick you up? I need to get on home too."

I kissed him again. "You can do whatever you want."

"I wish." He kissed the side of my neck.

I leaned back on the vinyl seat and stared at him, touched his cheek. "I love you." I jumped out of the car and leaned in the window, blew him a kiss. "See you at seven thirty."

"Have fun at the tea," he called out the window. Although he couldn't see me, I stuck my tongue out at the receding green Camaro he'd received for his sixteenth birthday; it was already rusting in the salt-laden air of Seaboro—an air that softened everything it touched, except for my mother's heart.

I skipped up the front steps and pretended not to notice Sissy glaring at me through the front curtain pulled to one side. Nothing would put me in a bad mood today. I had graduated and in less than three months I would leave for the University of South Carolina with Danny. Life had just started and even an uptight tea wouldn't spoil it.

I stopped in the front foyer when I heard my name; Mother was speaking to Uncle Tom. I adored Uncle Tom—Daddy's brother—who always took my side in family arguments. He'd even covered my tracks a few times when I'd snuck out at night. Mother was in mid-sentence. ". . . and I would have had five more children if I'd known they'd be like Sissy. But with my luck I'd have five more Meridys."

Uncle Tom laughed and my stomach plummeted like an elevator dropping out of control. I held my breath.

"You don't mean that, Harriet. I know you don't. She is so full of life and fun," Uncle Tom said.

"She's worn me out, Tom. Just worn me out. I'll miss her. I love her. But she is exhausting."

"Only because you let her be." I heard the sound of a kiss. "Only because you let her be."

"Oh, Tom. Always sticking up for her . . ."

Footsteps approached, but I froze in the hallway. My behavior, my exhausting self, had caused Mother to never have more children. Shame and nausea rose together. I lurched toward the door of the hall bathroom.

Uncle Tom came up behind me. "You okay, Meridy?"

"Yes . . ." I leaned against my uncle's shoulder. "I'm glad you're here."

Tom rubbed the back of my head. "You heard your mother."

"Yes, but I already knew that. I guess I already knew that about myself."

"Oh, she didn't mean it."

I let go of my uncle, stepped back. "Yes, she did. But that's okay, because I'm leaving in three months and she won't be exhausted or miserable any more."

"Only lonely. Now pay no attention to what she said and go in there." He waved toward the living room. "And open all those presents."

"I don't want them."

I ran up the stairs, taking them two at a time. The framed portraits of my relatives along the wall stared at me with their cold, disapproving glares. God, why didn't any of them smile back? Someone had once told me it was because everyone had bad teeth in those days. I believed they didn't smile because they'd all been taught that having fun led to a life of foolishness. First the smile, then eternal damnation. I reached the top landing, ran to my room and slammed the door.

I wouldn't go down and open the presents or face the family I had exhausted. I didn't want to look at my sister in her pressed linen sailor dress with her diamond engagement ring from Penn Warren on her right hand. Of course, Sissy had done it all correctly and been engaged before her junior year in college.

I pulled off my graduation gown and stood in my pink silk sheath dress in the middle of the room. An unnamed dread bubbled below the surface of my skin, and I believed it stemmed from Mother's words—I had exhausted her.

A discernible tug rose below my rib cage—a fight about whether to be the girl Mother expected me to be, or to ride the longing and freedom I constantly felt rising within me. I leaned into the mirror and stared at my graduated face. I wanted to run out to the backyard and swing on the tire swing hanging from the gnarled live oak until the wind washed Mother's words from my mind. Maybe there was a way to ignore the desire to find out what lay around every corner, to ignore the restlessness that rose with the sound of sea and wave, to ignore the want for more and more and more. But if there was a way, I hadn't found it yet.

I rubbed my face, pinched some color into my cheeks. I'd go downstairs and be the girl they wanted me to be, then run to Danny and we'd meet our friends at the old Lighthouse Keeper's Cottage to celebrate at Tim's party. Mother believed I was going to McCall Hampton's graduation party at the Seaboro Yacht Club, but nothing would be more torturous than that.

I opened my bedroom door and ran into Tulu, our housekeeper. She was as dark as the chestnuts I collected in a sweetgrass basket. "Sorry, Tulu . . ." I hugged her; I loved the way Tulu hugged back, as if she knew what a hug really was.

"You ready for your party, lil' one?"

I laughed. "I'm not a lil' one. . . . I graduated today."

She leaned her head back and laughed with the sound of pure unrestraint. Tulu always seemed to enjoy me, but at the same time hold a secret she was never willing to tell. "You might be all grown up, but you must never lose the heart of your lil' one."

"Is that another one of your proverbs?" When, I wondered, had I become too old to crawl in Tulu's lap and listen to a Gullah proverb or ghost story, twist her braids between my fingers?

"Not a proverb, just my truth." Tulu lifted a pile of folded sheets from the hall table.

"Well, if you listen to Mother, I've never lost the little one inside, can't seem to quite get grown-up enough, can I?"

"Getting grown-up is only part of the way life steals your heart."

"Not me, Tulu. Not me."

I walked down the stairs. Tulu's gaze burrowed into my back, and the odd dread I'd felt in my bedroom moments ago returned, bringing a wave of panic. I shook off the emotion and entered the living room, smiled at the family and lifted my cup of tea. Only four more hours until the beach and Danny and our friends surrounded me—I could make it through this to get to that.

I leaned into Danny's chest and he wrapped his arm around my shoulders and pulled me closer as he steered the car with his other hand. "How was the family party?" he asked.

"Same. Sissy was perfect. Mother was critical. Daddy smiled and had another Bushmills on the rocks."

"And you were your adorable self."

"Yeah, tell Mother that. She didn't like my hair down, she didn't like the way I talked to Aunt Maddy, and she definitely didn't like that I was leaving early."

"Well, we're almost home free . . . just a few more months." Danny drove the car down a dirt road obscured by palmetto bushes and clouds of Spanish moss filling in the cracks of light. Leaves and moss brushed up against the sides of the car until Danny parked among the other half-hidden cars and pickup trucks in the empty field behind the maritime forest that bordered the beach.

We had almost taken the Boston Whaler from behind Danny's house, navigating the Seaboro River to the sea, as the Lighthouse Keeper's Cottage sat on the end of a stretch of sand where river met sea. But we hadn't wanted to worry about the tides, so we'd taken Danny's car instead.

I jumped from the passenger side and stretched my arms to the sky. "Only three more months." My voice rose high and strong, and then stopped at the top of the oak canopy. Something wasn't right, something felt . . . shifted. I glanced over at Danny pulling a cooler from the trunk. Maybe graduation wasn't all it was cracked up to be; maybe I wasn't as excited as I thought I'd be.

"Danny?" He looked up at me, and my heart swelled with love.

"What?" He dropped the cooler on the gray dirt. A puff of dust rose, settled at his feet.

"Is something wrong?" My hands fluttered in the air. "I feel like there's something . . . wrong."

"Nothing wrong here, you?"

"I guess not." I moved toward him.

"Okay, then, let's get this party going." Danny walked around to the front of the car and pulled a cassette tape from inside. "Can you grab the tape player?"

I nodded and yanked the player from the backseat, stepped into rhythm with Danny and headed toward my friends' voices floating through the trees. The sea's full voice mixed with the distant cry of a gull. A cluster of our friends stood around a pit in the sand that Tim had dug out with a shovel. He threw clumps of sand at Karen, the girl he'd been trying to hook up with since eighth grade. It still didn't seem to be working, as she stomped away, rolling her eyes at him. Tim hollered instructions to our other friends as he organized his party at the beach. Bill Murphy piled dried driftwood to one side of the pit.

Tim nodded at us, shouted, "Welcome to my party." He pointed to a box in the sand. "I even bought firecrackers."

Danny dropped a blanket and cooler onto the sand, and then popped the tape into the player. As Boston blared with as much static as voice, everyone greeted us with lifted beers and "Where've you been?"

"Meridy's family had a . . . tea." Danny lifted a few pieces of wood and began to build a pyramid inside the pit.

Bill tossed a horseshoe crab shell into the woodpile. "Yeah, wouldn't want to come without her, would you?" He ducked, expecting at least a punch to the arm.

"Hell, would you?" Danny grinned and threw another log onto the pile.

Bill groaned and grabbed me by the waist. "You're lucky I love you guys so much or you'd make me sick to my stomach." He lifted his beer, guzzled and then crunched the can on his head.

"Bill, you're crazy." I ducked out from under his arm. "You're gonna get kicked out of the Citadel in the first week."

"If only I'd be so lucky." Bill turned around. "Beer, I need a beer, someone."

Tim—we'd all stopped calling him Timmy in eighth grade by threat of death and dismemberment—tossed a beer from the cooler. Bill caught the can in midair and yelled to the night sky, "We did it—we survived Seaboro High School." Then Tim lit the logs and drift-wood; the fire reached for the stars just like I felt I was ready to do—burst skyward.

At least thirty of our friends, who'd all said they were going to McCall's party, lingered around the coolers, the fire and the warmth of our common cele-bration. I thought of poor McCall staring out the door looking for all the people who'd said they were coming. She probably had her hair up in a bow and wore one of those dresses that looked like the material came from my grandmother's couch.

Fifty yards away from the roaring fire, the old Lighthouse Keeper's Cottage leaned toward the sea. The strip of sand the cottage stood upon had once been wider, longer. If I squinted, I could see the quaint cottage as it must once have been—white rockers on the railed porch facing the sea, a split-cedar shake roof sloping down to protect the lighthouse keeper and his family. Now the porch sagged and pieces of the roof had long since washed away like an old man losing his hair.

The cottage was located behind barricades of yellow tape that read CAUTION, metal signs warning trespassers of being prosecuted and a list of the dangers of the crumbling house. None of us had ever paid attention to the warnings. There was no counting the number of Seaboro teenagers who had lost their virginity on the disintegrating heart-of-pine floors, or the parties held in the wee hours of the morning when parents thought each child was spending the night elsewhere. The cottage held memories of guiding ships in the early 1800s, the Civil War, hurricanes, the encroaching sea and the hearts of Seaboro youth who found the cottage a refuge while growing up.

The wind had risen along with the song and drink. It was graduation night and the Seaboro police would probably ignore the sounds of partying coming from the area of the Keeper's Cottage.

Bill danced, swaying to music that someone had changed to something softer, dampening the mood and slowing down the party. Tim appeared to finally reach his goal with Karen, who moved with him toward the cottage in a half dance, half stumble.

I laughed and pointed at Tim, whispered to Danny, "Looks like he's finally got what he wanted. Only took him five years."

Danny squeezed my hand. "It's about damn time she woke up to Tim's better attributes."

"Which wouldn't be dancing."

Couples started to pair off in the darkening night. Others huddled and whispered and retold the stories of high school. Memories and gossip gathered in a farewell celebration that seemed as sad as it was joyful. We had survived, but survival also meant separation. Some were leaving for college, others staying to run family businesses, or to attend the local junior college. Everything either had changed or was just about to change.

We stood on the cusp of *before* and *after* and we all recognized it. Nothing would be the same and we made promises that we understood we couldn't keep—"Best Friends Forever" carved in the sand in a futile attempt to stay what would easily be washed away with the next high tide.

Bill sidled up next to Danny and me. "This is just so . . . sad."

"Really, you think so?" I said. He'd obviously had too many beers. "I think it's just . . . awesome."

"That's because you know what you're doing, where you're going and who you're going with. Not me. I have no idea what to do next."

Bill had been the quarterback, the homecoming king and the next best thing to a celebrity in Seaboro. But in the first football game of his senior year, he'd torn a ligament in his knee and dislocated his hip, and he hadn't been recruited for a single college team—his only goal.

"You'll figure it out, Bill." I hugged him. "You can do a million more things than play football."

"I don't think so." He lifted his head and howled at the moon, then looked down at me. "I really don't think so."

I wanted to cry for Bill, for his lost dreams, but instead he shouted, "Hey, let's get this party back on track." He ran back toward the cars. "What we have here is a dwindling fire and a dying party."

As cheers rose, I snuck closer to Danny's side. With ABBA playing in the background, with Danny breathing the same air, with friends laughing and mingling on the beach while deciding who was worthy of midnight kisses once the fire went out, I truly believed life would always feel this good, would always be so right. I sighed.

"You okay?" Danny asked.

"More than." I ran my fingers through his hair and it was his turn to sigh.

He wrapped his arms around me. "Come here, you." He nuzzled my neck, picked up a box. "Let's set off those firecrackers." He grabbed a handful. "Follow me."

I did; I always would. He led me to the edge of a sand dune that dipped toward a tangle of sea oats with a long stretch of fragile picket fencing meant to stop erosion.

Danny pulled me behind the sand dune, where we could hear but not see our friends. He wrapped his arms around me. "My sweet Meridy." We tumbled down to the sand.

Our love had always been sweet and stolen in the natural world that surrounded us, as if the land brought us together as much as the love buried inside us. He unbuttoned the top of my embroidered white peasant blouse I'd bought six months ago and saved for this night, ran his finger across my collarbone. Even with the evening sun still warming the sand, I shivered.

"Meridy, I can't believe we're finally here . . . done, graduation."

"Hmmm."

He ran his callused fingertips along my skin. "Remember the day we met?"

"Yes," I murmured.

"You know you woke up my heart that day."

Danny wasn't given to romantic words; he just loved me in the way he treated me, held me, took care of me. I leaned away from him. "That is the . . . nicest thing you've ever said to me."

He laughed. "Did it come out right? I practiced, ya know."

I punched the side of his arm. "Way to ruin the most romantic moment I've ever had."

"But I mean it. I've thought about it a lot this week . . . you know, with graduation and our whole life ahead of us and all that. I mean, who stays with the girl they fell in love with when they were twelve? Nobody. And I sorta started to wonder why we did, how we could. And the only answer I have is that when you jumped off that dock with that damned green dress flying over your head . . . you woke my heart up, so then you got to keep it."

I buried my face in his neck. "I love you. I swear you've saved my life. I don't know how I could've survived my family without you."

"Actually . . ." He kissed each corner of my lips, ran his mouth down my neck. "You probably would've gotten along a lot better without me. . . . I'm half the damn problem."

"No, you're the solution."

Danny ran his finger inside my blouse, lifted my frilled denim skirt to my knees.

I gently pushed him away. As much as I wanted him, as much as my heart stretched and reached for him, there were too many people around. "Danny, let's shoot off those firecrackers. . . ."

He moaned and pulled me close. "You make me crazy, Meridy."

"Good." I smiled.

Danny grabbed a handful of firecrackers. I stepped back; the things scared me, but Danny loved them. He buried a tube in the sand, lit the fuse and grabbed my hand as we ran back to watch it fly upward, sputter and explode in the naked sky in a spray of blue and white. The sparks fell to the sea and sizzled on the dark waves.

Cheers came from the crowd at the other end of the

beach as they watched our display. I looked at Danny's face lit in the scattered light of the gibbous moon and flying sparks of the firecrackers.

Finally he grabbed the last one, larger and wider than the others. "The monster," he said, handed me the lighter. "You do this big one. It's called a Typhoon—it has streamers. Should be cool."

I lit the fuse; a sense of freedom and daring grabbed me as we backed away. Danny pulled me farther back this time, toward the Keeper's Cottage.

Wind rose with the ascension of the firecracker, caught the streamers in its breath and threw the sparks and scattered embers across the sky, across the beach and to the roof of the Keeper's Cottage. I gasped, grabbed Danny's hand.

"Oh, shit." Danny released my hand, backed up.

It happened so fast—the fire, the screams—and I didn't know until later, much later, that at the same moment I'd lit the Typhoon, Bill Murphy had thrown a can of gasoline onto the bonfire in an attempt to reignite the dwindling flames. Nature joined forces in wind, flame and dark night to create a memory burned into my mind—a branding of guilt.

The flames fed off the rotting cottage's roof, and the embers landed on small piles of brush. Fire leaped off the cedar in dancing patterns, reaching like a tongue over the house.

Danny stared at me; the fire was spreading so quickly that I hadn't yet spoken a word. Danny ran toward the cottage even as I reached out to stop him. I screamed, but the wind and waves swallowed my voice.

I shivered on the top of the sand dune as Danny disappeared into the chaos of the night gone wrong. This was it—the cause of the dread in my belly before the party. In the dark-blanket night now filled with flame, the cottage leaned inward from the encroaching flames carried in whole pieces by the wind.

I ran to the side of the cottage where the fire now dominated the night. I ran into Lilly McIntyre—her mouth opened, closed. I grabbed her shoulder. "Go get help. Call for help."

Lilly's voice came strangled. "Bill . . . he threw a gas can in the fire and it went up as tall as the sky, I swear to God, Meridy. He was swallowed by the fire. . . . He won't answer me. He won't move." She pointed toward the sea. "He's just lying there." Lilly turned and ran toward the parked cars.

Fragmented sentences hammered into my mind like metal spikes. My feet carried me toward the cottage, toward the stench of burning wood and the screaming voices of helpless panic.

I lowered my head; I'd once heard that if you stayed below the smoke, you were okay.

Danny.

In the Cottage.

I ran around to the side of the Keeper's Cottage, crawled when I choked on the black smoke, the sand rising in the current of the fire. Smoke poured through the gaping wound of the side door to the kitchen. I pushed my head in the door, screamed,

"Danny . . ." Louder. "Danny!"

Only the sounds of hissing, creaking and a faint muffled human groan reached my ears. I pushed on, feeling my way past the cracked countertops and empty cupboards into the back hall leading to the two cramped front rooms. I crawled down the hall, inhaling only to scream Danny's name again and again.

I bumped into something hard, firm . . . a leg. I grabbed it. Danny. I pulled myself up. "Get out! Get out!" I screamed at him. I couldn't see him, but I knew him.

His arms reached for me, lifted me up, threw me over his shoulders. "Meridy, get the hell out of here. Now."

"Come with me, come with me," I hollered, pumped my legs against him. I choked, lifted my head to try to find his eyes, just his eyes, before the descending blanket of darkness completely enveloped me. I couldn't find his face, couldn't catch my breath as he ran carrying me.

He placed me down on the sand behind the dune, then turned again toward the flames. I reached for him and tried to find words inside my parched throat. "Stay with me," I said, but I heard only cracked sounds of desperation. And then the darkness became complete.

Sirens screamed inside my head; my throat ached for water. I tried to open my eyes but found them incapable of seeing more than a sliver of light. My hand banged against metal, voices came loudly through the fog of what felt like sleep but was something far from sleep.

Remembrance poured in like the smoke I'd sensed descending while I'd lain across Danny's shoulders. "Danny." I thought I screamed, yet nothing came out but a pure, raw animalistic wail. I forced my eyes as far open as I could; I was belted to a stretcher next to an ambulance parked in the sand. Strobe lights flashed against the night. Figures moved back and forth whispering to each other. No one looked at me.

I reached down and fumbled with the belt, undid its latch. A plastic mask fell from my face: oxygen. I was falling to the ground, jolted by sand and pine straw. The figures turned. Someone, I thought it was Karen, yelped and lurched toward me. My legs gave way beneath me when I tried to stand.

"Stop, stop. You'll hurt yourself." A woman in a blue uniform came into view and knelt next to me. "You must be still. You've inhaled too much smoke. . . . Be still."

I rolled to my right as if I could escape this woman telling me what to do. I grabbed Karen's ankle. "Danny . . ."

Karen sobbed, buried her head in her hands and ran away. Nothing else needed to be said. I allowed the darkness to come again—settled willingly into the blank space where I wouldn't face what waited for me in the light.

I wasn't able to attend Danny's funeral—the doctor said I couldn't. The smoke inhalation had turned to bronchitis, and the meds they gave me allowed me to slide down the long, narrow tunnel of darkness I craved.

Whenever I emerged to the fierce light of Danny's absence, the medication would take me back down and I went willingly, eagerly. In this place I found scattered, gentle-edged memories of Danny: on the boat teaching me how to hook a worm, in a hammock asleep as I lay against his chest, in the woods carving arrows out of broken twigs with his pocket knife.

My favorite memory came as the pain medication drew me under slowly, evenly, to the softer parts of my dreams. Here Danny, Timmy and I played manhunt, hide-and-seek in the dark, with the other neighborhood kids. We were thirteen years old. I crouched behind a palmetto tree that had been shattered by lightning. The branches, dead and dry, hid me in their shadows. The night had fallen dark and moonless; the stars concealed above low clouds. The thrill of manhunt came when you hid alone, hoping you'd be found, and hoping you wouldn't be found. I heard footsteps and held my breath. A body crouched down next to me. I whispered, "Hey, this is my hiding place . . . Move."

A hand reached out and touched my arm. "It's me . . . shh," Danny's voice said. Somehow he saw better in the darkness than I did. He'd scooted up next to me, shared my hiding place. We didn't say a word for the longest, most precious moments I'd known. We shared that one space under the leaves, below the blank sky. He reached up and ran his finger across my face where a piece of moss tickled. I couldn't see him, but I felt him and it was all I needed.

And it was all I needed as the pain medication drew me to him. I didn't need to see him—just sensed he was there. Each time I thought I drew closer and closer to him in the haze, I'd realize he was gone. Completely gone. But by the time the next medication was given, I'd believe I could find him again or that he'd find me in the darkness as he once had, and would stay with me until we were both found.

I lay in bed for three days, praying that whatever internal damage the smoke had done to my lungs would kill me. When I realized that it wouldn't, I still refused to open my eyes and face the knowledge of Danny's absence—a gaping hole I felt opening beneath me every time I came to consciousness.

On the third day, Doc Hamm came into my room and sat on the edge of the bed. "You're going to be fine, Meridy. Unlike some of the other kids, you're going to be fine."

"Who else died?" I asked with my eyes closed.

"What do you mean, 'Who else'?"

"Who else besides Danny?" My voice sounded monotone, depleted. Doc's eyes lifted. His bushy eyebrows moved together as one. "How did you . . . ?"

"I can feel it. He's gone. Who else?"

"Bill Murphy . . . I guess he's the boy who threw the gas on the fire."

"I didn't see it."

"Now that you're talking, can you remember anything? Can you answer some questions?"

How could I answer questions when there was nothing inside me but a black void? I had no answers, no questions, nothing at all. I shook my head; even words seemed too much of an effort in a world that made no sense, in a world empty of Danny, in a world that would allow a boy like him to die.

Mother's presence filled the room with a combination of cold and panic. I twisted away from her face. Then the bed tipped as Doc Hamm stood up.

"She's still not able to answer questions," he said to Mother.

"Give me some time with her." Mother whispered as if I couldn't hear her.

The bedroom door clicked shut and I buried my face farther into the pillow. Mother was here and Danny was not. There was nothing, absolutely nothing to lift my head for.

"Meridy McFadden, you need to listen to me."

Some younger, more obedient fragment of me rolled over and looked at Mother. "Yes, ma'am."

"You need to know what happened. We have to talk. . . . You will have to leave for a little while."

It didn't matter what Mother said or where I went in this new blank world, so I just nodded.

"Danny and Bill Murphy died in that fire. These are the things that happen when children are irresponsible and foolish, Meridy. I've warned you about this for a very long time. You cannot run around testing fate at every turn, acting as if you have no responsibility or that there are no consequences. I'm going to tell you what happened. Bill Murphy died immediately when the fire blew up in his face after he threw the gas can in the bonfire. All anyone can figure is that either he wanted to die or he was so drunk he didn't know what he was doing. The flames spread quickly in the wind to the cottage. Danny pulled Tim and Karen from the cottage, where they were trapped in an upstairs bedroom. I'm sure Karen's parents do not want to know what she and Tim were doing in an upstairs bedroom of a deserted, condemned cottage at one in the morning."

I rolled away, my emotions as flat as my voice.

"Young lady, roll back over and listen to me. You were part of this and you need to hear what happened."

Yes, that would be the punishment I deserved. I turned over and stared at Mother. "Yes?" I sat up.

"These are the bits and pieces of information that have come from your friends to the police. All of you trespassed, destroyed a town landmark—a historic landmark, for God's sake. All that is left of Seaboro's Keeper's Cottage is the foundation and part of the rear wall to the kitchen." Her face filled with a pained grimace—the look she had when a migraine arrived. "Anyway . . . Danny thought that some other kids were at the top, in the lighthouse tower. God only knows what they'd be doing up there. . . . That tower was threatening to crumble at any moment. All of you thinking that you'll live forever . . ." Mother then stood and paced the room, touching my horseback-riding trophies, my collectible china dolls, then my diploma resting on my desk.

The looming shadow I had avoided for three days now approached and smothered me in the darkening panic of the lost. Sobs rose. I clapped my hand over my mouth. If I started crying now, I'd never stop.

Mother turned back to me. "Danny went to the top of the lighthouse, but no one was there. Whoever it was must've come down on their own. Only one person saw what happened to Danny . . . little Weatherly Jones. She said that Danny stood on the top deck of the lighthouse, screamed down for Tim . . . then turned around and went back in . . . then came out again. They assume he was trapped up there. . . . Then the tower tilted, broke off from the back. Weatherly said it dangled there for a minute before Danny tried to jump from the parapet to the sea. But, of course, the water there is shallow, because of the sand they've deposited."

"Then what?" I found my voice, found my grief, found my desperate need to know.

"Well, it all gets a bit mixed-up after that because no one really saw what happened. Everyone ran from the falling tower."

"Who . . . found him? Where is Danny?"

"Today, this morning . . . they found him, Meridy. He—" Mother's hands fluttered around the air in an aimless, desperate attempt to tell me the unbearable. "His body washed up on Oystertip Island. They still don't know whether he was killed by the fire, the fall, or . . . drowning."

"It was the fall."

Mother turned in a sharp pivot on her high heels. "How do you know that?"

"I can feel it. I know. It was the fall. You can leave now, Mother."

"No, Meridy. I have some more—"

I held up my hand. "Can it wait?" I wanted to descend into the sorrow washing over me, taste it, swallow it whole and pay for my own part in it. There was something I needed to do, couldn't do until Mother left.

"Listen to me. We are going to send you up to Mawmaw and Granddad's in the mountains. You need some rest. It will be absolute chaos here. Everyone will try to find someone to blame. And we know you had nothing to do with it. But whoever took part in the bonfire will have to take responsibility for that. We don't want you mixed up with any of this. You leave for college in three months and—"

"You want to hide me. You're ashamed. I understand."

"We want to protect you. We know that you had nothing to do with building the bonfire that set the cottage on fire. . . . We know you didn't go in the cottage. You need to rest. We are protecting you, Meridy."

"I did go in that cottage and I helped Danny build that bonfire . . . and I set off—"

"No, you didn't." Mother marched toward the door. "No, you did not!"

I lifted an untouched glass of water on my ruffled lilac bedside table and threw the glass across the room. "Danny saved my life too. Mine too. I did go in

140

there . . . looking for him. And I wouldn't have left without him. He carried me out. I. Wouldn't. Have. Left. Him." Fear rose with the sorrow in a swelling silence. "He left me. I asked him to stay." But I said these last words so quietly, I was sure Mother didn't hear them.

Mother stared at the shattered crystal on the flowered carpet, then at me. "We must get you to Mawmaw's. I'll get Tulu to come clean this up. You rest now." She turned, left the room, closed the door behind her.

I rose from the bed, walked toward my dresser and stripped off my nightgown. I pulled on a pair of cutoff jean shorts with the peace sign appliqués—Danny's favorite—and a T-shirt. I looked at myself in the gilded mirror over my dressing table. Whoever the blond girl looking back at me was would soon be gone.

The door clicked, opened. I turned to Tulu's angelic face.

"Lil' one, whatchoo doin' out of bed?" she said in a voice that sounded like a soft song.

"There's something I need to do."

Tulu walked toward me, dropped the dust pail and vacuum at the door. "My precious child, 'Death is one ditch you can't jump.'"

"I'm not trying to jump anything." I fled to the bathroom and locked myself in until the vacuum's hum stopped and the click of my bedroom door signaled her departure.

I walked toward my bedroom window. I'd been in and out of that window so many times I had used it almost more than the doors. I slid from the windowsill to the roof, scooted down to the side pillar to meet a trellis of jasmine vines. I climbed on the opposite side so as not to disturb the flowers, then landed on all fours on the manicured lawn behind the house.

The grass felt alive between my toes. I didn't understand how it kept growing, how the birds still flew. Shouldn't everything stop? Even if the grass didn't die with Danny, shouldn't it stop growing? How could everyone and everything just keep blundering ahead? Mother was making plans; friends were being questioned; Danny's body was . . .

The pain was unbearable in a way I'd never known anything else to be. The only way to stop the grief was to get rid of my heart—abolish it. And there was only one place to take my heart: the sea.

I ran across the lawn to where it sloped from manicured grass to a thin line of the gray Lowcountry mixture of sand and dirt; then I turned toward the sea oats and river, which ran to the sea. I stood at the shoreline, the river in a waiting stillness as if it knew what I had come to offer. I waded in to my knees, to the gradation of sand I'd known since I was a toddler, where the river's firm floor sloped to greater depths. I dived in, allowed the water to surround my body, mind, senses and heart. The tide flowed out and I let it carry me. I'd heard that you could hold your breath longer underwater than above water, and I tested this theory to the limit.

I wasn't there for my body to die, only my heart. My

lungs burned and I swam farther out, to a place where I intended to leave behind all I'd ever been. I blew out the last breath resting in the bottom of my lungs and sank deeper. My body ached to pull in a breath, shoot to the surface, but I fought the urge and imagined my heart joining Danny's where I couldn't yet allow my body to go. I said good-bye to all wildness and all unrestraint, all pain and all joy, then envisioned a childlike Meridy sinking to the ocean's floor.

I floated to the surface and lifted my head above the waves, turned onto my back as my lungs gasped for oxygen. I stared up to the sky of so many different shades of blue that it hurt my eyes to look at it. Why wasn't it gray, overcast?

I kicked my legs toward the shore, tasted the salt on my lips, inside my mouth: tears mixed with sea. Then a surge of anger rose and I screamed, against the sky, against Danny's need to save the others. "Why didn't you stay with me? I wouldn't have left you!" I kicked against a dead love, a heaven I no longer believed in and a sea I would never again swim in.

My voice became raw in the mixture of tears, salt water, smoke damage and screams. Then other voices joined mine, panicked voices yelling my name. I flipped over; Mother, Sissy and Tutu stood on the shore hollering, jumping up and down in absurd motions. A figure swam toward me; dark hair and swinging arms cut through the water. For half a breath I thought it was Danny, but it was Daddy.

I moved toward him in a slow crawl until we came

next to each other. Daddy grabbed me, pulled my arm, as our legs dangled and kicked below us to keep afloat.

"Not you, Meridy. Don't let this take you."

"I'm not, Daddy, I'm not." I touched his face, unsure whether the wet was tears or sea. "Only my heart, not me."

"Swim in, Meridy . . . with me."

I nodded. "Daddy, don't let Mother send me to the mountains. I won't be able to breathe."

Sorrow wrenched his face in a way I'd never seen. There was nothing he could do to stop it, nothing anyone could do to stop anything.

CHAPTER NINE

"You need to take care of the root in order to heal the tree."
—GULLAH PROVERB

By the time I finished the story, Tim had wrapped his arms around me. He hadn't spoken a word through the entire telling until I sagged against him and sighed. "Now you know. I'm telling you because only one other person knows and he can't say a word—he gave his life so I didn't have to tell. But the silence is killing me just like the smoke killed him."

Tim whispered, "It was not your fault. It was a terrible accident."

"Well, I can't let you keep the blame just because you

gave the party, and I can't live with the silence and guilt anymore."

"Danny ran into that cottage to save Karen and me and whoever else he thought was still in there. I'm the one who told him I thought someone was in the top tower. Please tell me you did not come here to confess . . . or take the blame. It was a stupid accident a very long time ago."

"I know what I did, Tim. And no, I didn't come here to announce I set off a firecracker. It would destroy Mother, damage my marriage to a man I've hid all this from, a man who spends his life trying to uncover deception. But one of the reasons I came was to try and help."

Tim sighed. "Same sweet Meridy, trying to fix everything for everybody. I told you I don't need help."

It was as if I'd laid down a terrible burden and my body rose; I glanced away from Tim and stared at the water, and then walked to its edge.

He stood, but he didn't follow. "Meridy?"

I didn't turn to answer him. Water licked the edges of my sneakers, splashed my shin. I lifted one leg at a time and removed my socks and shoes, tossed them backward without looking at Tim. I closed my eyes, tasted the briny air and absorbed the heat warming the top of my head. I lifted my face upward, walked into the water until it reached my knees and the hard surface of the cracked shells softened.

Sand wrapped around my toes; a kiss of fish or moss tickled my shin as I moved forward until the water

145

hugged my waist. I hadn't put my head below the sea since that day. I took a deep breath and lowered myself into the water until the swell of wave surrounded me. I sank lower, pumped my legs, swung my arms in the even strokes of a rhythm I'd never quite forgotten.

I lifted my head for a breath and glanced across the drops of sunlight scattered like jewelry on top of the water—nothing but water and sky. My clothes sat heavy on my body and I longed to pull them off beneath the water, yet I continued to swim. Something primal and young and discarded pulled me forward even as I knew Tim watched me from the shore. No fear enveloped me, although I waited for it. I turned and flipped on my back, floated facing the sky.

Danny, poor sweet Danny. "I loved you, Danny."

"I know." The voice wasn't aloud, but it was as real as my sodden clothes against my body, as real as the sky floating above me in massive infinity.

"I'm sorry. I'm so sorry." But nothing came back to me this time. I closed my eyes.

Water filled my ear canal, dizziness rolled over my body, and I curled into a ball, sank into the water. I twirled under the surface, drifted. Silence, as familiar as the smoke that surrounded me the last time Danny held me over his shoulder, surrounded me. I had fallen into that silence fighting, kicking, gasping for breath. This time I let it enfold me willingly. But it wasn't like hiding under the broken palmetto tree; here I couldn't see him and I couldn't feel him. Danny was gone.

I swam back and reached the shore and the two men

staring at me like I needed serious medical attention. Tim shook his head, glanced at Revvy. "Told you . . . crazy as a loon."

Revvy threw his head back and laughed, then looked at me. "Thought you might've needed some help. . . . He told me you were fine."

"I'm just . . ." I cleared my throat. "Fine, just fine."

Tim reached for me, but I held up my hand. "Really."

Revvy smiled, walked back to the dense forest. "I'm gonna check on a couple things. We'll leave in a few minutes."

Tim handed me my shoes. "You know when you asked me if I missed Danny . . . that first day you saw me?" I said.

"Yes."

"I told you I didn't think about him. But I do miss him, every single day, and I just realized it. But you know what I miss more? Who I was *with him*. I miss the me with Danny." I bent over with the weight of all I had hidden even from myself.

Tim let out a breath with a groan. "Okay, this is probably why I'm divorced. . . . I'm terrible at this stuff. I want to say something really profound for you, but I'm sitting here like a moron."

I laughed. "God, you could always make me laugh."

"That's worth something, right?"

"Everything." I leaned into his shoulder, not wanting this moment of contentment to end. Even if the salt water was starting to itch my head, even if mascara ran down my face, and my shirt stuck to the tummy I never could get flat again, I wanted to stay at the shore's edge.

Revvy's voice came over the trees. "Time to get out of here . . . tide is going out."

Tim spoke low and soft. "You will not tell anyone what you told me, Meridy. It doesn't matter anymore and you didn't do anything wrong.

The sound of broken branches and crunching earth came from behind us. Then Revvy stood next to us. "Y'all ready?"

Tim and I looked at each other. "Ever," he said.

I drove home sitting on a towel from the back of Tim's construction truck. I crossed my fingers that Mother wouldn't be home to witness my state of disarray. It didn't work—she stood at the back door and watched me walk toward the house with her nose screwed up like she smelled something dead.

"Meridy McFadden, what have you been doing?"

"Mother, it's Dresden and I've been swimming in the ocean."

"In your clothes?" Mother rolled her eyes, slammed the back door. I stared at the closed door, and then threw it open and walked into the kitchen. "Mother?" I called out.

She turned. "Yes?"

"Let's sit and talk."

"Meridy, right now your hair is dripping salt water all over the heart-of-pine floors."

"Okay, Mother. I'm going to take a shower. Then I was wondering if maybe we could make one of those gorgeous shell lamps we used to do together. I've collected an entire basket of white shells and I thought . . ." It seemed very important to once again establish common ground with Mother—as if it were the only thing I'd come to do.

"I haven't made one of those in . . . years." Mother stared out the window.

"Well, good. Let's do one today." I walked out of the kitchen before she could argue.

When I returned, dressed in a floral skirt and white T-shirt with pink rickrack trim, Mother still stood in the same spot gazing out the window. She looked so alone and suddenly old. My heart skipped in my chest; my hand fluttered to my throat. She was a woman living alone in a house where she'd once raised a family, been married to a vibrant man. Now I saw why she spent so much time away from home doing busywork.

I hugged her, although she stood rigid. "Mother, it must get too quiet here sometimes."

Her face fell. "Oh, oh." Her hand quivered in the air, landed on her middle. She shrugged off my arm.

"I'm glad I'm here to spend some time with you," I said.

With her back turned, Mother said, "Where's that basket of shells?"

I reached into the walk-in pantry and pulled out the sweetgrass basket Tulu had given me, which now stored the shells I'd been collecting on my morning walks. "I saw a lampstand in the shed last week. I'll go get it." I placed the basket on the kitchen table.

Mother nodded and I let the screen door swing closed behind me.

When I returned she had spread out the shells, set out newspaper and two hot-glue guns. I smiled. "This looks like old times. . . . I used to love the way the hot glue stuck to my fingers, the way the lamp would look all lumpy; then all of a sudden it would be beautiful when I stepped back from it."

Mother looked up at me. "You used to love doing this?"

I tilted my head. "Yes."

"I don't remember that. . . .

"I do." I almost hugged her again.

We sat down and began to work without speaking. Mother hummed. I lifted up a white shell and shot glue onto the convex portion. The odor of hot glue filled my nose, replacing the sting of salt water. At length Mother asked me where I'd been all day.

"I went to Oystertip Island . . . where they found Danny's body all those years ago."

"Why did you do that?" Mother laid down her gun, her shells. "Why *would* you do that?"

"Well, I didn't know I was going at first—I probably wouldn't have. Tim took me. But I needed it, Mother. It was important and I'm glad I went."

I felt warm inside—my hair wet, my face free of makeup, my hands on the shells.

"That Tim is nothing but trouble."

I laughed. "Trouble?"

"Yes. He's always gotten you in so much trouble."

"I got myself in trouble, Mother."

"Yes, you did."

"Didn't you get in trouble *ever,* your entire childhood?"

Mother evaded the question. Instead she picked up a large shell, turned it over. "You should have left this one on the beach. It's cracked."

"Okay, cracked shells stay on the beach. . . . You didn't answer my question."

Mother squeezed the shell and it broke beneath her frail fingers; she opened her palm and let the pieces tumble to the kitchen table. "You don't want to know about my childhood."

"You've got to be kidding. I'd love to know about your childhood." I stood and swept the broken shell pieces into my palm, then walked to the trash can and threw them away. When I turned back to the kitchen table, Mother stared right at me.

"You know how I grew up, Meridy. Living on a farm is hard work." An edge of bitterness tainted her words. Mother turned away and spoke to the far wall. "I didn't have *time* to get in trouble. Dad could barely keep the farm going and we all worked the land. Mom cleaned houses for the rich folk in town. I helped her. The Donnelly family—who we cleaned for—took pity on me and paid for my college education when they found out how high my grades were and how Mom and Dad could never afford to send me to college." She spoke fast, clipped.

"Mother . . . how come I never knew about the Donnellys? I never knew things were so hard. I'm sorry."

"I don't need your pity, Meridy. I'm telling you this because you asked." Her voice softened. "I met your daddy in college and I was lucky he fell in love with me. All the girls wanted him. . . . He was quite the catch."

"I'm sure."

"And I wanted to make sure his children and our family would never have the kind of hard life I grew up with, that no one in Seaboro would ever know that Dewey McFadden married poor."

"You are not poor, Mother."

"I don't need you telling me what I am or am not." She tapped her forefinger on the table, accenting each word. "I'm telling you what I *was*."

"But . . . we're always part of who we . . . were, aren't we?"

"No. We are not. You're not."

"What does that mean?" I peeled some glue off my finger and stuck a shell below the one Mother had just placed.

"Look at you now. You have this great life with this nice man and a nice son in a gorgeous house . . . and you were wild as they come."

"I was not that wild. Please stop saying that."

"Yes, you were."

"Did I ruin that reputation you were trying to build?" Although I knew the words were harsh, I said them softly across the table.

Her head snapped up, her mouth opened and closed. "Don't you judge me, young lady. I was trying to make a good life for your daddy, keep you girls in line." She stuck a shell a little too hard against the base.

She had been trying to build a life for her family, not ruin my good times in childhood. The difference between these two motivations now seemed as stark and obvious as day against night. "Mother," I said in a whisper, "thank you for telling me. I'd love to know more about those days."

She nodded and glued. "There's nothing else to know."

There wasn't a way to tell this woman, who had spent her entire life building and shouldering a reputation and image as protection, my responsibility for the Keeper's Cottage ruin.

When the lamp was finished, she picked it up and placed it on the counter. "Well, well, that might be one of the prettiest lamps I've ever done." She glanced over at me. "*We've* done. You can take it back to Atlanta for that fancy sitting room you have in your bedroom."

I smiled. "It's nice. Thanks, Mother."

She raised her eyebrows. "Oh, I forgot to tell you. I called Mr. Cragg this morning at the historical society and told him about your art festival idea."

"You did?" I jumped up from the table. "What'd he say?"

"He said it sounded like a mighty good idea and that he'd love for you to come share it with the society."

"Really?"

She nodded. "Yes."

"You did that for me?"

Mother screwed her face up in a question mark. "For

you? I thought you wanted to do this for the cottage and Seaboro."

I blushed. "I do . . . but thank you for talking to Mr. Cragg. Thank you, Mother. What about Charlotte Hamlon?"

"Ah, just ignore her naysayer doom. We all do."

"Will you go with me?" I grabbed Mother's hand.

She smiled. "If you want me to."

"I do. I do." I hugged her.

"Well, I told Mr. Cragg you'd probably still be here. I wasn't really sure when you were going home." She stared at me.

"I don't know either. I need to talk to Tulu at least one more time. I'll call Beau at home this evening and see what his schedule is. Maybe he can come here. . . . I've only been gone a few days."

Mother nodded and left me alone in the kitchen to admire the lamp we'd created with the shells I'd collected. I ran my hand over this art we'd completed together—over the gift she had just given me that was more than this lamp. She'd handed me a hidden piece of who she was and the reasons why she cared about the things she did—why she was the mother she was with me.

I couldn't imagine how hard it must have been to prove herself worthy at all times. I took a sharp breath—yes, I could; I was doing the same thing.

I turned and caught a wavy reflection of myself in the bubbled-glass cabinet holding the family china; I looked a disorganized mess with limp hair, no makeup and sloppy clothes. I looked . . . eighteen.

I ambled up the stairs to my bedroom. I grabbed the curriculum folder and began to organize it. I needed to get information on stories, medicine, sweetgrass baskets and burial customs. Yet after a minute I set the folder aside. I squatted down and reached underneath my childhood bed for the wooden box Tulu had returned to me. I ran my fingers over the dolphin, under the rusted hinges, and placed it back under the bed. I didn't need to know what my dreams and goals were then. I needed to figure out what they were now.

The phone in Mother's library stared at me with accusing black-numbered eyes. I picked up the handset and dialed my home phone number with a shaking finger. How would I tell Beau about the fire? A jumbled mess of thoughts, about not understanding why the star moved away from the moon every night, the truth of the fire, a desperate need to run away and a rising longing that went along with remembering who I'd been, filled my head. I took the portable handset into the drawing room and curled into the plush green chair I'd once sat in for hours reading *The Secret Garden* over and over.

I glanced at the grandfather clock against the wall while the phone rang—seven p.m. Then Beau's voice came alive over the phone and into the room; I almost saw him standing in our kitchen next to the family desk.

"Hey . . ." I stumbled into my hello.

"Hey, sweetie. How's it going down there in the life

of luxury?" He laughed.

I didn't. "Okay . . . how about there?"

"Well, the house is empty as hell and I'm a little sick of eating out . . . but everything's fine."

"Anything new with the trial?"

"Damn, they're killing me. I'm so sorry you've had trouble catching up with me. We're in meetings all day, then all evening, and when I get home I don't want to wake you or your mother by calling so late. It'll be worth it when it's over. . . . But surely you don't want to hear about my work. Are you almost done with that curriculum?"

"I'm making progress."

"When are you thinking you'll be home? It is so terrible here without you. Nothing gets done."

Did he miss me or what I did for him? "Beau . . ."

"Yes?" The clatter of a glass, the slamming of the refrigerator door, came through the line.

"You know those forsythia bushes behind the house?" I said.

"Yes."

"When I left two weeks ago, I was looking at them and they were climbing over the back fence. I was looking at them and they're all green now . . . and I never even noticed them turn yellow in the spring."

"Okay . . ." He coughed. "What's wrong? Is something wrong with your mother or the house?"

"Beau, I don't know what's wrong. I just don't know if we've noticed anything in our lives in a very, very long time."

"I really don't have any idea what you're talking about," he said in between blank spots of sound that I recognized as the call-waiting on our home phone. "Listen, someone's trying to call in. . . . Can you hold on while I make sure it's not B.J.?"

"Sure." I leaned back against the chair cushions.

He came back on the line, his voice tight, controlled. "Meridy, Ashley is on the other line—some important news on the case. I have got to go. . . . I miss you."

"Ashley?"

"You know—the junior partner . . ."

"I know, Beau. The tall blonde who's there to take care of things."

"What is that supposed to mean? This is work."

"I know it is."

"Meridy, I've got to go. . . . I love you."

"You too, Beau. You too."

I pushed END and dropped the phone in my lap; the hope of some connection and communication sank into the darker places of my heart and the anger rose. As I probed and discovered the girl I used to be, I wondered: Was Beau finding a new place for himself? I turned away from the emotion that had no grounds for arriving; Beau hadn't done anything wrong. I had no right to be mad at him. I leaned back against the chair, closed my eyes.

I curled my legs beneath me and let sleep wash over me; it was better than the wondering and disillusionment that came with my first attempt at some real talk with Beau in as long as I could remember.

The dream came before I was fully asleep. I wandered through a house, or maybe it was a cottage, but I did know it was mine. I was looking for something—but I wasn't sure what. I'd know when I found it. The rooms were clean, the hardwood floors were polished, and the paint was unmarred. I flowed from empty room to empty room, opening doors, then shutting them again. I stood in a long hallway, framed photographs lining the wall with faces I might have recognized, but I wasn't quite sure. Then I remembered—the large room at the end of the hall where I'd stuffed everything. I ran down the hall, opened the door at the end and stared into a room crammed to capacity with furniture, boxes, paper and pictures. I reached to pull down a wooden box when a long vibrating ringing sound caused me to drop the box, jump.

I woke abruptly, jumped up from the chair in the drawing room, the phone tumbling to the ground. I grabbed it from the floor and pushed the ON button. "Hello . . ."

"Hey there, little sister, how's it going in Seaboro?"

"Sissy?"

"Sounds like I woke you up. . . . It's seven thirty in the evening, Meridy. What's up with that?"

"You didn't wake me up. . . . How are you? How are Annie and Amanda?"

"Good, great. Guess what? Penn just bought me a new Jaguar."

"That's fabulous, Sissy. I know you've always wanted one."

"Yep. So, how's Mom? You taking care of her while you're there?" Somehow Sissy had managed to move from *Mother* to *Mom* in our older years—I'd never made the transition.

"Mother doesn't need to be taken care of. There are more people here taking care of things . . . and she's busier than any woman I've ever seen. She's never home."

"You could still help, take her out or something."

"Trust me, Sissy. Mother does not want me taking her out."

Sissy's silence was more agreement than I'd hoped for. "Did you call for a reason?" I asked, rubbed my temples and cursed the phone.

"Just calling to tell Mom about the new car. Penn and I thought we might come and visit in the next week or so . . . but I wanted to make sure I wasn't intruding on your time with Mom."

"No intrusion." I was wary of the undertones in her voice, in our relationship.

"You mean you're staying longer?" Sissy's question had a hundred other questions behind it.

"I don't know. Hold on . . . I think I hear Mother coming in. I'll have her call you right back." I hung up before Sissy had the chance to answer or wait.

I wandered to the front porch and stared out at the winding driveway that led to the street, and as if I had the gift of prophecy, Mother's white Mercedes turned into the driveway. I waved at her as she pulled into the garage.

I met her in the kitchen. "Sissy just called."

Mother's face lit up as if there were an internal lantern for Sissy's name. "How is she?" Mother pulled a lavender cardigan from her shoulders, placed it over the chair.

"Fine. She wants you to call her when you get a chance."

Mother went straight to the phone and picked it up. I was sure Sissy was number one on the speed dial. I walked outside, headed toward the beach to watch the remainder of the day disappear behind the line of sea and sky.

CHAPTER TEN

"The thorn in your foot is temporarily appeased, but it is still in."
—GULLAH PROVERB

I awoke to face a window full of honey-colored light. I lifted the window and held my hand out into the open air that felt as though it waited for me today—an expectant day holding its breath. Or maybe it was only I who was expectant; Cate was coming to visit. After Mother had finished talking to Sissy, I'd had an intense need for some connection, a friend who knew me well in my present life. I'd called Cate and invited her to come spend the day with me. Although she'd been surprised to hear I was in Seaboro, as I hadn't told her, she was only two hours away and promised to be here before lunch. I'd then called Tim to beg him to show my best friend the better parts of Seaboro—the water.

I opened the bedroom closet. I hadn't worn any of my matching outfits or laced sundresses except to the Ladies of Seaboro luncheon. I leafed through the sundresses and had the odd feeling that I was peeking in someone else's closet, trespassing on the wardrobe of a woman who was much more together than I was.

I yanked a pair of wrinkled shorts from the laundry basket, dug around for a clean T-shirt and went down to the kitchen. Mother sat at the table waiting for me. She had always been beautiful; I had no doubt that Daddy assumed he was as lucky to have her as she thought she was to have him. Even now a stunning face lingered behind the sagging skin, the age spots and wrinkles, as if it were all a tissue veil over the beauty underneath. Her hair had once been blond as the sun at midday; now it was silver and still long and consistently pulled behind her head in a severe knot.

Her hair was down again, which meant she had no plans for the morning. "This is nice," she said.

"What?" I asked, and poured myself a cup of coffee.

"Having you here for breakfast every morning . . . I'm getting used to it." And she actually smiled.

Although I felt I should say something profound and loving in return, I only grinned like a goofy five-year-old who had just been told her scribbled artwork was a Picasso. I walked over, leaned down and kissed her cheek.

She squinted at me, glanced up and down at my

161

outfit. "What are you wearing?" she asked.

"Clothes." I laughed.

"Meridy, surely you have some better clothes than that."

"Well, I invited a friend from Atlanta to come visit today and—"

"A friend?" She stood. "To stay here?" She swept her hand across the kitchen.

"No . . . just for the day. Cate—she's in Wild Palms."

She sat, breathed out. "Well, will she be coming for lunch?" I nodded. "Is that okay?"

Mother lifted her chin. "Of course it is. I just need to prepare something."

"You do not need to prepare anything . . . really. It's just Cate and we'll be gone most of the day."

"Well, you still have to eat," she said.

I laughed. "Yes, we do."

"Well, where are you headed this morning? Not out with that Tim . . . are you?"

I half lied. "No, I'm headed to Tulu's this morning. I'm hoping to wrap up this curriculum today. I've done as much research as I can and I just want to ask her a few more questions."

"Good. I wouldn't want you to . . . with Beau not here and everything, I wouldn't want . . ."

"I wouldn't either." I reached for a biscuit. I wasn't sure what mother didn't want to happen, but I might as well agree.

"Lil' one," Tulu said, "you see, the songs are more

162

than the songs. They too are the story." She spoke to me on her front porch. I leaned back in a rocking chair, absorbing her melodic voice. She'd sung a few spirituals, told a ghost story. "The story is always what matters. Our lives are a story; you're a story."

I laughed and leaned forward. "No, Tulu, I'm a character in someone else's story, that's all."

"Well, then, there's your problem. This is your story, child."

Past her lawn, two children across the street stared and pointed at me, giggled as they ran behind some bushes. My story? I was more worried about how I fitted into everyone else's story. "Tulu, I swear, you drive me crazy. I came here to get some information on the Gullah music and ghost stories. You've turned it back around again." I handed her a piece of printed paper with a list of proverbs. "Here are the proverbs I've found. I remember some of these; some I've never seen."

"You go to the Penn Center?"

"No. I got these off the Internet before I left Atlanta."

Tulu leaned forward. "Let you in on a little secret . . . my great-grandmother was a slave child and was set free and went to the Penn Center. It was once called the Penn School and was part of the Port Royal Experiment—a school to educate Sea Island slaves freed at the beginning of the Civil War."

"Tulu, that is amazing. I can't believe how much of your history I didn't know. So those proverbs . . ." I tapped the piece of paper on her lap. "Was this how y'all talked to each other?"

"We just call the proverbs the 'palm oil with which words are eaten.'" Tulu leaned back in her chair and smiled.

I wrote down what she said, scribbled across the pages. "Thanks, Tulu. I never want to misrepresent any of this. . . . I just want to give it in a form the children will enjoy and understand."

"You was always wanting to teach. . . . As long as you could speak, you wanted to teach children."

I tilted my head. "No, I didn't. That must have been Sissy."

"You're joking with me, right?"

"No, I went to college for business—"

"I didn't say what you went to college for. I was talking about what you wanted to be, what you walked around pretending to be with your notebooks and fake blackboard and pretend school-room in the corner of the bedroom. That's what I was talking about."

"I didn't . . ." I halted in confusion. Had I really set up a pretend schoolroom?

"Yes, you did." Silence ran between us. "You looked into that box yet?"

"No, there's no need for that right now," I said.

"There will be." She rocked, with tiny pushes of her feet against the porch. "You asked yourself what you want?"

"Want?

"Yes, want. Do you know what you want?"

164

It had been so long since anyone had asked me that question that I wasn't even sure I had an answer. "What do you mean, Tulu? I want to write this curriculum, spend some time with Mother and Tim. Get the arts festival off the ground. Go home . . . I don't know."

"Beyond that . . . beyond those doings, beyond those chores and then all the way to the being."

"Being?"

"Who you're wanting to be."

"Just me, just Meridy." Wasn't that what I wanted? It seemed the right answer.

"Ah, who is that?"

"I'm sitting right here. But I know. I need to go home. Talk to my husband, find out what is . . . missing. Running away never solved anything. No lectures, please." But I smiled when I said this.

"You don't talk to someone to find that, Meridy. You go inside for that." She leaned her head on the back of the chair, closed her eyes.

"I'm sorry, I've made you tired." I stood.

"It's not you, lil' one," Tulu mumbled.

I leaned down and kissed her forehead. "You need anything before I leave?"

She shook her head. "My son, Will, he arranged for someone to bring me my groceries and now I'm just getting lazier and lazier." Her head drifted backward and the soft sound of sleep whispered through her lips.

I leaned my forehead against the glass pane of the

side panel to the front door, gazed out to the empty driveway. Mother came up behind me. "Staring out the window every two minutes will not get her here any sooner. You are *still* so impatient."

I laughed. "Thanks, Mother. I'm just worried—she's late. She called from the road and said she'd be here by eleven."

Mother glanced at her watch. "Ten minutes late, Meridy. Come in the kitchen and have a cup of tea with me."

I nodded and turned just as the sound of a car motor purred up the drive. I threw open the front door; Cate's Mercedes appeared. I waved, ran to the car and hugged her before she even fully emerged from the driver's seat.

"You're here," I said.

Cate laughed, stumbled on the crushed shells. "Yes, I am." She nodded toward the house and Mother standing on the front porch with her hands on her hips. "This is where you grew up?"

"Yes . . ."

She leaned her head in, whispered, "You made it sound like a place you never wanted to come back to, but this is paradise."

I nodded. "I know. But sometimes appearances are deceptive."

She nodded back. "I do know that. Come on, show me around this place."

After a formal tour of the house, Mother, Cate and I sat down for lunch. Mother placed Wedgwood china in front of us with her Waldorf chicken salad, poured iced tea into the large handblown glassware she hadn't used since I'd arrived.

"So"—Mother sat—"what are you ladies doing today?"

I glanced sideways at Cate. "What do you want to do?" I attempted to make a be-quiet face, but Cate didn't catch the hint.

"Thought we were going out boating and fishing with your friend Tom."

"You mean Tim?" Mother asked, placed her fork back on the table with a clatter of emphasis.

"Yeah, that's it," Cate said, oblivious to Mother's tone of voice.

I held my fork up in the air. A glob of chicken salad landed on the table. I grimaced. "Tim offered to take us out in the boat and I thought Cate would love to see the water, the river and all."

"Oh," Mother said, wiped up the fallen food.

In stiff conversation, we finished our lunch, telling Cate about the idea for the arts festival and sharing local gossip about people she'd never met. She laughed and smiled, but looked sideways at me with the left side of her lip upturned in an expression of curiosity.

Finally Mother stood to clear her plate; I grabbed the other dishes and placed them in the sink. "Okay," I said, "let's get going." I grabbed Cate's hand, nodded toward the door.

Cate spoke to Mother. "Thank you for such a lovely lunch. It's been a long time since someone cooked for me."

"Oh, you're welcome." Mother brushed her hand through the air. "You two go have fun now."

After Cate changed into shorts we walked to my car. She grabbed my hand. "Now, what the hell is going on?"

"What do you mean?" I tossed the car keys in the air, caught them.

"I haven't felt undercurrents like that during a meal since the day Harland came home and told me he had something very important to talk to me about. I thought it had something to do with money or investments or family—but nope, it had to do with a mistress and divorce."

"Mother has that way about her. She can make you feel something is . . . well, wrong when nothing is."

"Are you sure?"

I glanced at Cate. "This is a very long discussion. Can we have it some other time?"

"How about the CliffsNotes version?"

"Mother thinks something is going on between Tim and me . . . and there's just a lot of misunderstanding between us. Nothing to do with you."

"Is there?"

"Is there what?" I stopped next to the car.

"Something going on between you and Tim?"

I opened the driver's-side door, looked at Cate. "No."

She held up her hands. "Okay, okay. Just had to ask."

I nodded and got into the car, took a deep breath as Cate climbed into her seat. "Come on, let's show you Seaboro," I said.

● ● ●

River swells banged against the hull as Tim's boat rocked back and forth with the rhythm of the tide. Cate and I stood on the splintered dock; she dug her sunglasses out of her bag and I called Tim's name.

His head popped out from the galley. "Hey." He jumped up onto the dock, held out his hand to Cate. He wore a faded blue bathing suit and a bright red T-shirt; a baseball cap was pulled low on his forehead. His curls poking out from beneath the hat made him look fifteen again. "Hi, Tim Oliver."

Cate blushed and tucked her hair behind her ear. "Hi, I'm Cate Larson."

I raised my eyebrows as she used her maiden name. "Better known as Meridy's lifesaver," I said, stepping between them in an instinct I didn't understand.

"You two ready?" Tim grabbed the towels I held in my arms.

"We are," Cate and I said in unison.

The boat cut through the water, and the waves separated in a V as the cloudless sky reflected light off the whitecaps the boat created in the water. The motor hummed a soft lullaby and I leaned my head back on the seat, closed my eyes.

Cate touched my arm; I looked at her eyes. "This is so beautiful," she said. "You are so lucky you can do this every time you come home."

Tim laughed, pushed the throttle forward.

"What's so funny?" Cate glanced at me.

"I didn't go out on the water until last week," I said.

169

"What do you mean?"

"I haven't been out on the water since I moved away . . . until last week."

"You have got to be kidding," Cate said, then looked at Tim. "She's kidding, right?"

"Sorry to say—she's not. But she's reformed now." He glanced over his shoulder at me. "Right?"

"Reformed?" Cate asked.

"Something like that . . . ," I said.

Tim leaned back in his seat, steered with his knees as he grabbed three beers from the cooler and tossed one to each of us. Cate popped hers open, then glanced at me as I took a long swallow of mine. "I don't think I've ever seen you drink a beer," she said, pulling her sunglasses down to stare at me.

"Really?" I said. "That can't be right. . . ."

"No, it's right. I've never, ever seen you drink a beer."

I shrugged my shoulders as Oystertip Island came into view on the left side of the boat. Cate took a deep breath. "Oh, that is absolutely beautiful. What is that?"

And, as one does on the water, while waves and wind soothe the rougher places of life, I answered before I gave it much forethought. "That's Oystertip Island. Remember when I told you about my high school boyfriend, who died on graduation night? Well, that's where they found his body."

Cate gasped. "What? You never . . . well, you implied something terrible happened to him, but . . . not . . ."

"It was terrible," I said.

Tim looked back at me, winked, then pulled back on

the throttle. The boat idled as he reached behind the seats for the fishing poles. "This is a perfect fishing spot for whiting. Or at least it was yesterday." He handed Cate a pole. "You ready?"

Cate shrugged her shoulders. "I guess I'll try."

In the deeper silence of tide and nature the three of us sat and hooked the bait, threw our lines over the side of the boat. Tim threw me another beer.

Cate glanced over at me, her line tangled in her hand. "Meridy Dresden, are you having a second beer?"

I glanced down at my hand. "What?"

Cate shook her head at Tim. "I can never get her to have that second drink. I bet you can even get her to be late to a party or wear shoes that don't match her outfit."

"Not me. I've never been able to make her do anything, ever. Meridy's always done exactly what she wants to do."

"Well, there must be two Meridys then. . . ." Cate lifted her knotted line in the air. "I think I need a little help here."

Tim laughed. "Never done this before?"

Cate shook her head. "Nope. But perfectly eager to learn." She glanced at my pole, steadied between my legs with one hand, droplets of water dancing on the nylon line. "Where in the hell did you learn how to fish?" she asked.

"I grew up with it," I said.

"My God, where have you been all this time I've known you?"

"What does that mean?"

"Where has *this* Meridy been?"

"Right here," I said.

The afternoon passed in the glorious haze of two friendships, each of which defined the separate parts of me. Cate left Seaboro before dinner to make the two-hour drive before dark. When I hugged her good-bye, she pulled back, stared at me. "We never talked about what is going on with you . . . and Beau."

I shrugged. "There really isn't anything to talk about. I just needed a day like this—to enjoy you, the water. You know? I've really missed you and somehow just being with you puts things in perspective. We didn't have to talk about anything."

She placed her hand on my cheek. "Well, if you need to talk about anything, you know I'm here."

I nodded. "I do." I glanced over at Tim, who sat in his truck waiting for me—he'd said he wanted to show me one more thing.

Cate nodded toward the truck. "You two have a very . . . unique relationship."

"I've known him since . . . I don't remember not knowing him."

"You're lucky."

"Yes, I am. I have you." I hugged her again and she climbed into her car, waved out the window until she rounded the bend at the end of our driveway. I jogged over to Tim's truck, climbed in the passenger seat. "Okay, let's go. Where you taking me this time?"

Tim's truck pulled up into his driveway. "Your house?

172

You wanted to show me your house?" I opened the passenger door.

"One of the things . . ."

We walked up to the front porch and stood in front of Tim's double front doors. I ran my hand across the carved wood. In the top right of the door, a dolphin curled around the corner, pointing his nose to the sky. If I could have reached to touch it, I would have, but Tim's doors were at least nine feet tall. I pointed to the dolphin. "Did you carve that?"

"Yep. Remember . . . when all three of us threatened to get dolphin tattoos after we found out that a Celtic dolphin stood for the power of water?"

"We snuck out that night and drove to Savannah—to that tattoo parlor. My God, what were we thinking?"

"Well, I think it was Danny who finally pushed us out of the tattoo parlor. So I made y'all a box with the dolphin instead."

His boyish eyes were still open wide, as if he was always ready for something good. "You remember that?" I asked.

He laughed. "I sure do. You probably lost that thing by now."

"Not entirely . . . come on, show me this gorgeous home."

Tim pointed out the heart-of-pine floors, hand-carved banister, twelve-inch molding, until we stood in the kitchen. A window as large as the wall opened out to the sea. Bloated clouds sat motionless, waiting for direction from the wind. The top halves of the clouds were bleached and puffed cotton, the bases gray and expectant.

"It's like you live outside but inside," I said.

"That was the idea."

"You know"—I took a deep breath—"you're the only one who did exactly what you said you'd do—build houses."

"No one does exactly what they said they'd do. I never said I'd get a divorce. I never said I'd live on Mom and Dad's property taking care of them, barely scraping by—life just happens."

"Okay, Mr. Philosophy." I held my hands up in surrender. "Where else did you want to take me today?"

Rain skidded across the tin roof of the Keeper's Cottage and broke into shattered drops denting the sand. I didn't shield my eyes or wind-whipped hair from the downpour, which the latent clouds had released along with the stinging sand whipping my legs. In the late-evening light, I stared at the Keeper's Cottage or actually at an exact replica of the cottage that the town had built two miles inland. The porch was missing, the tower gone; only the left side was painted. I stared at a building that might be a half-finished dream or nightmare.

"You okay?" Tim touched my back.

"Yes . . ." I turned to him, stared at him through my own memory of that horrid night. He'd been thinner. His hair had touched his shoulders, despite his father's disapproval. His mouth had been fuller but with the same smile. "Why are they doing this?" I squinted at the cottage; it really was quite miraculous. "It's like traveling back in time. Why are they trying so hard to reconstruct it?"

"They started the reconstruction about a year ago, then ran out of money. There are a lot of reasons to build it, but mainly because it is a historic landmark for our humble town. There are also a couple families who actually had ancestors in the Civil War who died while disassembling the lighthouse so the Union troops couldn't use it. Those soldiers took the Fresnel lens out and buried it in the sand a few miles away. They were shot coming home, so the families want the cottage as a tribute. Also it is, or was, the oldest Keeper's Cottage in South Carolina. . . ."

"None of this . . . restoration is a tribute to the fire, is it? To Danny?"

He closed his eyes, let out a long sigh before he opened them again. "The fire is only one more tragedy associated with the cottage. There are quite a few of them. I even heard about a time in the early 1900s when a plantation owner gave huge parties here for hunters' escapades. One of his guests got drunk and fell off the tower. There's more. But this committee seems to think that restoring it or saving it is more of a tribute to the people who survived than to those who didn't. I agree."

"So do I."

"I wanted to show it to you before you went home. I knew you hadn't seen it. Let's get out of the rain."

I ignored his suggestion. "Can we go inside?" I pointed to all the yellow caution tape surrounding the cottage.

"No, the floors haven't been reinforced yet."

"Will they put the tower back on?" I pointed to the roof "Where the light was, where he fell off?"

"Yes." Tim took a deep breath. "God, I should have gone up there with him." He groaned, dropped his head. "I ran with Karen, tried to help her out. I ran toward the woods, away from my best friend. I wish I knew what happened to him . . . you know?"

"I know," I whispered.

"I mean, did he get trapped? How exactly did he . . . die?" Tim didn't look at me as he spoke, as though he spoke to the regret and sadness surrounding the cottage.

"I used to lie in bed at Mawmaw's and stare out the window at the mountains and use them as a backdrop like a movie screen to picture the different ways Danny could've died. I saw him flying through the air. I saw him collapse on the tower. I saw him try to swim and be pulled under." I closed my eyes. "But I think he died from the fall . . . I don't know why I think that. It was just what I saw most in those days when I'd try to . . . imagine him."

"I guess we'll never know."

"I guess it doesn't really matter," I said.

"Or maybe it does because maybe I could have stopped it."

"No, you couldn't have. You had no idea the tower

would collapse. . . . I passed out on him. I left him alone too. I'm the coward—I never returned, never faced any of it."

"Damn, Meridy, there is enough blame to go around. None of it goes to you."

"Yes, oh, yes, it does." I kicked at the sand. "Hell, yes, it does."

Tim threw back his head and rain scattered across his face. "Did little Miss Perfect just curse?"

"Did you just call me 'perfect'?" My mouth dropped open. "That's what Alexis called me. What are you people talking about? I'm a jumbled mess of a woman right now."

"A perfect jumbled mess." Tim leaned down and kissed my forehead, as if I had a fever. "Come on, let's get out of this rain."

CHAPTER ELEVEN

"Promising talk don't cook rice."
—GULLAH PROVERB

The Seaboro Common Square was empty in the hushed morning as Mother and I parked the car in front of the antiquated library, which now held the Seaboro Historical Society. The grass was low and newly mowed, the fountain gurgling in a lonely echo across the lawn. Together, Mother and I walked into the building and toward the last room at the end of the hall. The structure carried an odor of all old buildings in

Seaboro—a mix of mildew and sea, moist and human. Everyone greeted us as we sat down at a cedar conference table, crafted from a tree that had fallen in a hurricane and blown through the side windows in the early eighties.

The mayor had appointed the ten seated men and women to the society. Mr. Cragg seemed as old as the historic building itself. "Now, everyone." He clapped his hands together once. "Meridy McFadden . . . Dresden has come to our meeting with an idea I think is fabulous. Meridy?" He lifted his palm and motioned toward me. "What would you like to say?"

In the largest voice I could muster, I told the society about my idea for an arts festival to raise money for the Keeper's Cottage.

"Now, Meridy," Mr. Cragg said, "this fundraising idea has much merit, but why do we need to do this when it appears that Tim Oliver will donate the money?"

I stood, a million wings fluttering against my ribs. "I think it would be more . . . beneficial to both the city and the reputation of the cottage to have an arts festival." I leaned forward, placed my palms on the table and looked each person in the eyes. "Listen, you are constantly trying to get the outside world to notice Seaboro's merits, of which there are many. Bringing in artists from all over the Lowcountry would seem to accomplish a dual purpose. The Oliver family has already lost so much; Tim has finally built his business. Forcing someone to pay for the renovations seems to affect the . . . spirit of the building." I took a deep breath. I'd practiced that speech.

A few men and women cleared their throats; Charlotte Hamlon leaned back in her chair. "I think it's a waste of time—we could never raise that much money at a festival. And that Tim needs to pay for what he did."

Mr. Everett, my old history teacher, stood. "Well, I think Ms. Dresden has a valid point. It's as much a tourist and reputation issue as a money issue. The PR for something like this would be great for the city and county." He winked at me. Ever since I'd built a Roman city out of Popsicle sticks, he'd been on my side.

"I've held an arts festival five years in a row for our private school at home," I said. "I could help you get it organized, show you how, and . . . you could have it on the Fourth of July, when you have so many visitors already. My voice vibrated in the room; I was talking too loudly, the way a child does when trying to talk parents into something they've already said no to.

Lansing Manning, an old friend of Mother's, tossed her head as if she still had shoulder-length curls. Now a scarf surrounded her head—the only indication of the cancer she fought. "I want to head up this project." She nodded toward me. "This is a magnificent idea for our town. The arts and the Keeper's Cottage together—we can bring in every kind of artist: writers, storytellers, sweetgrass basket weavers. It is a fabulous idea."

Then voices overlapped, caught up in the excitement. Yes, now we could make the lists, assign the duties, and I could stop thinking about the past. I could once again forget, if I wanted to.

Mother reached under the table and patted my leg, indicating I should sit. I smiled at her and obeyed.

Charlotte Hamlon stood. "I think this is a ridiculous idea. How in the world will we get that many artists to come in under a month?"

I straightened in my chair. "It would have to be for next year."

"See, it's a ridiculous idea. We're not willing to wait that long to make a few bucks when we could do all of it right now," Charlotte said.

"You've already waited twenty-six years. Surely another year of planning won't harm the cottage," I said.

"Humph," Charlotte muttered, but had nothing else to say.

"Now, I can't head this up," I said, "but I can tell Mrs. Manning how to do it. And I'll always be available by phone for consultation. I have an entire notebook on how to organize, run and set up an arts festival." I motioned toward Lansing Manning.

Mrs. Manning clapped her hands together. "This is so wonderful."

"Should we take a vote?" Mr. Cragg stood.

The historic society's voices rose in nine ayes, and one nay from Charlotte Hamlon, who then stomped out of the room and slammed the door behind her.

I thought Mother stifled a laugh, but the buzz of

conversation overwhelmed the sound and I wasn't quite sure.

The afternoon after the historical society meeting, I made two more phone calls to home. When the answering machine came on—again—and Beau's secretary told me he was unavailable—again—I realized I needed to go home. I must leave and discover what it was I was avoiding with Beau. I couldn't hide here. I left a message on Beau's voice mail: I was coming home in the morning.

My suitcase lay open on the bed. Clean clothes were stacked around it, ready to be packed. I sat down on the mattress and it tilted under my weight. Beau knew I was coming. B.J. had decided to stay in Nashville for the weekend as usual—he loved it there. I was headed home without understanding how I felt about Beau at all, understanding only how I felt being here—more alive and open. Maybe I could find what I'd lost and bring it home with me.

I sighed and walked downstairs—I definitely knew I couldn't fly down now. I was grounded in my responsibilities and commitments.

The arts festival committees were being formed under the direction of Lansing Manning; the curriculum was almost done. There was nothing left for me to do here. I stood on the back porch, the wood warm on my bare feet, the breeze a caress on my cheeks. This was the place where my memories gathered: this house, this beach, this sea-soaked air. These memories frolicked and talked to each other, passed stories and secrets. I felt they were just beginning to whisper to me, tell me their mysteries. Long ago, I'd left them all here and I would do so again.

CHAPTER TWELVE

"If you hold your anger,
it will kill all your happiness."
—GULLAH PROVERB

I belonged here. In my very marrow I understood I belonged here: in our kitchen, cooking Beau's dinner, folding the laundry, organizing the calendar for the family and addressing correspondence. I didn't need to be diving in the sea, tramping through the woods, lifting my face to the wind with the bow of a boat cutting through the water.

I ran my hand across the kitchen counter and then leafed through the pile of mail on my desk. Beau had divided the mail into piles of magazines, bills, personal mail and junk mail. I had once told him to never throw away junk mail; his idea of junk and mine weren't quite the same.

I hadn't decided, until this moment, what a fool I was for thinking I could stay away. This was my home and my husband and my family. The past and Tim could take care of themselves. I lifted a picture of Beau, B.J. and me standing in front of the house posing for a Christmas card three years ago.

The hum of the garage door slid into the kitchen; I smiled and waited for Beau to walk in. He sprang into the kitchen calling my name.

"I'm right here," I said.

He held out his arms. I went to him. "I'm so glad you're home." He wrapped his arms around me and hugged me so tightly the air squeezed out of me.

I laughed. "Beau, let go."

"Never. Don't you ever go leaving me like that again."

I stepped back and stared at him. The stress of the trial lay on his face in dark circles under his eyes. His hair fell back as he smiled, leaned in for a kiss. I closed my eyes and tasted this kiss, the one I'd known for twenty years but hadn't really tasted in a long time. He pulled back from me. "You look great, honey. Tell me everything about the trip. How's your mother? Sissy?" He walked toward the wine storage and pulled down a bottle of Merlot.

"It was really great, Beau. I missed you." Then the words rushed out that I'd kept tucked under my heart with hope. "Maybe we could go back together . . . in a few weeks or so. They're organizing an arts festival I'd like to help with and I love the beach and the tides and I saw old friends I'd like you to meet—"

He held up his hand. "Whoa."

"Well, Mother just seems so lonely and Sissy and Penn are coming to visit and . . . I'd like to see Tulu one more time—"

"Who is Tulu?"

I sat down at the kitchen bar and reached for the glass of wine he'd just poured me, let the liquid run warm to my middle. "She's our old housekeeper, the one I've been interviewing, and I'd love it if you'd go with me, Beau. I've been very . . . empty here and there is some unfinished business there . . ."

"What is that supposed to mean?"

"Nothing more than what I just said."

"Are you unhappy with us? With me?" He made a pouty face and sat next to me at the bar.

"To be unhappy, you have to feel something. I've just been kind of . . . empty. At least until I got there."

"I don't understand." He took a long swallow of his wine.

"I don't either. I'm trying to talk to you about it." I leaned forward. "I keep thinking if maybe I talk about it—with you—I'll come to understand how I feel, what I want. Don't you feel like something is gone? Like we're not really here or that everything is fake or just ridiculous? Like we don't notice anything anymore?"

"I'm too busy to feel any of those things. . . ." He shook his head at me as if I had way too much free time on my hands, as if I were worrying about something as trivial as what color sandals to wear to the garden party.

I picked up my wineglass in perfect synchronicity with the ringing phone. Beau rose and picked up the handset. I was stunned by his action—I was in the middle of trying to tell him how I felt. I tamped down my anger, hoping that Beau would understand—help me breach this distance between us.

After his brief hello, he looked at me and motioned for me to pick up the other line. "What?" I mouthed.

He shooed his hand toward the library, where the other portable phone was. I ran and picked it up.

". . . my friends posted bail . . . ," my son's voice said.

I walked back into the kitchen with the phone to my ear and heard Beau's voice in the room and over the phone line. "How long did they keep you?" Beau motioned for me to be quiet with a finger over his lips.

"Overnight. Dad, it was so terrible. God, I am so sorry. I've ruined everything. If Coach finds out, he'll suspend me from the team. If the school finds out, I'll lose my scholarship. I've screwed up good this time." His voice caught. "I swear, Dad, I drove because I was the most sober. . . ."

"You don't drive because you're the most sober, son. You drive because you're just plain sober."

"I know, Dad. I know."

"Okay, here's what we do." Beau paced the kitchen. "I'll call Harland. He'll handle the legal side—his brother is the best DUI lawyer in the state. I'll have Coach Mac call the college. We'll work this out."

"I don't know if we can, Dad."

"Son—you did screw up. You did." Beau leaned against the counter. "But I know this isn't what you normally do. I know this isn't . . . how you are. We'll figure it out."

B.J.'s voice broke. "I'm sorry, Dad. I know what you're going to say—I can hear it: I have to pay for what I've done."

"I'll call you later. I'll call Harland."

Beau hung up the phone and stared at me. "Shit."

I ended the call on the other handset and set it on the counter. Beau turned away from me and walked toward his office, where he'd do what he did best—use his contacts and friends to accomplish a goal. If all mistakes were to be paid for, if everything had a consequence, how would he make our son pay?

You can't get straight wood from crooked timber, said one of the many Gullah proverbs I had typed and listed in my file. I sat back on the barstool and stared at my warped reflection in the stainless steel refrigerator. Maybe I should have seen something like this coming—just because we ignore things does not mean they disappear. They hide in the deeper places and emerge when we need them the least.

I hung up my clothes and sank onto the bed. With the suitcase unpacked, it was time to read the mail. Beau had been on the downstairs phone for two hours and hadn't once come up to talk to me, explain what was going on. My sweet son in a cell for DUI. The news sat on my chest heavier than the disinterest that seemed to come from my husband, weightier than any of the confusion I'd felt during the past two weeks. Normalcy was unraveling; life was coming apart at seams that I'd thought were sturdy.

I stood and walked to the bedroom door, bumped into Beau entering the room. He regarded me with what appeared to be disapproval. "You're not ready?"

"For what?"

"We're having dinner at the club with Harland and Alexis and . . . all the rest. I told them you were coming home today, and they all want to see you."

"Beau, you did not tell me this."

"I guess I forgot while you were telling me I make you unhappy, and B.J. was telling me about his DUI."

I leaned against the doorframe, feeling drained and empty. "That is not what I said. Please tell me about B.J. Tell me what happened and who you've been on the phone with for hours."

"Let's get ready. We're already late and we'll talk in the car."

Beau brushed past me and I stayed still until I heard the shower running. Then I went into the closet and stared at my wardrobe. I chose a pair of baby-blue wide-leg pants with a simple white button-down. I slipped on my clothes and stared in the mirror. I needed to fix my makeup, and the shirt could probably use some ironing, but some small Meridy inside me rebelled. I swished on some lip gloss and went down to the kitchen to finish my wine. What else was there to do?

I needed to talk to my son. I picked up the phone and dialed his cell. His voice came warm over the line and I closed my eyes, imagining him next to me in the kitchen, wearing his baseball uniform and smacking his gum while he told me about his day.

"Mom . . . I'm sorry," he said as soon as he heard my voice.

The strictness of my mother within me rose and I opened my mouth to lecture him about responsibility and wise choices, but I opened my heart instead. "B.J., I love you. It'll be fine."

"I was hoping you'd answer the phone—I tried your cell."

"Why?"

"I wanted to . . . I don't know. . . ."

"Did you think I wouldn't tell Dad?"

"Maybe that's what I was hoping for." He sighed. "But I know . . . this time . . . you'd have to."

"Yes, B.J., I would've."

"I know. . . . I've just completely screwed up."

"We all make mistakes. This is just one of the bigger ones. One that has much larger . . . consequences. But no one was hurt. The car wasn't wrecked."

"You and Dad don't make mistakes."

I laughed across the phone lines and wished, desperately wished, I could reach out my arms and wrap them around my adorable son. "We don't? You have got to be kidding."

"I can't think of one you've made," he said.

"Okay, my goal this week will be to make a list of all my mistakes. . . . You'll enjoy them."

"Yeah, like you forgot the butter at the grocery store or something terrible like that, Mom."

"No, like I was grounded half my senior year, that your grandmother caught me asleep on the beach after she'd called the police because she thought I ran away, that—"

"No way, Mom. You're making all that up."

I stared across the kitchen and out the window to the backyard. How many times had I sat out there on the teak chairs and watched B.J. hit baseballs, talked to him? Had my pretense and facade been so intact that I'd never shared anything real or honest with my son? The thought nauseated me.

"Not making it up. Ask Grandma," I said.

"I will." He laughed. "Hey, Mom, thanks for calling. I've been pretty . . . down. I feel like I've screwed up all my dreams."

"No, Beau. You've learned a lesson."

"I love you, Mom." B.J. said this so rarely that his words filled my heart to overflowing.

"I love you too." I hung up the phone and leaned against the window. The Lady Banksia roses were in bloom.

"Who was that?" Beau's voice startled me. I turned to him. "What?"

His face was all screwed up in the look he had when he was sick with the flu. "Who did you just say 'I love you' to?"

"Our son."

"Oh." He grabbed his car keys from the counter. "Let's go, okay?"

"Who did you think it was?"

"I don't know, Meridy. You'd just finished telling me how unhappy you are with me, how you want to leave me, and I just—"

"That is not what I said. You didn't hear me, Beau. I

didn't tell you I was unhappy with you."

As Beau drove the car down the driveway I touched his leg. "Please tell me who you called about B.J. Is it going to be okay?"

"I don't know. Harland said his brother would defend him. His alcohol content was the minimum, so he said he should be able to help. I did talk to his coach and there is a chance he'll lose his slot. But he's had absolutely no other demerits. He's never even been late to practice. His coach said he's been the perfect rookie—doing everything that was asked of him and more. He even helped the other guys who are his competition for the lead pitcher spot. He'd been perfect until now."

"We taught him that."

"Taught him what? To drink and drive—please, Meridy."

"No, to be perfect."

"What?" He turned in to the valet, put the car in park and stared at me.

"Nothing." I opened the car door and stepped out.

He walked ahead of me into the dining room, where we greeted Harland and Alexis, Betsy and Mike, at the same table as the last time we ate there. Alexis hugged me. "I don't think I've ever seen your hair down—it looks nice."

"Oh . . ." My hand flew to my hair; I pulled on the ends of it. I felt misplaced, crooked, as though someone had dropped me into the wrong picture.

Betsy hugged me next. "How are you?"

"Great. Just great." A numbness washed over my thoughts—almost as if I were watching myself from the golf course through the window.

I sat down at the table and asked all the appropriate questions, smiled in all the right places. They began to discuss vacations and children, and Alexis asked Betsy, an interior decorator, what she could do about the hideously ugly wallpaper Harland's ex-wife had put in the master bathroom. Should she paint over it or rewallpaper?

I thought Harland would certainly flinch or show some emotion at the mention of Cate in such a derogatory way. But no one except me seemed to notice. It was as if she'd never been there, as if Cate was just some old homeowner who didn't use the right decorator, instead of who she was: a friend and a wife. My hands shook beneath the table, my mouth went dry as I realized that it could just as easily be I who was replaced. Now you see her; now you don't. I could just as easily disappear from this vaporous world I thought so important and they'd discuss how I had never picked out the right shoes to go with my skirt.

Betsy patted my hand. "Meridy, you're so quiet tonight. Tell us about your beach trip."

Alexis tossed her hair behind her shoulder. "Did you finish the thingie you were working on?"

"It's a curriculum—and I've almost finished. I'll probably go back there. . . ." A need to escape overcame me. "Excuse me, I need to make a quick phone call." If I said I was going to the ladies' room, which was where

I was going, Alexis and Betsy would follow me.

I opened the handicapped bathroom stall, where there was a bench. I slumped onto the paisley seat and lowered my head into my hands. I hadn't even been home for five hours and here I was hiding in the bathroom.

The slam of the outside door caused me to look up. Women's voices came to me in my hiding place.

"What's up with her?" It sounded like Alexis.

"I don't know. Maybe she's just upset B.J. got a DUI." That was definitely Betsy. I leaned toward the stall door. Nothing like overhearing a conversation while one hid in the bathroom—pitiful.

"Well, her poor, adorable husband. God, I would never leave him alone for a week. He told Harland he thought she was only going for the weekend . . . but then she just kept staying away. Harland said Beau seemed really irritated . . . and now she says she's probably going back. Something is up with them. Well, I guess people aren't always what they seem—she's always been so perfect, but you never know what goes on behind closed doors."

An electric tingle began deep in my throat. I stood up. I started to open the door when I heard Alexis say, "Well, if Beau gets lonely, I know someone who will have no problem taking care of him." She laughed.

"Alex, that is not funny . . . ," Betsy answered.

"Well, obviously perfect little Meridy is falling apart. Did you see what she was wearing? Her hair is a . . .

mess and it looks like she just rolled out of bed."

"I like her hair down and she's probably upset about her son and she just got home. . . ."

"She'll ruin Beau's chances if she's not careful. You can't have a son in jail and a wife who runs away all the time and be a senior partner. I think it looks like she just woke up and——"

I threw open the bathroom stall door; it banged against the far wall. A botanical fern print fell to the floor. Both women gasped, stepped back. "I did just wake up. Thanks, Alexis."

Alexis stepped toward me, touched my arm. I shoved her hand off my shirt and walked toward the door as gracefully as I could on my stiff legs. On the threshold I turned back around. "Will you please tell my adorable and lonely husband that I have gone to get the car?"

I walked through the corridors of the country club in a fog of anger and embarrassment. Nothing, absolutely nothing, was making any sense. I didn't belong here; I didn't belong at home anymore.

As the car pulled up to the curb, Beau came up behind me. "What are you doing?"

"Didn't Alexis and Betsy tell you? I'm falling apart." The anger that I'd hidden now came out full and ugly.

"What are you talking about? You can't just leave in the middle of dinner."

"Yes, I can. You can stay or come home with me. I'm leaving."

"Okay, let's calm down here." Beau waved the valet away with his hand. "You can't just walk away."

"Am I messing up your job opportunities?"

"That is not fair, Meridy. What is going on here?"

"I've made a terrible choice. I need to go back to Seaboro. . . . I've let a friend take the blame for something I did, and just because he says it's all right . . . it's not. Telling the truth is part of who I am, who I'm supposed to be, so I can quit just faking it."

"You're not making any sense at all."

I stared at the man I'd been married to for twenty years. This was not the place to tell him everything I carried within me. He wanted to go back inside.

"Beau, I'm going home now. You can stay and talk to your friends or come home and I'll try to tell you what I'm going through."

"I can't just walk out without paying the bill. I can't just leave Harland when he's helping with B.J.'s DUI and . . . that would be beyond rude."

"What his wife just said about me in the bathroom was beyond rude."

"This is about Cate and Alexis?"

"The substitute wife? No, it's about everything, Beau, everything before and after Alexis." I grabbed the car keys from the valet and got behind the wheel. I didn't even look to see if Beau was coming. He wouldn't be. Maybe it was an unfair test. Utter humiliation washed over me.

I returned to a house that was incredibly full of things to do, demanding my time, yet it was also completely empty. Yes, Alexis was gossiping, but she was right about one thing. I looked like I'd just woken up—I stared in the mirror at the wrinkled cotton shirt, my hair down and unstyled. But I'd woken up inside too.

My mind turned to my son. What if something worse had happened to B.J.? Mrs. Garrett's face flashed through my mind. Danny's parents' distress and grief must have been more terrible than I could ever imagine. Danny was an only child, as was B.J. I doubled over with the grief that must have surrounded them, probably still did. There was something I should have done a very long time ago: go see Danny's parents.

The phone's ring startled me. I stared at it as if it might bite me. Mother's voice came over the line. "Tulu is in the hospital, Meridy."

"What?" Her voice seemed to come from underwater.

"She's fine. I think. She fell off her porch today. I'm not sure I got the entire story, but she was unconscious for a few minutes, so they took her to the hospital. They are just keeping her overnight for observation. She's refused any X-rays or tests, but the doctors say she's going to be okay."

"Oh, Mother, I'll be there tomorrow. Will you tell her I'll be there tomorrow?"

"Meridy, you can't come back tomorrow. You just got home."

"I was coming anyway . . . I think."

"What?"

"I'll be there tomorrow. Of course, if it's okay with you."

"Yes . . ."

I hung up feeling the weariness that comes of emptiness, finished the laundry and packed. I crawled into bed wanting the Beau who'd knelt before me on a portico and proposed, who'd stood in the front lawn with a cold margarita and an obnoxious palm tree shirt, who'd rushed out into the field to hug his son who'd just pitched a no-hitter.

But when Beau came home, a cold tension saturated the room. My suitcase sat sentinel at the bedroom door to roll out in the morning. He pointed to it, opened his mouth, closed it, then turned away from me and walked into the closet.

"Beau?"

He turned to me but didn't answer.

I sat up in the bed. "Tulu fell—she's in the hospital. I'm going back to Seaboro tomorrow. I'd like it if you went with me."

"You know I can't do that. You know that." His hands were in tight fists at his sides.

"I need to . . . go see her."

"Meridy." He slammed his fist into the doorjamb. "You were going anyway."

I searched for words to say to him to alleviate this situation, to please him, to make him understand. All the times in my marriage when I had struggled to explain how I felt seemed to have drained me of any

196

words that might remain now. There was nothing to say and everything to say. I rolled onto the pillow feeling I needed to start with the truth and the past and work toward the present.

Water ran in the sink. Beau getting ready for bed sounded familiar and comfortable until he walked out of the room and I heard the guest bedroom door click shut. His anger prevented him from coming near me, prevented him from listening to me even if I did speak. Then I waited for the dawn, which lingered beyond the horizon longer than it ever had as I searched for the truth. I was as much and even more than who I was when I'd set off the firecracker. And now I would not be less.

PART III

"Do you wish to be great? Then begin by being."

—SAINT AUGUSTINE

CHAPTER THIRTEEN

*"You can recognize a person's tribe
by the way he cries."*
—GULLAH PROVERB

Sissy's new white Jaguar was parked under the live oak, moss brushing the leather convertible roof. I groaned. Just what I needed—I thought she and Penn weren't coming until next week. Mother hadn't said a word about Sissy being there.

I had planned on telling Mother about the fire, but not with Sissy's honey-laced curls straightened into a bouncy bob and her lip-lined pout and Chanel suit on a two-hundred-degree day. Somehow the moisture and heat here never affected Sissy, while my hair wilted and my clothes sagged before I reached the porch.

I opened the front door and called out for either Mother or Sissy. A rustling came from the library and I opened the double French doors. A gasp stifled itself in the base of my throat; Sissy was crumpled on the edge of the couch. Her hair fell in loose curls to her shoulders. She wore a pair of jeans and a wrinkled peach button-down blouse.

I entered the room, whispered, "What's wrong? Are the girls okay?" All I identified was something completely amiss.

Sissy looked up with swollen eyes, a red-blotched face. "Penn has a mistress. An honest-to-God-lives-in-a-condo-he-bought mistress."

I placed my hand over my mouth. "Oh, Sissy."

She lifted a crushed lace handkerchief to her face and blew her nose. "You want to know how long?"

I shook my head. No, I did not want to know how long. I glanced at Mother sitting upright in the green velvet chair, a glass of sherry in her hand.

"Five years. Five shitty years," Sissy said.

A laugh bubbled up from my throat. Mother gasped. Sissy had never cursed in her life as far as I knew.

"It's not funny." A sob broke free from Sissy's distorted face.

I stood amazed at how much of the McFadden family's facade was falling away, as if some seismic shift had taken place. I went to Sissy, wrapped my arms around her. "No, it's not funny." I hugged her. "I'm so sorry. What happened? How did you find out?"

Mother stood. "I'm sure it is much too painful for her to repeat." Her face was blanched. It would be better if this were happening to me—at least that, Mother could understand. But not Sissy.

Sissy's stare bore into Mother. "I can answer for myself, Mom."

Mother placed her hand over her mouth.

"I found his skinny blond girlfriend on top of him in the back of his BMW in the parking lot of his office complex." She shivered. "Could you throw up? I'd gone to drop some papers off for him that he'd forgotten at home. There they were in the parking deck. My God, you'd think if he'd bought her a condo, he could've at least made it there, not the parking deck."

"Oh, God, I'm sorry, Sissy."

She lifted her own glass of sherry. "What are you doing here?"

"Didn't you tell her I was coming?" I said to Mother.

Mother took a long sip of her drink. "I forgot to mention it—Sissy is having a crisis here. We have to figure out what to do. . . ."

I sat down on the couch. "Doesn't matter why I'm here. What can we do? Where are the girls?"

Sissy softened; her shoulders slumped forward. "Upstairs. I think they're actually scared to death. I didn't tell them what happened. I just threw them in the car and came here. They don't need to know. . . ." She burst into sobs again. "It'll ruin them forever."

"No, children do not need to know disgusting things like this," Mother said.

I stared at the ceiling, seeing the similarities in the way we protected our children, shielded them. "So we just let them think we're all perfect and then they never understand why they're not?"

"What?" Mother's and Sissy's voices said in unison.

I waved my hand in the air. "Okay, what can I do to help, Sissy? What do we do now?"

Sissy wiped her face with the handkerchief. "I can't think straight—I don't know. Right now I'm going to go talk to the girls. Then . . ." Her voice cracked. "Then . . . I have no idea."

"We'll figure it out. We will definitely figure it out." I patted her knee.

"What are you doing here? Beau's not . . . ?"

"No. I just have some things to take care of. And—" I glanced at Mother, who definitely could not take one more shock today; the symptoms of a hysterical fit were etched all over her tight face and listless eyes. "I'm going to go get my bags. . . . Are the girls in my old room?"

"Yes . . ." Sissy stood, then sat, then stood again as if she couldn't figure out even the simplest motions. "I'll move them to the guest room in the attic cove."

I nodded, almost feeling the unopened wooden box under the bed in my hand, my tattered quilt over my body.

"Meridy, don't be so selfish. Let the girls stay where they are," Mother said.

Sissy rolled her eyes. "Mom, let Meridy have her room. For God's sake, there are a lot more things to worry about than that. The girls don't care and neither do I. They don't like sleeping in the same bed anyway." Sissy stood, walked out and slammed the door.

Mother and I exchanged raised eyebrows. "Okay, then. I'll be getting my things. Do you have any more news about Tulu?" I asked.

"I think she's fine. I heard they let her come home this morning."

"You didn't go see her?"

"Well, I was going to, but I heard she's okay."

"I'll go see her tomorrow." I glanced over my shoulder as I moved to leave the room.

"Oh . . . how come my family is falling apart now . . . and Dewey not here?" Mother lifted her glass, then set it on the side table. "I never thought these kinds of things would happen now. . . ."

"Why not now, Mother?"

"Because I felt as if I'd already got through the worst parts. . . ."

"The worst parts?" I left to grab my suitcase, laptop computer and papers. Yes, the worst parts.

My bedroom swallowed some of the loneliness and battered emotions. But a deeper fear arrived—Cate and now Sissy. Was I better than them? No, much worse. So why would Beau be any different than these men who had seemed so . . . devoted?

I slipped on my tennis shoes, walked down the hall and knocked on Sissy's door, not knowing what I could or would say, but knowing I had to try to find some words to comfort her.

She opened the door in her white cotton gown. "What are you doing?" she asked, glanced at my shoes.

"Want to take a walk on the beach?" I whispered, nodded down the hall.

She backed into the room, slumped onto her bed. "Meridy, I don't even have the energy to take a walk down the hall. No."

I sat next to her. "I'm so sorry you're going through this, Sissy. I really am."

She looked up at me. "See, here's the problem—I just don't get it. I've tried so hard to do everything right, to be so good, and look where it got me. You never tried that hard . . . and you're fine. It's so backward and unfair and—"

"I don't know what you're talking about. . . . I try too." Anger attempted to rise, then sank in the empathy I felt for my sister.

"Maybe now you do . . . but you didn't when we were kids." She lay back on the bed, sighed.

"Why do I feel like you're picking a fight?" I said, but smiled and tousled her hair.

Sissy rolled her head toward me. "I'm sorry. . . . I'm just so pissed off. It's not you. You walked in the room at the wrong time. I'm sorry. . . . Your life is so . . . perfect and mine is all screwed up now."

I laughed. "Maybe it's time we had a little sister-to-sister chat."

"What do you mean?"

I grabbed Sissy's hand, squeezed it. "Nothing . . ."

"I really thought that if I did everything right, nothing like this would happen to me. Isn't that ridiculous? Like being good is insurance on love."

"Maybe the love we need or want isn't the kind we deserve. . . . It isn't a prize or . . . something. I don't know. I'm still trying to figure it out myself. Let's just find out what would help you right now."

"Sleep, sleep would be good." She closed her eyes and curled into a ball.

I lay down next to her and held on to her hand. And at that moment there weren't words to be said, or platitudes to offer, or even a parable to quote—only a hand to be held. After a while, her breath softened, then evened out into the rhythm of sleep I'd heard from her my entire childhood.

CHAPTER FOURTEEN

"I have a lot of songs for children,
but I have no child."
—GULLAH PROVERB

The long overdue desire to see Danny's parents awoke with me the next morning. I called B.J. on the way to the Garretts'—the thought of losing my only son had been more than I could fathom when I was eighteen years old, but now it was unimaginable.

"Hey, Mom." I knew his sleep-soaked voice.

"I woke you." I stopped at a red light before the bridge.

"That's okay. I wasn't sleeping well anyway."

"I just needed to hear your voice," I said. A car behind me honked as the light turned green.

"Where are you?" He sounded more alert.

"Crossing the bridge in Seaboro."

"That's my favorite part of the trip to Grandma's.

"Me too," I said with the slightest tickle of relief that I had handed down something sacred, something of beauty, to my son along with the things I regretted.

"What are you doing there? Didn't you go home yesterday? I'm confused. . . ."

"I did, but an old family friend is . . . well, was in the hospital and . . . enough about me. How are you doing?"

"Feeling pretty bad about all of it. Such an idiot. But I talked to Dad and he said Mr. Finnegan's brother would be my lawyer and was planning on proposing that I pay for my DUI by giving educational training at the local high school, on the dangers of drunk driving, taking a defensive-driving class and losing my license for a year—and the worst, being benched for the first three baseball games of the season. He says that if we show I'm willing to pay for what I've done . . . well, you know the deal."

"I do." I focused on the road; I would not cry on the phone with my son. I was driving toward a family who'd paid the ultimate price.

"I've gotta go, Mom. Thanks for waking me up. . . . I've got to meet with Coach."

I hung up and drove until I reached Sun City—a retirement community forty minutes from Seaboro. The clusters of homes seemed to squat and protect themselves from the open sky and sun and were arranged so that everyone had a golf course view. I rechecked the address and then stood in front of number 206. I knocked on a door exactly like the twelve others running down the sidewalk.

Bee Garrett opened the door with a smile that dropped as recognition spread across her face. She had changed, but not beyond remembrance. Her face was much thinner, her body fuller and her blue eyes faded, as if the tears had washed the deeper colors away. I was ashamed. Yet she still stood as straight as the columns on her old front porch.

She whispered. "Meridy?"

My gaze dropped to the WE ONLY PLAY GOLF ON DAYS ENDING WITH Y foot mat. I couldn't look her in the eyes.

"Yes," I said.

"Oh, my dear."

"I know—I should've called." Then I felt her arms around my neck and her cheek next to mine, and Chris Garrett appeared in the doorway. Bee's hug made my knees buckle, my heart leap from my chest. I think I hugged her back while Chris squinted at me through his bifocals.

"Is that you, Meridy McFadden?"

Bee released her grip on me, but grabbed my hand. "Yes, it's her. Do you believe it? Look at this beautiful woman. . . ." She beamed at me. "Look at you. We've wanted to see you for so long . . . and look at us—we're a mess." She ran her hands over her hair, which fell to her shoulders in thick silver waves. "We didn't expect guests at all."

"I'm sorry. I should've called," I repeated.

Chris stepped forward, placed his hand on my shoulder; I thought I might collapse beneath its familiar weight. I tried to speak and a childish sound came out that sounded something like "Sorry."

They glanced at each other; Bee wrapped her arms around my shoulders. "Come in, come in. Please."

I walked into the house and noticed some of the same furnishings, picture frames and knickknacks I'd once known—in a different place, in a different home. I said to Bee, "I've been in town and I just wanted to stop by, say hello . . . I've been thinking a lot about you and—"

"Sit, sit." Bee patted the couch. "Chris, go get her some iced tea, please."

I took a seat on the beige cotton muslin couch. Bee sat next to me. "How are you, my dear? We think about you so much. Please catch us up on your life."

"I've been good, really." Then a strength I must have been garnering through the weeks, through each truth, came over me and I sat up straighter, fuller. "Until a few weeks ago when I sort of . . . woke up.

Bee nodded as if she knew what I was going to say and just waited. Chris appeared at the side of the couch, but I couldn't look at his face—the face Danny would have if he were alive now, wide, full, handsome in that way that makes you stop to figure out why.

I squeezed Bee's hand. "You know they're reconstructing the Keeper's Cottage? The foundation was still intact and—"

Bee spoke. "We've tried to stay out of it, dear. We have to be . . . done with certain things."

"I wasn't trying to say you should help. . . . I'm messing this up, aren't I? I just needed to tell you something."

"Tell us what, dear?" Bee wrapped her arms around me again and I wanted to stay there for a few minutes longer.

I took a deep breath. "That night was *all* my fault. Danny and I were lighting firecrackers. . . . I lit the one that hit the roof. It wasn't the bonfire like they've always thought."

Bee gasped. Chris jumped up, then sat.

I stood as well. "I know you must not want me in your home and I'll leave, but I had to tell you in person—it's part of the . . . way it should be."

Bee looked up, but she smiled. In the face of this woman's pain and loss of her only son, my petty accomplishments and concerns over what happened to my family reputation and marriage felt hollow and inadequate.

"Sit, Meridy. Please." Bee's voice cracked and I had no choice but to do as she said. "Wait here. I'll be right back."

Chris followed his wife to the end of the hall, leaving me alone. I looked around the room, but the details blurred. I covered my face and waited for what Bee had for me, or wanted to say to me.

She returned with a large black book, sat next to me and dropped it in my lap.

"What is this?" I held my hands up in the air as if it might burn me.

"Danny's scrapbook. Take a look at it."

"No, I can't." I turned my face away. "I just came to tell you about what really happened that night. I didn't want you to blame Tim or Danny or . . . anyone else but me." The weight of the book on my lap felt heavier than my entire body. I grabbed Bee's hand. "I have an only son too, Bee. I would die if I lost him. . . ."

"Look at the first page, Meridy."

I opened the top and flipped open the first page. Danny and me at the prom—I wore a baby blue dress of raw silk that rippled to the floor in waves. Danny wore a white tuxedo with blue ruffles at his chest.

"He loved you, Meridy," Bee said. "He made a choice to go into that burning cottage. I've prayed, since the day he died, that you carried no guilt. I didn't think I should contact you if you didn't want to see us. Now I see I should have. If you've carried this guilt with you—it must have killed you."

No, only my heart.

"He was always the strong one . . . I wasn't."

Chris sat on the other side of me and grabbed my hand. "Strong one? Who came to my front porch and stood up to Danny Garrett at twelve years old? You were always strong, Meridy. Bee's right. . . . It was Danny's choice to go back in—we are proud of him. He did the right and terrible thing."

I whispered and held Chris's hand. "I loved him so much . . . and I forgot and then I remembered, and when I remembered I couldn't think about anything else. It all came back to me when I heard they were trying to make Tim pay to renovate the cottage. I wanted to do something, anything." I looked at Danny's parents, whom I had once thought I loved more than my own.

Bee tapped her finger on the edge of the scrapbook. "That book is as full of pictures of you as it is of him. He loved you too, Meridy."

I turned the pages: Danny in his football uniform, Danny standing in front of his Camaro in bell-bottom jeans with a lopsided grin, Danny and his dad on the back dock holding a whiting up for the camera. Then I turned the page to Danny's senior picture—we'd stood in line in the cafeteria, which had smelled like spaghetti and bland tomato sauce with a slight twinge of chocolate milk. Danny had winked at me right before the picture and in the photo his left eye was half open.

"It smelled like spaghetti and chocolate milk." I tapped the picture.

"What?" Bee asked, touching the scrapbook.

"That day we took our senior pictures . . . in the cafeteria. I'd forgotten about that."

Bee nodded, squeezed my knee.

I took in the pictures—ones I'd thought I'd forgotten, but remembered with each turn of the page, each beat of my heart. Bee whispered, "You have lived a life since then, Meridy. Please tell me you have not lived with guilt all this time."

"I've tried to live the best life I can. . . . I've tried so hard to make up for it, do . . . good."

"Oh, child. Do you think Danny died so you could live a good life or a full life?"

"Full," I whispered, and understood this truth.

CHAPTER FIFTEEN

"Any kind of crying will do for a funeral."
—GULLAH PROVERB

I drove the car faster than was necessary down 278, gambling that the cops weren't out for their daily quota of tourists driving four miles over the speed limit. More of who I used to be drew me forward: the box beneath my bed.

I ran up the stairs of Mother's house, dropped to my knees next to my bed and grabbed the box. I lifted the lid; rust dust scattered on the flowered carpet and the back left hinge fell off. The box was no bigger than a postcard—intricate in its design for a boy of sixteen who'd once carved it and now built houses. Yellowed pieces of paper and two upside-down photographs rested inside the box, wavered in the light of my over- head pink crystal chandelier. This was the first time these papers and photographs had seen the light in twenty-six years, and they danced as if they wanted to jump from their coffin of dead dreams.

I closed my eyes as the feel of the day Danny and I had written on these papers rushed back at me. The rain had come in torrents all day, sideways and twisting with the odd green light of a Lowcountry storm. It had been the kind of day when the latent smell of mildew leaked from the house, and Tulu seemed frantic with her lemon cleaner in case Mother wrinkled her nose. Danny and I had stared out the window like the two kids in the *Cat in the Hat* book, not knowing what to do when almost everything we usually did was outside in the dense nature—away from Mother, away from criticism.

The box Tim had made for my seventeenth birthday sat on the coffee table in the drawing room. I'd turned away from the window and picked it up.

Danny joined me. "Damn, Tim gave you a nicer present than I did." He walked over, cuddled my neck.

"Never," I said. Danny had given me a charm bracelet with a single shell on it. I held my arm up and shook the bracelet. "Never."

"Well, you can put all your favorite stuff in here."

"Our stuff," I said, and found his lips.

Then somehow we spent an entire afternoon writing our dreams for the future on small scraps of paper and stuffing them in the box. We took our two favorite pictures of each other and shoved them in there also. Tulu came in twice and laughed her pure laugh.

"Now," Danny said, lowering me to the floor. "When we are old and gray, when the kids are grown, we can look back and see if we've made all those dreams come true."

I pushed him off me. "Danny, Mother will be home any minute. Get up." I jumped up and laughed. The mere thought of Mother discovering Danny and me together would ruin anything special about it.

Now I ran my fingers across the old papers as if they

might disintegrate. I pulled out the first torn sheet. "Be a vet," it said in all capital letters. That was how Danny had lived his life: in all capital letters.

The next piece of paper contained my crooked, loopy handwriting with a heart for the dot of the letter i. "House on the beach with porches galore."

I took the papers out one by one: dreams of a boy and girl long, long gone. "Have a boat," he'd written; "Teach kids," I'd written. "A big bed overlooking the ocean," he'd written. "A library overflowing with books," I'd written. We'd made wishes for cars that weren't even made anymore, for friends I'd since forgotten about.

I had known what I wanted so surely that I had written it on scraps of paper and just believed it'd happen. The naïveté of the pitiful girl who had no idea of the tragedy awaiting her shone through the carefree dreams she believed were possible.

Inside this box were two entirely unlived lives, but one of us was still alive.

A slicing pain cut through my middle and I bent over the carpet and lay down. So I had accomplished my goal—when Danny had died, so had this girl. But she really hadn't, because here she sat on her childhood carpet reading her childhood dreams.

I reached inside the box and pulled out the first picture—of me on my sixteenth birthday at a surprise party my parents had given me at the roller-skating rink when skating was the in thing and I owned a pair of pink leg warmers. Light surrounded my hair—stick straight and pulled into a barrette in the back. Although I couldn't see the clip, I remembered it was red plastic with a small hole in the middle. My hair fell to my chest, and light surrounded me from a disco ball above me that wasn't visible in the photograph.

Danny had loved this picture—said I looked like an angel—and now, at forty-something, I agreed with him. Ah, to look like that again. More important, to feel like that again.

I stared at this girl and I felt it all—I was sixteen; I loved my leg warmers; I loved Danny; I loved my friends; I loved when the skate DJ played "Maybe I'm Amazed" by Wings.

I pulled out the picture of Danny but held it upside down for a moment. I fingered the paper, savoring the moment, and then flipped it over. I took a sharp breath and felt a quiver under my lungs. I tasted the salt air, heard his fingers whisper across my skin moments after I'd taken this picture. We'd been on a family picnic on the shores of Seaboro Beach—the McFaddens and Garretts attempting some type of bonding, although the families were as different in origin as the sunrise and sunset.

In the picture, Danny stood at the edge of the sea, his hand outstretched to me, his palm flat. His mouth was open and I remembered what he'd said: "Put down that camera and come swim." I'd stepped back and shot this picture and then he'd splashed me. I'd dropped the camera on the beach blanket while pretending to fight his attempts to pull me into the ocean.

214

Of course he'd won; I'd let him.

The warmth of the sea, the feel of his skin next to mine, our families laughing at us.

I curled into a ball and tucked the picture into my palm. I closed my eyes and let sorrow cover me, not only for this boy who was gone, but also for the girl in the pink leg warmers who wanted to "teach kids" and have a "house with porches."

A rustle of silk and the soft vibration on the floor told me Mother had entered my room. I jumped up.

"Meridy, are you okay?"

"Yes, yes." I wiped at my face; the photograph fluttered to the floor.

Mother advanced to the photograph I'd dropped, and picked it up. A long moment of silence spread across my room like the hum of a vacuum. She didn't look up when she spoke. "You can't live in the past."

"I'm not living in it. I'm . . . remembering it, mourning it maybe." My voice came out in a whisper, although I hadn't meant it to. A wave of emptiness rose. "Or maybe just looking at it."

"You have to worry about what you have now, Meridy. You can't just throw it away . . . Don't."

"I'm not throwing anything away, Mother." I waved my hand toward the scattered papers on the floor.

"All it does is bring pain and bad memories and—"

"It doesn't bring just bad memories. It brings back great memories too." A thought came to me, as though looking at these things of the past gave the memory permission to return with joy. "Remember when Daddy

215

took Danny and me out on the boat, and we got lost in the fog and landed on a sandbar and had to wait until the tide came back in to go home? We laughed until our faces hurt. Remember when Danny tried to help you out by cutting the back lawn because the gardener was sick, and he cut down your dormant prize rosebush because he thought it was dead?" I was whispering now. "There is so much good in the past you want me to forget."

Mother bent over and picked up the photograph of me. "Your sixteenth birthday."

"Yes."

"Oh." She rubbed her finger across the picture. "You were so beautiful that day, so gracious to your guests, so . . . poised."

"What?

"I was so proud of you that day, proud of the woman you were becoming."

I didn't remember the day exactly like that. "I was grounded the next day for breaking curfew that night."

"Probably." Mother looked up at me.

I looked out the window; an osprey dipped below the tree line and rose again with a fish dangling from its feet. Alive—everything was so damn alive here. At home I'd stare out my back window into my neighbors' fence line and the tip of their pool slide. "You know," I said to Mother, "I had very simple dreams. I wasn't all that complicated." I indicated the scraps of paper. "I didn't ask for an Oscar or dream of a Pulitzer . . . or a house big enough to hold a clan of families."

"That was the girl you were then. . . ." Mother held up the picture. "Then."

"The girl I was then is part of the woman I am now." I understood it only as I said it, and a sensation appeared in the middle of my heart—the kind I felt standing next to rivers—the possibility of change, of life.

The phone rang in the hall and Mother turned toward the door, then back to me. "You should let all this go, Meridy. Danny is—"

"Dead. I know. Danny is dead."

"I was going to say *gone,*" she said.

"But I'm not."

Mother closed her eyes. "Thank God." And then she turned and walked out of my room.

"But I'm not," I repeated.

The curriculum papers lay heavy in my hands. I stood on Tulu's porch and listened to her footsteps labor down the narrow hallway. When she opened the door I was already holding the packet out like a gift I was in a hurry to give.

"Hello, lil' one." She hugged me while ignoring the papers. "You came back."

"Are you okay, Tulu?" I touched the side of her head where a white bandage, the size of a credit card, covered a shaved spot on her head.

"Oh, I'm such a klutz. I fell on the porch and . . . I'm fine. They made me stay in that nasty place overnight just to prove I'm okay." She touched her head.

"Mother told me you refused tests. You should've let them at least x-ray it."

"Why? So I can spend my children's money on something unneeded? No. I'm fine. What are you doing back here?"

"I came because I heard you were in the hospital."

"That is the only reason?" She winked.

Of course it wasn't the only reason—I needed her. "There's more. I wanted to give you this curriculum—see if I've covered it all. I really want to do this right. I want the children to see the culture the way it really is—*all the things of the past that still matter.*" And just like Tulu's, the words I spoke were as much about me as about the papers.

"Come in, come in." She swept her arms across the doorway.

I wanted to sit outside on the porch, away from the reminder of her poverty and dilapidated house and furniture. Porches always seemed so much more friendly and . . . equal. I didn't have a single porch on my house in Atlanta; I had a deck, but not a porch—there was a difference.

"Can we sit out here?" I pointed at a chair.

"Sure," Tulu said.

We sat facing each other in shredding wicker rocking chairs. I watched her face as she flipped the pages and read through my work. The curriculum was still handwritten and I felt like I was ten years old and waiting for her approval on how well I had made my bed.

Finally she raised her head. "Lil' one, this is wonderful. You have captured the essence of the Gullah culture. You have a gift—you know that—of communicating in a way a child can understand. We must always know the entire story to understand any of it. You used everything I told you and made a story—you know how to tell a story."

My heart swelled. "Really?"

"Really, really. But do you mind if I show you one thing more? I feel that you've left out a few important things." She stood.

"I'd love to see something more. . . ."

She had me drive to the curved edge of Seaboro where a Gullah graveyard sank into the ground between a disintegrating iron fence and the riverbank. Here the river ran wild, fast and alive, full of songs to the sea. Trinkets lay on gravestones: broken pots, bowls and stopped clocks. Fresh plants and herbs were scattered among the over-grown weeds and thick rush grasses. Tulu held my elbow as we walked toward the graveyard's center.

I spoke first. "When we were kids we'd dare each other to come here at night and touch the stones."

"I know."

"Of course you do." I laughed and immediately felt irreverent. "Sorry."

"Stop being sorry. Stop now. You must laugh again—stop hiding your laughter. Do you know why we build our graveyards by the water, by this river?"

"No . . . ," I said.

"So that our souls will be carried across the sea to our home in Africa."

"Home . . ."

"Yes. The river runs past this graveyard and out to the sea. The most dangerous part of the river is where it meets the sea—where the tides run in and out and create a dangerous current."

I nodded, but she didn't look satisfied.

"Ah, I can't make you see, can I?"

"See what?" I looked past her to see if there was something behind her I was missing.

"See that the river is our life, a flow that takes us home. And where it meets the heart, it is the most turbulent."

My breath caught in the bottom of my throat. I stood very still. I hadn't let life reach my heart in a very long time. It was too dangerous, risky and turbulent. I had let meager trickles of water run by and had withheld the remainder.

"I do see," I said, my voice as soft as the moss below my sandals. But I needed to absorb this revelation alone, not discuss it in the middle of the graveyard. I took a deep breath and leaned down, touched a broken clock.

"And the clocks, trinkets and containers . . . what are those all about?" I asked. "I bet kids would love to know about that."

Tulu retreated from the quiet moment as well. "Most of the items are water symbols. And the clocks are usually stopped at either twelve—for Judgment

Day—or at the time of death. I wanted to show you one more thing. . . ." She ran her hand over a small tombstone. "This was my first child—she lived only two days."

"Oh, Tulu."

"Her name was Anyika. The only thing I feel you've left out of your class lectures is the meaning of names—one can easily lose the right to a name. Names have power." She tapped the gravestone with her forefinger. "My child's name meant 'She is beautiful.' "

"Oh. I'll definitely include a section on names."

"You can see that we respect our graveyards and our names. We believe the dead are still with us—that their souls go to God, but their spirits stay on earth."

"Tell me you don't believe in ghosts, Tulu."

"Do you know the ghost story from the Keeper's Cottage?"

"Not Danny . . . ," I whispered. "Not about him, right?"

"No . . . back in the mid-1800s, the lighthouse keeper had a daughter, Lilly. They say she was as beautiful as the flower she was named after. A man commissioned from the government came to check on the lighthouse and fell in love with her. He was married and though he promised to one day return for her, he never did. They say Lilly still wanders the tower looking for him over the sea."

"The tower is gone. . . . It fell that night."

"Yes, it did."

"She can't look for him anymore."

"He wasn't coming back for her," Tulu said.

I stared off toward the river, which ran into the sea a few hundred yards away. "What are you trying to tell me? Tell me in plain words, Tulu."

"Stop looking for something you already have, Meridy. Stop looking for a ghost of the past to give you permission to fully live your life. Stop wandering and waiting, or you are no better off than Danny or Lilly—ignoring what is alive and here for what is dead and gone."

Anger that often comes with painful truth ran over my arms in a chill. I gritted my teeth as I spoke. "I'm not waiting for permission or someone to come so I can live my life. I am living my life. . . . I'm here to do that."

"Then do it."

Tulu appeared exhausted, faded. I shivered in the warm afternoon. "Are you okay?"

"I'm fine—it is you I worry about. You can't continue this way with a dead heart. I see nothing of you any-more—you might as well be here." She spread her hands across the hand-carved stones.

"No!" I think I screamed the word.

Tulu smiled. "There you are, Meridy. Let's go home." She ran her hand again over the top of her baby's gravestone.

When we arrived at her house, I sat in the rocker on the front porch. "Thank you for this." I held the papers up to the air. "Thank you."

"See what it is telling you."

"Okay, I'll try. Tulu?"

"Yes."

"I opened the box."

"And what did you find?"

"A bunch of stuff I'd wanted when I was seventeen years old."

"No, Meridy." She leaned forward and her eyes came awake, sparkled. "Those are the smaller pieces that only add up to who you were. Take the sum total of what they tell you. It is not things or accomplishments you wanted. It was a value. Those pieces of paper won't tell you what to do, but they just might tell you who to be."

"No, they just told me all the things Danny and I wanted. You know, houses, jobs, porches . . . all that."

"No, those are what came from who you wanted to be. Those were just the result of the being. One tree does not make a forest—look at all of them."

I turned away, confused again. She placed her hand on my shoulder. "Lil' one. I need you to promise me something."

"Yes?"

"I need you to promise me that you will allow the river to reach your heart, not stop life's flow as you have."

"What?"

"Just promise me."

"Okay. I promise." Frustration overwhelmed me. Enough of the proverbs and half-told truths. I stood, leaned down and kissed her forehead. "Thank you for everything, Tulu." A porch board beneath my feet crackled; I jumped back. "Tulu, you can't live . . . like this." I grabbed her hand.

She didn't need any help. "Oh, dearest lil' one, you always thought it was me who was the poor one. You thought it was me when it is your heart that is asleep— it is you who is poor."

Poor, I'd never once thought of the McFaddens as poor. "We were the poor ones," I said, closed my eyes and leaned my forehead to hers.

"Only in spirit and truth," she whispered.

I sat in the car for long moments before driving away; I felt that I needed to go tell Tulu one more thing, or maybe hear one more thing. I shook off the thought and stuck the key in the ignition and drove back to Mother's house. Maybe we McFaddens really were the poor ones all along.

CHAPTER SIXTEEN

"I've been in sorrow's kitchen
and licked out all the pots."
—GULLAH PROVERB

I drove home from Tulu's slowly. I passed the Seaboro Library and made a sharp turn into the parking lot. Mother didn't have Internet access and I wanted to discover what my name meant, what power my name might have.

Nothing, my name meant absolutely nothing, because I couldn't find *Meridy* in a single search engine on the computer. I rushed home to ask Mother where my name came from.

"Mother?" I opened the door to her bedroom. She sat in the bed with her head back on a satin pillow, a novel facedown on her lap. The lights were dim; the room was full of the rosewater fragrance that caused childhood memories to rush back at me.

"I have a migraine," she said, her eyes closed.

"I'm sorry." I lowered my voice.

"Do you need something?"

"I just wanted to ask you a question—is *Meridy* a form of *Margaret* or *Mary*?"

"What?" Her eyes opened. "Neither. It's just *Meridy*."

"Why did you name me *Meridy*?"

"I thought it was . . . pretty."

I walked toward her bed. "Well, *Margaret* means 'pearl' and *Mary* means either 'rebellious' or 'wished-for child,' and somehow it seems important to know which."

A tightness of her jaw showed me that my voice was increasing her headache. She whispered, "It came from the name of the woman who paid my way through college. Her name was Meredith Donnelly. I should've used my mother's name—but I used Meredith's. I have no idea what it means. It doesn't matter."

"Yes, it does."

"I didn't mean it to be anything other than a pretty name. . . . Why don't you pick what you want it to mean?" Mother rubbed her temples with her forefingers.

"Can I get you anything? Water, tea, a pill?"

"No, I'm fine. . . ." She waved her hand toward the door, which I took as my sign to go. I kissed her forehead and left.

Sleep came in sporadic shifts after my visit with Tulu. There seemed to be multiple pieces of a puzzle in each word she spoke, on each piece of paper from the box, and I couldn't figure out how to put them all together. There was a picture forming that floated above and beyond my consciousness. I drifted off before dawn and again dreamed of the day I met Danny on my twelfth birthday. But for the first time in twenty-six years, the dream ended differently. Before Danny turned to leave, smoke at his edges, he handed me the dolphin box. I clutched it to my chest. The sharp edges of the rusted hinges scratched my forefinger; the latch squeaked against my hands.

When I awoke, Tulu's words came back strong and full: *You will know you have come out on the other side of the sacred when someone gives you something in a dream.* I sat up in the bed, felt Tulu's presence in my room as if I could reach out and touch the rough and smooth pattern of her braids between my fingers. I spoke aloud. "I haven't come out on the other side of anything at all."

I rose and stood at the window and scanned the sky for a whisper of dawn. Sissy had gone home to try to talk things out with Penn. Beau hadn't answered the phone at either his office or our home, although I'd left messages. B.J. slept alone in his dorm room hours away. Mother was curled in the eerie quiet of painkiller sleep, and I was more alone than I had ever been since the night Danny died.

Light crept over the back roof of the house and spilled onto the lawn in the thin strips of a new day. I slipped on a pair of shorts and a T-shirt and headed for the beach—through the front door, not the window.

I walked the shoreline, dragging my thoughts through the sand. Why had Danny given me the box? What did I need to come out on the other side of?

Tim's voice came from behind me. "What are you doing up so early?"

I stumbled and my bare feet splashed into the incoming tide. "You scared me." I kicked a spray of water at him.

He jumped back, but the water hit his legs. "Well, you're scaring me. I saw you from the deck—wandering up and down the beach mumbling to yourself like a madwoman."

"You spying on me?"

"No, couldn't sleep. I always watch the ocean when I can't sleep—it never sleeps either. We have a deal. It'll stay up with me if I ask it to." He grinned.

"You think I'm a madwoman? You have a deal with a body of water. . . ."

Tim made a growling noise in the back of his throat. "You drive me crazy. . . . Seriously, when did you come back?"

"A couple days ago. I was gonna call you today. I

feel like I have this huge puzzle to solve, but all it does is get more and more complicated, like one of those awful calculus 'problems of the week' that Mrs. Greene used to give us. Tulu tells me all these strange things in proverb and story, and I keep thinking I'm on the edge of understanding something . . . and then it disappears."

Tim nodded. "I wish I could solve this one for you, Meridy."

"I don't think anyone can. It's almost like something I have to—I don't know—find. I feel my marriage slipping away and at the same time I feel some part of me coming back—like they're moving in opposite directions. Does that make any sense?"

"Completely."

As we walked in silence back toward Mother's land, Tim reached out and took my hand. "Meridy McFadden, I've known you since you were four years old and I know how strong you are. You'll be fine."

In a world that echoed with loneliness, I gripped Tim's hand tighter. When we reached the corner of my childhood home, I stopped short. A man stood on the back porch, his hand shading his eyes, his face twisted away from us.

"Who's that?" I pointed.

"Hell if I know—it's your house, not mine."

"It's . . . what time is it?"

Tim shrugged his shoulders. "Six, maybe six thirty."

"This can't be good—what man comes to Mother's house at dawn with anything but bad news?" The man turned, squinted against the morning and looked directly at us.

"Beau." I took a sharp breath.

"What?"

"Beau, my husband, Beau." I released Tim's hand, hugged him. "I have to go talk to him."

Tim stepped back, tilted his head. "This would probably not be the best time to meet him, huh?" He laughed.

"Go on." I punched his arm, then ran toward Beau.

When I reached the porch, I threw my arms around him; he stood rigid, taut as a wire stretched from Atlanta to Seaboro. I stepped back and asked, "Honey?"

"I drove all night to get here, to see you and talk about what the hell is going on. Now I know what the hell is going on." He stepped backward, banged into a column.

"What?" His words made no sense to me.

"What's his name, Meridy? Who is he?"

"Who?" I reached for his hand. "What are you talking about?"

"What am I? A moron? Do you think I didn't just see you walking down the beach holding that man's hand? I saw you ten minutes ago, but couldn't believe it was you. Then you got closer and by God it was you. Were you just leaving his house, his—?" He turned and kicked the column, slammed his fist against a wicker table. "Why didn't you tell me all this was about someone else . . . not some curriculum or school project or not noticing the forsythia or some shit like that?"

"No." Panic confused my words and all I felt I needed to tell him, to show him. "It's not what you think . . . at all. He's a childhood friend—Tim."

"You've known him since childhood?"

"Yes. And there's nothing there—well, there's everything there." I grabbed Beau's face to make him look at me, but he backed away, kept his face averted. "I'm making this worse. Please . . . please give me ten minutes to explain and then you can run as far away from me as you want. Just give that to me. . . . Just *listen* to me for ten minutes."

He slumped onto the rocking chair and his head fell into his hands. "You should've told me the truth."

"That's what I'm about to do, Beau." I sat across from him and took his hands. "Tim is an old friend—a neighbor. I've known him since I was four years old. Once, a very long time ago, I was a headstrong child who had a best friend named Tim and a boyfriend named Danny. I loved them both. . . ." I took a deep breath and used what Tulu had told me—turning the pain and harder parts into a story. I told Beau everything about Danny, about the fire, about how I felt, who I was and what I'd done—nothing edited, nothing obscured.

Beau didn't say a word and I spoke as fast as I could out of pure fear that I would run out of time, or he would stop listening, or I would decide to hide some of it.

"So then Mother called and told me about the cottage and how they were trying to make Tim pay for the renovations, and I wanted to help. I thought that a little fundraiser and some money would make it all right. And I knew I had to see Tulu again—find more of what she has been trying to tell me. Then I tried to go home—go back to normal and I couldn't. My heart was all stuck up in my throat. I couldn't breathe. Alexis and Betsy saw it and so did I—I didn't belong and they saw right through me; I was faking it."

"So you thought you'd run back here and not tell me why—just come back." He stared out to sea, his voice robotic and empty. "You couldn't tell me. You didn't trust me enough to tell me."

"No, that is absolutely not it. It wasn't a matter of mistrusting you, but of not wanting to hurt you any more. B.J. got that DUI and you were devastated—I couldn't get through to you at all. You were completely inside your own shell—busy with your case and worried about our son."

"I wasn't too busy to hear this." His face crumpled in an identical pattern as B.J.'s when he was a young child.

"Yes, you were. But I'm not blaming you. I had twenty other years I could've told you about Danny and the fire. I'm just trying to explain to you why I had to come back. And Beau, I know how you feel about these kinds of things—I understand what you're thinking without you saying it—I have to pay for what I've done. I know that. You taught me that too."

"I taught you that? That you have to pay for what you've done?"

"Of course." I leaned back in the chair. My neck and back ached with the effort to tell this man I loved that I was nothing like what he believed I was, but that I loved him anyway. "I love you, Beau. I didn't want to hurt you or . . . make things worse at home. You were already dealing with B.J. and I didn't want to be a burden."

"A burden?" His head came up. "A burden? What are you talking about? Is that some excuse for lying to me?"

"Lying? I didn't lie to you." I snapped back as if he'd hit me. "I was trying to—"

"Not telling me is lying. Same thing." Yes, in his eyes omission was the same as commission.

I dropped my head into my hands. "I'm so sorry. I haven't been thinking straight and—"

"I came to talk to you—I've missed you terribly and I find you on the beach with a friend you *can* talk to, and I find out this is about the memory of some high school love who died while saving lives? You're here for that?"

"No . . . you didn't listen to me, did you? I'm here for . . . me. You're not hearing anything I'm saying to you."

"What do *you* want to do, Meridy? What do you want *me* to do?" His voice echoed across the porch.

I closed my eyes. The answer to this question seemed as important as any ever posed. Then the pieces of all Tulu had told me, of all the notes in the box, settled into words. My eyes shot open. "That's it, Beau. It is not what I want to *do,* or want you to *do.* It is who I want to be, who I was meant to be."

"And who is that, Meridy?"

I still didn't have an answer. "We're disconnected, too busy. We have reasons and lists for everything. We don't make mistakes or if we do, we pretend we didn't. We hide behind pretense and image. I want something worthy, something of sacred value. I want an open heart; I want connection—with you. I want to touch lives. I want to live, not just do." My voice rose with each sentence until I was as close to yelling as I'd come in years. "No faking it." The answers were coming slowly, but arriving nonetheless.

Beau opened his mouth. I held up my hand. "Give me a minute here to find the right words."

He licked his lips and leaned back in his chair, waved his hands at me in a "Go ahead" movement.

I paced the porch. "I want to be someone who takes the dare, isn't scared of what others think, helps others, appreciates nature, loves to teach. Someone who listens to the longing and doesn't squelch it every time it shows up just because it *might* be inappropriate. Because if I listen to longing, it just might show up again and again. I want to be someone who laughs loud, says what she thinks and not what others want to hear." I reached for him. "Am I making sense?"

He crossed his arms with knotted fists. "You still haven't told me what you want to do. I'm totally confused, Meridy."

"You see, I've been looking and looking for all the things to do—like organizing the arts festival, writing the curriculum, as if these 'doings' could wake my heart. But when Tulu told me how the river and sea meet in the most turbulent current, I understood. I hadn't gone there in so long—to the turbulent parts of me where all the longing and desire are dangerous and lie below the painful memories. It's dangerous because love can disappoint and hurt. But it isn't better to just be safe anymore."

"Are you trying to tell me you don't love me? That you've used me to be *safe?*"

"Absolutely not. I'm trying to tell you that I love you completely and now I want to live that way."

He released his fist, planted his hands on the arms of the chair. "Let me tell you what I hear you saying, Meridy. You don't feel you belong at home with me anymore because it isn't where you can be yourself. You loved another man much more than you've ever loved me. You trust and care about what is here more than what is at home. You couldn't be your full or real self—whatever that means—at home, with me. You don't want what I have spent twenty-odd years building. You think all we've built together is fake. And most important—you lied to me. That is exactly what I hear."

None of what he said was true, wholly true, but none of it could be argued with. He was a good lawyer: summing up the entire story from his own perspective and leaving no room for dispute.

He stood, hesitated before he moved toward the door. All I'd feared was true—he would not accept me.

I chased after him, caught him by the arm. Now was not the time for pride or pretense; my heart stood naked and exposed. "I know I've ruined everything—I know, but I don't want to ruin us . . . not us."

"There was a time, probably quite a while ago, to tell me the truth. Not about the stupid fire, but about who and what you loved. I don't see how this can't hurt us, Meridy. You don't love me—you are in love with some adorable ghost of the past who *might* have been the perfect husband. It is utterly absurd that you believe this confession about the fire was bad enough to keep from me—this is about how you love him, not me."

I held up my hand. "No," I cried out. "No . . . that is not true. This was about the terrible way I protected my heart. It's not about you."

"Protecting your heart is all about me. I am your husband. What else do I need to know?"

"That I do love you." I bowed my head. "Please stay."

He spun around. "You know I have to go home. You know how important this case is and—"

"I know how important we are."

"You do?"

His tone sounded sarcastic and my heart lurched forward. "Yes, I do. Please just stay one day. . . . It can't hurt the case that badly. You can meet Tulu—"

"Meridy, I'd love it if I could stay—you have got to understand that I can't. I came to get you to come home with me because I love you, because I can't stand being there without you, but you're . . . otherwise occupied here."

"I am not."

"Yes, you are." This time when he walked away, he did not turn back.

I sank to the bottom stair of the porch believing it would be a very, very good time to start crying. But what came were not tears—just pure anger and frustration. I kicked at the ground with my heels. Moments later, the engine of a car purred and gravel popped beneath tires as Beau's car left the driveway.

I looked up to Mother standing on the top stair landing, looking down at me. "What happened, Meridy?"

"I ruined everything. You can go back to bed, Mother. You were right—I've ruined everything with my own irresponsibility." I walked into the house past Mother's broken looks and into my bedroom. I shut the door behind me.

I had talked with a man who thought I didn't love him anymore because I had withheld the truth of who I really was. Once again, approval was so attached to love that the separation was impossible—like the sweetgrass baskets Tulu wove, they knit in and out of each other in an inseparable thread.

My actions had shown him that I didn't love him when, in truth, it had been the opposite, the complete opposite. I had meant to prove how much I loved him and our life together, and how I didn't want to ruin it. But motivation had no say now—only the consequences.

CHAPTER SEVENTEEN

"If you throw ashes, ashes will follow you."
—GULLAH PROVERB

I ran up to Tulu's front porch, needing to check on her, tell her all I'd discovered in my conversation with Beau. The sun ascended behind the roofline. I lifted my hand to knock. It was early—eight a.m. Maybe she didn't rise at this hour. But I couldn't contain the knowledge she'd imparted to me. I needed to tell her that she'd shown me the way.

I knocked, called her name and listened. Silence met my calls. I knocked again, but there was no answer. I turned the knob; the door was unlocked. I cracked open the door and hollered her name one more time. Silence filled the house and stretched through the front door and onto the porch.

I stepped into her house and swore I heard Mother's words: "Don't enter people's homes uninvited." But I ignored her voice for the first time in years and found my own voice: "Go, find Tulu," it said.

The cramped living room was empty as I crossed the hall to the kitchen in the back of the house. The backs of Tulu's braids were visible as her head rested on the kitchen table. Relief spread through my body and I took a deep breath. She'd fallen asleep at the kitchen table just like she fell asleep in chairs when she talked to me. I touched the back of her head.

"Tulu?"

A chill ran up my arms, through my body. Tulu was gone. I stumbled backward, tripped on a broken chair and fell to the hardwood floor. I curled in on myself. "No!" I screamed into my legs. This was what happened when I cared too much about someone. The old fear of loss I'd once buried on my swim into the sea rose again. "No," I said again. This was where the river met the sea, where life met the heart in chaotic currents. My heart reached for Tulu and found her love.

I scooted backward to the wall, grabbed the phone off the counter, dialed 911 for an ambulance. Then I sat next to Tulu and took her hand off her lap. I grasped her cold fingers and rubbed them.

"I came to tell you I understand. I see." Tears started as if the sorrow I'd held back through all the years gathered here, in Tulu's kitchen. "You pointed the way for me, but now you can't go with me." I held her hand and waited. "You see, I've been looking and looking for all the right things to do—as if something will wake up my heart to feel again if I find just the right thing to do. But it was never anything I could do. I've spent so much time trying to do everything so damn right. When you told me about the river . . ." I choked, tears flooding my words.

The paramedics arrived and filled Tulu's kitchen with squawking radios. A man knelt before me, attempted to take Tulu's hand from mine.

"How did you find her, ma'am?" the paramedic asked in a soft voice.

"Just like this." I didn't let go of Tulu.

"What were you doing here?" He gently took her hand and nodded at the other men to take Tulu. They lifted her as if she weighed no more than one of the baskets on her shelf, placed her on a stretcher.

I dropped my useless hands into my lap. I felt the paramedic still kneeling before me. "Ma'am, I know this is hard, but I need a couple statements from you. Like your name."

My tears flowed of their own volition without sound. "I am Meridy McFadden Dresden. I came to visit Tulu this morning, and when no one answered, I let myself in the unlocked door and found her exactly as you saw her."

The man nodded. "Thank you. Do you know how to contact her next of kin?"

I shook my head. "I don't. But I know the sheriff will—Tulu told me her children kept in close contact with him." I headed toward the front door, loss overwhelming me: Beau, Tulu. The love I'd offered both of them combined with a dangerous current, threatening to take me under, drown me in its power. My heart didn't know which grief to allow in first or second.

In my car I followed the flashing lights of the ambulance until it took a left toward the hospital and I took a right to Mother's home. I had so many things to say to Tulu. I needed to hear so many more things from her. I longed to call Beau and tell him about this death, my grief, but I wouldn't have been able to bear his cold anger.

I was gasping for breath, falling farther and farther below the rapid waves of grief. When I arrived home, Mother stood on top of the stairs as I walked in the front door. I stood still, a hovering sensation drifting past me, as if I were rising above the scene. She descended slowly, as though she floated down the stairs in her white gown.

"Oh, Meridy." She came to my side.

"Tulu is dead, Mother."

"I know. The sheriff called me, told me you found her."

The curved staircase spun before me in a dizzying pattern. "These days with her have been the most unusual gift I've ever received. She showed me so many things—I ran to tell her I saw, that I really saw what she'd been trying to tell me. And she was gone."

Mother made the clucking noises of pity and wrapped her arms around me. "Tulu was a mighty fine woman."

"And more," I said, walked up the stairs to my bedroom, where I would allow the fast-moving current to carry me away for a few hours.

The news of Tulu's death washed over Seaboro like the rain flooding the roads after the marsh has been saturated. An undetected blood clot in her brain had caused a stroke and instant death. Grief consumed all those who had known her and needed more of her, who regretted the time not spent with her. A day and a half had passed since I'd found Tulu in her home. As her family and the town planned her burial, I'd buried myself—as I'd taught myself to do—in the dutiful busyness that kept pain at bay.

Sissy and the girls had moved into Mother's house for the time being, but I hadn't seen much of them, as I'd secluded myself in the darker places of mourning and confusion. My neck popped as I stretched and attempted to release the muscles that had been scrunched as I'd bent over the computer. The bedside clock blinked obnoxious numbers in red: 4:07 p.m. It couldn't be right—I'd sat down after breakfast to work on the curriculum. The clock's batteries must be going. It clicked over silently to 4:08.

I lifted my hand and stared at my watch. I had been working on the Gullah curriculum for over six hours and noticed neither pain nor hunger. When was the last time I had been so absorbed in anything? It always seemed that when I was doing one thing my mind was rushing on to the next. *Move on—move on,* was usually the singsong voice in my head. *You're wasting time.* And somehow this work had silenced that voice long enough for me to lose track of time and forget the emptiness waiting to grab me.

I stood and stretched. The work was good; I felt it. The curriculum was damn good. In my mind I saw the kids absorbing the information, writing Gullah stories, weaving baskets, learning about a cherished heritage. God, I wished Tulu could see it finished, that Beau could read it. The makeshift wall of duty fell—the grief rushed in, washed over me.

I forced my mind back to the task at hand. The printer, which seemed to date back to the days before I wore spandex, grounded out the pages slowly, noisily. Mother had dug the printer out of Daddy's office and I'd attached it to my laptop. I was anxious to hold the pages—read them outside the flashing screen.

Watching the document printing wouldn't make it go any faster. Hunger had its say now; I went down to the kitchen. I peered into the refrigerator, grabbed a cold piece of chicken left over from last night's dinner, and ate standing up.

"Meridy, sit down when you eat." I looked over my shoulder at Mother. She stepped into the kitchen wearing a pale blue linen suit, a jeweled bag in the crook of her arm. "And you'll ruin your dinner that way."

"I'm famished. I haven't eaten all day," I said as I sat at the table.

"What have you been doing?"

"I finished the curriculum: I think it's good. I really do." I took a huge bite of the fried chicken and glanced around for a napkin.

Mother grabbed a paper towel and handed it to me. "Slow down."

"I'll mail it off to Williams Prep tomorrow and be done with it."

Mother sat, placed her purse on the chair next to mine as if the bag deserved a seat too. "If it's that good, why don't you see if some of the schools around here want to use it too? Seems Seaboro would be much more interested in the Gullah culture than your private school in Atlanta would be."

I only nodded, stunned that she thought something I'd done was worthy enough to show. "Okay, I'll send it off to them. That's if you don't mind."

"Or I could drop it off at the school board offices when I go into town today," Mother said.

"If the printer is finished this century."

Mother rose to her feet, ready for duty. "Do not talk with your mouth full," she said, but she smiled. "I know you're preoccupied and upset right now, darling. But the historic society is meeting about the arts festival again tomorrow, and they called last night to see if you'd come."

"No problem," I said.

Then Mother's heels clicked as she walked out.

My heart ached like an old bruise and I needed to talk to Beau. I took a deep breath—I'd try one more time to find that connection, that thin thread that might still exist.

I dialed my home phone number. "Dresden residence." A woman's voice answered the phone.

"Who is this?" I said. My skin prickled in warning.

"This is Ashley Murray. May I help you?"

"Ashley?" My fingers went numb; I fumbled the phone; it fell and banged against the wall. I grabbed at it, placed it back to my ear.

"Hello? Hello? Is anyone there?" A purr lay underneath Ashley's voice—like a contented cat.

"Ashley—where is Beau?" My lips were now numb.

"May I tell him who is calling?"

"His wife." I stuttered into the phone, blood now leaving various parts of my body.

"Oh, well, hi there, Meridy. I hope you're having a good time at the beach while we're all here working." She laughed, but the sound contained no humor at all.

"Where is Beau?"

"Oh, he's in the shower. Can I have him call you when he gets out?"

"What are you doing in my house?"

"I'm working on this case too. . . ."

"I know that. What are you doing in my house?" My voice rose.

She laughed again. "Working . . . didn't you hear me?"

"I heard you."

"Well, someone has to take care of Beau. Poor man."

"Will you please have him call me as soon as he's out of the shower?" I leaned my forehead against the wall—weak and nauseous.

"Sure thing . . . and—"

But I didn't hear what she said as I hung up the phone and collapsed into a chair. I reached for some kind of assurance in my mind and heart that Beau wouldn't pay me back for not telling him about Danny—he wasn't that kind of man. But I found only a white hissing sound of panic.

Was this how it had started for Cate? How it had ended? With a static of white noise and another woman's voice?

Within minutes the phone rang and I yanked it from the cradle. "Hello."

"Hey, Meridy. You just called?" Beau's voice sounded overeager.

"Yes, I did and it appears that you've moved your business into the house."

"What is that supposed to mean?"

"What is Ashley doing in my house, answering my phone, when I'm not there and you're in the shower?" My voice rose in a crescendo with each question.

"Could you excuse me for a moment, please?" Beau's words were muffled.

"What?" I asked.

"I was talking to Ashley . . . Hold on," he said.

The sound of footsteps and the shutting of a door came through the line. Then Beau came back on the phone. "Meridy, calm down. Ashley dropped off some files and I didn't hear her come in. We go to trial tomorrow and I've done nothing but work. . . . Just relax and let me explain."

"Relax? You did not just tell me to relax."

"You don't sound like yourself at all." He spoke so low I was having trouble hearing him.

"Or maybe I do sound like myself—just not the me you're used to hearing. If you only want the perfect wife, the one who does everything right . . ."

"What are you talking about?"

"Beau, if you wanted to go home to—"

He interrupted me, his voice tense and low. "You want to stay there to see some old friends and raise some money for a cottage—but you know what? Bringing back that cottage will not bring back your old boyfriend." His bitterness and anger were palpable, as if I could reach out and touch them, taste them.

"No." I took a quick breath. "I'm not trying to bring Danny back. I'm trying to bring myself back."

"Then come home."

"I have Tulu's funeral tomorrow."

"What? Your old housekeeper—I thought you said she fell."

"She died, Beau. She died the morning I sat on the back porch with you trying as hard as I could to explain how I felt, how much I love you. But you needed to run back to . . . ?" I told him the horrid story of walking into her house, finding her.

Silence fell around me and for a moment I thought Beau had hung up. Then he said, "I'm sorry. That is terrible."

"It was horrible. Tomorrow is the funeral. And . . . I know you're angry and want me to come home. . . ." Exhaustion overwhelmed me and it seemed irreversible.

"I'm sorry Tulu died. I am sorry."

"No, I am. I'm sorry you had to run back to . . . Ashley and the case that will make your career . . . and whatever is there for you that you couldn't stay with me for a day or a minute longer."

A knock resonated in the background, a muffled voice. Beau hollered, "Hold on," then returned to the phone. "Meridy, I am late for this dinner with the firm. We'll be up all night preparing for trial tomorrow."

"I know . . . you have to go. So do I."

I hung up the phone and ran, in the instinctive memory of other times when life had become too much to bear in Mother's home, to Tim's house.

CHAPTER EIGHTEEN

"Empty sack can't stand upright alone."
—GULLAH PROVERB

I knocked on Tim's door before my head told me exactly what action was appropriate. Tim opened the door in a pair of jeans and no shirt, a towel in hand. His wet hair dripped onto his shoulders.

"Oh, I'm sorry . . ." I backed up. "I interrupted you."

"Nope." His smile was wide. "Just getting ready to go out." He opened the door wide and made a sweeping gesture. "Come in, Meridy. What's up?"

I shook my head back and forth, unable to find words for my anger—yet.

He threw his head back and laughed. "My God, this is like traveling back in time. Look at you. I can tell you're mad as hell. What'd you get in trouble for this time? What did your mother say to you?"

"It's not Mother. . . . It's Beau."

"Damn, I'm such an insensitive idiot. I already warned you about that." He spread his hands open. "Come in . . . now."

I walked into the foyer, ran my hand across the wood table, plopped down on his leather recliner in the living room. I looked around the room. "Tim all grown up," I said, and glanced at the evidence of a man I'd known only as a boy with Danny. "Who do you think he would've grown up to be? What do you think he'd have been . . . like?"

"Beau?" He pulled a T-shirt over his head. "I've never even met him."

"No . . . Danny."

"You changed subjects on me there, changed men on me." Tim sat on the arm of the chair. "I think he would've been amazing, would have done all the things he said he'd do. Been smart, funny, still our best friend. Wise. Good-looking . . ." He tousled my hair. "Or maybe not. Maybe not any of those things. That's the advantage he has over us. . . . He gets to be frozen in that perfect time."

I nodded. "That perfect, adorable time. I guess I still envision him as eighteen, full of promise."

Tim nodded. "Promises he might or might not have been able to keep."

"I can't imagine he wouldn't have kept them . . ."

"He probably would have. But that's not why you ran here. What's up?"

"I called home. A woman answered my phone."

Tim put his hand on my shoulder. "Did you know her?"

"Yep, she's the new junior partner in the firm, helping with this huge negligence case along with Alexis, who's been plugged into my best friend's spot."

"Alexis is your best friend?"

"No . . . absolutely not. You met my best friend, Cate

. . . she was Harland's wife. Then he lost twenty pounds, bought a vintage Mustang convertible and decided that his paralegal was much more interesting than his present wife. So he swapped cars and wives. Just plugged a new one in each slot. And I'm supposed to let the new one be my substitute friend. You know, like in school when a teacher comes in because your teacher is out sick, and you're supposed to treat the substitute with as much respect? Just like that. Now I call my house and this other woman answers my phone. I guess she wants to plug into being—" I groaned, slumped in the chair.

"Could you be jumping to conclusions, my dear?"

"Maybe . . . but Beau was in the shower and she was purring." Tim jumped up, clapped his hands together. "Get up. This is crazy. We're going out. Now."

"Out?" I looked down at my shorts and rumpled T-shirt. "No way. Not looking like this."

"Where do you think I'm taking you? The Seaboro Yacht Club? No, we're off to an oyster roast and some cold beer. Weatherly's husband is running for office and is having an oyster roast down at the public beach. We're going. No more moping around."

"I'm not moping," I protested.

"Oh, you're moping all right. In fact if you don't get your mopey butt out of my favorite chair, you'll win moper of the year."

I laughed and he joined in. "There is no such thing," I said, jumped up, thinking that oysters and beer sounded like the absolutely best thing I could think of.

"But there is one thing I want to do before we go."

"No, you may not go home and change into nicer clothes or do your hair or—"

"Do you have a computer, Internet access?"

"Of course."

"Do you mind if I use it real quick? Mother doesn't have it and I wanted to look something up."

I followed Tim to two closed wood doors. He hadn't shown me this part of the house and as I drew closer, I realized it was his office. He pushed the door open. An oversized pine desk filled the center of the room; three carved chairs covered in leather scattered around it. Papers, books, framed pictures and rolled blueprints filled the space.

A flat-screen computer sat on his desk. "How come you never showed me your office?" I asked him.

"It's a mess."

"A beautiful mess." I walked over to the computer. "It is so full of you.

He walked up behind me and clicked a button, and the Internet glared from the screen. "Yeah, so full of me that my ex-wife couldn't find room for herself here."

I typed in a search engine, looked up at Tim. "No, she could have found room just like I could have found the words to tell Beau the truth. If you really need or want to find something . . . you will. Even if it is too late." I sighed, typed in, "Name meaning Meredith," and stepped back from the computer.

Tim read what I wrote. "What are you doing?"

"I want to know what my name means." I punched a

few keys until I found the name *Meredith* and clicked on it. *A Welsh name meaning "sea lord"* flashed on the screen.

"So you're a sea lord. That makes a lot of sense, except your name isn't Meredith," Tim said.

"Mother said my name came from *Meredith.* I asked her after Tulu told me that names have power . . . that someone could lose the right to their name."

"Well, I don't believe you've lost the right to your name. You've always been . . . I don't know . . . part of the sea."

"Used to be."

"Was, is, still are . . . whatever. You're still lord of the sea even without someone else to tell you. Now let's go—we'll miss watching Weatherly's husband make a fool of himself. He and his opponent each get to talk about why they want to be mayor . . . should be interesting."

"Okay, then, let's go." His elbow brushed my shoulder as I turned off the computer; his hand reached down for my hand as I got out of his chair. "You heard about Tulu, right?"

Tim nodded. "I'm sorry. I know you cared a lot about her."

"I feel like we weren't done. She had so much to give."

"I know." He nodded.

"I ran to her house. I thought she'd like to know that I'd figured out some of what she'd been trying to tell me. I knew she'd have more and more to say. Before she died, she tried to warn me that opening up my heart would be dangerous. Maybe she knew."

"Knowing Tulu, she probably did know she was leaving. But I guaran-damn-tee that she didn't want you to close up your heart." He hugged me and we left his house.

Tim drove his pickup truck and it wasn't until I had walked over the new boardwalk and tossed down a plaid blanket on the sand that I realized we were on the same beach where we'd celebrated graduation those long years ago.

The Keeper's Cottage that had once squatted on the end portion of the beach was missing. Blankets, tents and tables were scattered across the beach. On the firmer ground of grass and pine straw a large stump from a once-proud live oak stood with a tent over it. Streamers hung down the sides of the tent and danced along the ground. I pointed to it. "What's that for?" I asked Tim.

"Weatherly's husband, Mitchell, will get up there to make his speech—try to make us all feel like this is an old-fashioned political party where the candidates get up on their 'stump.'"

"Very clever." I sank to the blanket and stretched my legs out. The day's heat was now hidden in the deeper parts of the sand, and a tepid breeze—the most we could hope for—whispered in from the sea. "I might not get up from here all night. This is so . . . nice." I dug my toes into the sand.

Tim sat down next to me. "Nothing like a little sea

and sand for some perspective, huh?"

I nodded. "Everything seems upside-down lately. Everything. I never thought Harland would leave Cate, you know? Never. She's funny and smart, and like me, she never forgot what she wanted or who she was. And Harland just decided he'd try something new. I never thought I'd talk or think about the Keeper's Cottage again. I never thought I'd come back to Seaboro . . . You just never know what's going to happen or what people are capable of doing."

"Meridy, I have a very hard time believing that you would've fallen in love with a man who is capable of cheating on you."

"You know what? I probably didn't. But people forget who they are. . . . I've seen that. The numbing quality of life makes us forget who we are, and then we're doing things we never would've done otherwise. After Danny died, I thought I'd never fall in love again. Ever. I'd resigned myself to that. Then I met Beau. . . ."

"And you fell in love."

"Not at first. In the beginning I admired him. But I remember the day I knew he loved me." I closed my eyes and felt it, remembered the feel of my dorm room quilt under my legs. I opened my eyes. "You don't want to hear this, do you?"

"Oh, yes, I do." He stretched and leaned back on his elbows. "If I've missed all this, at least I can hear about it."

"It was my junior year at university and I'd been elected by my sorority to run for class president. I was

253

scared to death. I was incredibly nervous about my speech in front of the students and faculty at the Student Forum Center. This was not the kind of thing I asked for or even wanted. I called Beau—he was in law school at the time and I told him I didn't think I should've been elected to run. He told me my magnetism bubbled under the surface and that other people saw it too but didn't know what it was. . . ."

Tim nodded. "Yep."

"I told him I'd been chosen because of my grades and volunteer work, but he told me how I had no idea, that I was so much more than the sum of my grades and accomplishments. And then I knew he loved me—really just me. You know?"

"I know," Tim said.

"But then I kept trying harder to earn this undeserved love from him. You'd think trying to be good would make you a better and better person, but all it did was make me obsessed with my image and pretense, and then I couldn't find any feeling at all, besides the feeling that I cared what other people thought of me. And now that I want to get past that, through that falseness, I might have lost him. And even though I'm sure it's my fault for letting him think I was more than I really was—I set myself up for the fall. I wish there was a way back to my heart without ruining who Beau and I are together. Does that make any sense at all?"

"You make his love sound like some kind of reward. Like you won his love with good behavior or something."

A seagull dived, emerged with a fish dangling from its mouth. "I don't know."

"Meridy, this is exactly what happened to me; my wife left me when I wouldn't conform to who she wanted me to be. It doesn't have to be that way. It just doesn't."

"Well—I guess it is." I dug my toes into the sand. "Ugh, enough of this . . . go get us something to drink."

Tim jumped up. "Yes, ma'am."

I leaned back on the blanket and stared out to the sea I was definitely not the lord of. What I didn't tell Tim was that I had also known then that I loved Beau.

I lay back on the blanket and closed my eyes. And Beau had loved me well. This restlessness had nothing to do with how well he'd loved me or taken care of me.

Sand scattered across my skin and I startled, sat up. Tim and Weatherly looked down at me.

"Hi there, Meridy, long time no see," Weatherly said in a cultured voice she'd mastered by sixth grade.

I stood up, offered a hug. "It's good to see you, Weatherly. How are you?"

"I'm just exhausted." She ran her hand through her coiffed and blond-streaked hair. "This campaign has been so much more grueling than I thought and . . . oh, it's boring. I'd heard that you were back in town. I was hoping I'd get to see you. Then I heard you left again."

I held my hands up. "I'm here." I smiled, but my lips shook. I was acutely aware of my wrinkled shorts and T-shirt next to Weatherly in her floral lime green ironed sundress with matching purse and earrings—something

I would've worn if I was at home in Atlanta.

"Well, it is really good to see you. There are so many things to catch up on," she said, touched my hand.

Tim edged away. "Okay, I'm leaving you girls alone to yap. I'm gonna go help the men crack open the oysters. Can't have a grumpy, hungry crowd when it's speech time." He winked at Weatherly.

"Maybe you shouldn't help build the fire." I elbowed Tim.

"Very funny." He feigned a punch to my shoulder and left Weatherly and me staring at each other in the awkward initial moments of attempting to fill vacant years with conversation.

She smoothed her sundress and sat without causing a single wrinkle. "Sit, Meridy. Tell me how you've been."

We exchanged common chatter about children, where we lived and the facts that allow conversation to keep moving. Weatherly leaned in closer. "When was the last time I saw you?"

"I think at the Fourth of July parade a few years ago."

"You know, Mr. Cragg told my mama about your great idea for the arts festival to raise money for the Keeper's Cottage. Fabulous. I can't believe none of us thought of that. I thought it was terrible, all that pressure they were putting on Tim when it would've wiped him out."

"Thanks, Weatherly, but I had a selfish motive too."

"You know what, Meridy? I've tried to remember that night a thousand times and picture you in it, but I never can find you. I know Danny was still there, but I don't remember where you were."

"I was with Danny. . . . Then I passed out and then they rushed me to the hospital . . . or that's what they told me anyway."

"So you didn't see . . . Danny after that?"

"No." I cringed and Weatherly must have seen my face.

"I did," she said.

"I know. . . . Mother told me you saw him at the top of the tower before it fell."

She touched my arm. "I saw him fall off."

I stiffened in surprise.

"I saw Danny fall from the tower. . . ." She looked away when she said this, as though the Keeper's Cottage still stood on the beach.

"I couldn't do anything though, Meridy. He landed in the most horrible way . . . all twisted and . . ." Her mouth became a thin line as she pressed her lips together. "And then the tower fell on top of him and there was chaos and smoke and a policeman dragged me away and Danny was just . . . gone. And they couldn't get to him and they couldn't find him . . . and he was gone."

"He died when he fell," I whispered.

She nodded.

"Why didn't you tell me this before?" I asked.

She shrugged her shoulders, lifted her eyebrows "When? You never came back and you never called anybody ever again and . . . I called your house a hundred times back then, and I finally figured you didn't want to talk to me. I told your mother to please tell you to call me. . . ."

My first impulse—to blame Mother—was replaced by a feeling of empathy. Mother had been protecting me the best she knew how. Complete denial, complete shelter: it was how she'd survived and how she felt she'd help me endure the tragedy.

I placed my arms around Weatherly's shoulders. "I never knew you called. And I'm sorry I never called. Thank you so much for telling me this. . . . I've always wondered exactly how he died. But you know what? I knew anyway. I knew before you told me. I saw it in my mind."

She nodded. "You would. . . . That's how you two were."

"Let's get some oysters," I said, squeezed her hand.

We jumped up from the blanket. "Yes, let's," she said, and hooked her arm in mine, and I laughed, remembering how badly I wanted to be invited to her birthday party in fifth grade.

The remainder of the evening, for long moments, I forgot Ashley's voice on the phone, forgot Tulu was gone, forgot anything except the joy of the beach, the sea and this party with old friends. In one moment I stood back and looked at the beach through my adult eyes, stared at all of us grown and yet still gathering to celebrate life's moments at the curve of the beach where the river ran to meet the sea.

The stump speeches were given and applauded; oysters were baked over an open fire; chilled wine and beer flowed. I laughed more than I had in as long as I could remember.

Tim found me sitting in a sagging lawn chair, staring out to the sea. "Whatcha doing?" he asked.

His face wavered in front of me. "I definitely, most definitely, had too much cold beer."

He laughed. "And when was the last time that happened?" I groaned. "I have no idea."

"Only one way to work that off—dancing." He swooped me up into his arms and with the rest of Seaboro we jived to beach music until I collapsed, sweating and dizzy, onto our blanket.

I held up my hands. "I give. I'm done. . . ."

The night had crept up on us and the half-moon provided the remaining light. Tim held his hand out to lift me up. "Okay then, let's go"

He walked me to his truck, opened the side door, but stood still, blocking my way to the door. "What?" I whispered, leaned against the truck, pushed my hair out of my eyes.

He touched the side of my face. Then his hand remained on my cheek. The fog of beer, dance and moonlight cleared. He leaned forward and for the first time in all the years I'd known this man, I wanted to kiss him. But what I wanted to *do* was not who I wanted to *be*. The distinction was clearer than the blazing stars overhead.

Tim ran his thumb along my bottom lip and I think I let out a sigh, or maybe it was a whisper that said, "No."

He tilted his head. "This would not be a very good idea, would it?"

I shook my head. "A long time ago, it might've been."

He nodded. "Maybe." And he lifted his hand from my face, mussed my hair with a wink.

I stood for a few moments and stared at the sky— alone. I allowed the briefest moment of want for Tim Oliver to pass by and over me. I didn't understand why I craved this kiss, except that the feeling was some part of the closeness that existed when someone knew who you had been and who you were, then cared about you anyway. It was an unearned love and I craved it desperately.

Tim started the car as I climbed in. He patted my leg. "Let's get you home."

"I'm not really sure where that is . . . ," I said.

The true silence of night filled my room: an owl call, a soft murmur of wave, branches scratching the roof outside my window. Sleep came nowhere near me and I doubted it visited Sissy either, two doors down the hall. I slipped out of bed and pulled on a pair of velour sweatpants and a T-shirt. I tapped my fingers on Sissy's bedroom door; she opened it before I'd finished.

I grabbed her hand, whispered, "Come with me."

She held up a finger, reached back into her room and grabbed some slip-on tennis shoes. She was dressed in silk pajama bottoms and a tank top. I led her to my room, closed the door. She sat on the bed. "Oh, I

260

thought we were going outside. I thought I'd get that beach walk you asked for last time."

"We are." I walked over, lifted my window.

"You're crazy," Sissy said. "We can just walk down the stairs and go out the front door—we're not little kids sneaking out."

"Oh, yes, we are." I jumped up on the windowsill, slung my legs around and planted my feet on the roof. "Come on, prissy Sissy."

"Ooh, I hated when you called me that." She came to the window, placed her hand on the sill as if testing for firmness. "I was not that prissy."

"Prove it," I said, squatting on the roof.

She laughed. "If you're finally trying to kill me, it just might work, because right now I really don't give a flip."

I motioned for Sissy to follow me down my well-etched path over the roof, down the back of the trellis and to the soft ground.

Sissy landed with a grunt and sprang back up. "Have you always done this?"

"Since I was twelve."

"How could I not know that?"

"Because that's what sneaking out is all about—no one knows."

Sissy shook her head in the moonlight falling into the backyard through scattered clouds. She glanced up at the sky. "You can see the stars so much better here than in the city."

I nodded, started walking. "Yep."

261

"Where were you tonight?" Sissy asked. She walked ahead of me, talking over her shoulder.

"Tim took me to a party. . . ." I felt I needed to give further explanation, begin with the phone call to Beau and how I ran to Tim's house, but I hesitated.

"And?"

"And nothing . . . that's where I was."

"Is something going on . . . with—"

I held up my hand before she could finish her question. "Sissy, don't even ask me that."

"I'm sorry, I guess I see the monster of infidelity behind every tree and bush."

"Me too, sis, me too."

She twirled around, walked backward in front of me. "You too?"

"Sure."

Sissy stopped, waited until I came up next to her; then she swiveled and fell into step with me, as if my admission of seeing the same monsters allowed her to walk next to me.

"It's kinda scary out here at night . . . like the world goes on forever," she said.

"No, it's awesome." I flipped my shoes off and ran my toes into the moonlit froth at the edge of the wave. "Just awesome."

"Well, look at us—here we are. I've completely screwed up my life and you're the one that's all fine now. How the hell did that happen?"

"All fine now? Hardly."

"You know, I just don't get it. You never did anything

right when we were kids, and everyone liked you better—Tulu, the boys, the neighbors."

"Not Mother."

"That's not true. She just . . . got frustrated."

I ran my toes along the edge of sea and sand. "The tide is coming in."

"How do you know?" Sissy crouched down, ran her finger in the sand, and I could envision her at ten years old showing me how to dig fast enough to grab the ghost crabs scurrying below to hide.

"I just started noticing again. . . ." I squatted down next to my sister. "Did you know Mom had a really hard childhood?"

Sissy turned to me. "Well, I knew she grew up on a farm in south Georgia."

"She was telling me how hard it was, how she sacrificed so much of herself to make sure we never had a life like she had. Here I thought she was being so selfish, always worried about her image, when part of the way she acted was nothing but her idea of protection for us. Nothing is what it seems anymore, is it?"

"Yeah, look at Penn. A mistress for five years. Spending our family money on a condo, clothes and I don't want to imagine what else, while he gave me a hard time about signing the girls up for horseback-riding camp because it was too damn expensive."

"I'm sorry, Sissy. I really am."

"Well, now that I've spilled all my trash, why are you here?"

"Well, I originally came home a few weeks ago to

write a curriculum for our private school. But now I've come back to tell the truth and also—I know this sounds lame—figure out who I want to be. I've lost that knowledge through the years and I'm thinking that telling the truth might help me find it."

"What does that mean?"

"Do you really want to hear it?"

"As long as it doesn't have anything to do with Penn or family or marriage or money . . ."

"That's a wide variety of topics there. No, this has to do with the fire."

Sissy sighed. "Terrible night. I still can't believe it happened. Still . . . Danny . . . all that."

I looked up; the sky spun above me in crystal-dotted chaos. "Danny and I were sending off firecrackers—the ones Tim bought us for the graduation party. One landed on the crumbling roof that slanted into the bedroom on the right side." I closed my eyes and saw the flame run across the cedar shake shingles. "So it was never the bonfire. It was the firecracker I set off that hit the roof. And I never told anyone. Only Danny knew and he's . . . gone."

Sissy ran her hands through her hair. "You never told . . . anyone this?"

"I was a coward."

"No, you were probably scared. Have you told Mom?"

"No.

"Damn, Meridy. Just damn."

"I know. I'm reaping what I've sown—I know."

264

I felt, more than saw, Sissy shiver. "That is not what I was going to say. Is that what you think of me? That I would say . . . that?"

"Yes . . ."

"Oh, my God, I have been the most terrible, judgmental sister known to man." Sissy grabbed my hand. "I was going to say . . . you are so brave and it wasn't your fault. Mom and Daddy sent you away. You were eighteen—what else could you do?"

"Tell the truth."

"How? No one would've believed you. Mother wouldn't have let your confession out as much as they wouldn't have let accusation in."

"Mother will have to get over it. I'm not sure Beau will."

"Of course he will. He loves you."

"Sissy, his life is completely built upon integrity, honesty and making sure people pay for what they've done—especially if they've hidden their culpability—and I'm using his words here, if you can't tell. He came here a few mornings ago and I told him."

"How did I miss that?"

I shrugged my shoulders. "He came and went . . . quickly. But this blame not only goes against all he believed about me but all he believes about life in general. I'm not sure he can . . . love me even if he wants to. We were on two completely different planets as it was—then I told him about this and it didn't help at all—trust me."

"I think we train them that way, Meridy."

"What?"

"We train men not to accept the weaker parts of us. We show them just how perfect we are, so then they fall in love and marry us and then we can't show them who we really are . . . because then they might not love us. It's all so insane and stupid. . . ."

An opening appeared in my heart—the water-rushing kind of feeling that comes with revelation. "Exactly."

"But me? I'm wrecked."

I glanced at her face in the opaque light—at her beautiful bone structure handed down from Daddy's Mc-Fadden family. Her face required no further adornment.

Sissy sighed. "Damn, we're just falling apart, aren't we? The whole fam-damily is falling apart."

"Yes, yes, we are." A laugh bubbled from inside me.

We walked together as I told her of my reluctance to let everyone in Seaboro know about my part in the fire. I didn't want to ruin Mother's reputation after how hard she'd worked to get here, how far she'd come—to this place in local society.

"You see"—I faced Sissy—"it doesn't matter who I am now, because it's all come back."

"Is that why you tried to kill yourself the day you left?"

"Kill myself? I never . . ."

"Then why did you swim all the way out in the ocean? You completely freaked us all out." Sissy waved her hand toward the waves.

"I wasn't killing myself. I was . . ." I held my palms up in denial.

"Then what were you doing?"

"Leaving my heart out there."

"What?"

"Shutting down so I wouldn't feel anything like Danny's death again. I guess that is the best way to explain what I was trying to do. And it worked for a while—but not anymore."

By now we had wandered past Tim's house. I pointed up at his porch, lit by gas lanterns.

She looked up too. "Tim was so cute in high school."

I laughed, poked at her. "You thought he was a hellion."

"A cute hellion." She went on.

"Look at me now. I married a man I don't even know. We've lost over half our money; my girls are doing terrible in school; I can't think or sleep. . . ." She stretched, looked at me. "So I might as well have snuck out at night, smoked cigarettes, dated the hellions, got a B instead of an A. . . ." She pulled off her tank top, yanked down her pajama bottoms and ran naked toward the ocean. "And skinny-dipped in the middle of the night," she hollered, and disappeared beneath the surface of the sea. Only a circle of disturbed water showed where she'd gone under.

I opened my mouth to laugh or yell, but neither came out. I jumped up, flipped my sneakers off, rolled up my pants and waded into the water. Sissy's head popped up five feet out; then she stood completely naked and stretched her arms out to the sky. She squealed and disappeared back under the water, then reappeared.

I threw back my head and laughed.

"Get in here, Meridy McFadden."

"No way. You're nuts."

"I dare you."

Daddy's words washed over the waves: *Now you know—Meridy will always take the dare.*

I pulled my T-shirt over my head, yanked off my sweatpants and underwear and threw them toward shore, then dived into the vast sea. An emotion bubbled up from below my ribs and I recognized its face: the freedom and daring I'd last felt before I set off the firecracker. The face of these sensations had not risen since then. I immersed myself in them, under the water, and let the emotions surround me completely until the fear dissolved into the ocean floor.

Sissy's laugh echoed under the waves, and then vibrated across the night as I came to the surface. She bobbed in the water, only her face visible. "I knew I could get you in here with a dare. You always take the dare."

"I haven't lately. I can tell you that."

"Then you haven't been yourself."

"Exactly."

For a few minutes, we swam in the dark sea, diving, turning and floating on our backs. Then I swam toward shore, which Sissy reached before I did. She ran toward her clothes and yanked them on in frantic, quick movements. I slipped my own clothes on and we plopped down next to each other. Sissy curled her knees up under her chin.

"Well, then," I said.

"Yes, just well, well."

The sound of the incoming tide washed over us. I whispered, "Sissy, I can see the difference now—this huge difference between *living* my life and *doing* my life. After Danny died, I *did* my life—one thing to do after another, always something else to do. Because you don't need a heart to *do,* but you do need one to live."

"Who's there? Who is that?" A screeching voice, not unlike a cracked ambulance siren, shattered across our conversation. A beam of light skipped across the sand, landed on Sissy's face.

She held up her hands. "Mrs. Hamlon, it's just Sissy and Meridy."

Charlotte Hamlon swung her flashlight, and the light landed on my face.

"You're on my property," she screamed.

Sissy stood, stepped forward, wiped her hair off her face. "Mrs. Hamlon, calm down. It's not your property. . . . We're at the ocean and it's just Sissy and Meridy."

Charlotte approached us—a dent in the darkness with a beam in front of her. "I've been watching you from my deck," she said, swung her flashlight with her words, creating a dizzying pattern. "You were skinny-dippin'—I saw you. This is completely inappropriate, absurd. I've already called the police." She trained the light firmly on our faces. "I always knew your family was crazy, completely *crazy*—should've never married outside Seaboro, for God's sake."

I shrugged my shoulders at Sissy, wished I could see her facial features to know if I should laugh or *cry*. My sister had just been called "inappropriate" for probably the first time in her entire life.

Sissy's voice came wrapped in a stifled laugh. "She called the police . . . on me. I knew something like that would happen if I hung out with you." Full laughter poured out and we both ran back toward our own home.

We collapsed on the thin strip where sand met grass in back of our house, attempted to catch our breath.

"She called you inappropriate." I lay back and stared at the sky.

"She doesn't know what inappropriate is until she's seen another woman riding her husband like a damn horse."

I let out a strangled sound that came out something like "Gross . . . ughh."

Sissy rolled on her side toward me. "Now, that is what I call inappropriate."

A slight rustling sound came from behind us before we heard our names. "Sissy? Meridy? Is that you?" Mother called to us.

"Yes, Mom," Sissy called out.

We stood and walked to the porch, where Mother sat in a rocking chair. After we'd settled in our own chairs with afghans Mother brought from the house—Sissy had refused to change clothes, wanting to stay wet and sandy—we told Mother about Charlotte.

"Sorry, Mom. Really . . . sorry," Sissy said as though she were five years old and had just broken a china plate.

"Ah, don't be sorry. Charlotte is always looking for something wrong with the family. You just gave the poor woman something to talk about."

"What is her problem?" I asked.

"She dated your daddy before he left for college. . . . She has had it out for me since the Thanksgiving he brought me home to meet his family."

I laughed. "You're kidding. How come you never told us this? It explains a lot about the woman's consistently sour face."

"There are many things young children do not need to know about."

I laughed and there, as one day turned to the next, with my sister soaked from the sea and Mother at my side, I sat content. A tepid breeze blew off the water and crossed the porch, whispered across my cheeks, rustled the hair around my face. I sighed, remembering the feel of Beau's finger running across my cheek on the day we met, and I wondered if I'd feel that soft touch again.

CHAPTER NINETEEN

"A good run is better than a bad stand."
—GULLAH PROVERB

Mother's kitchen brimmed with the morning light as I sipped coffee and willed the slight headache to release. I could not drink that many beers anymore. Today was both the historic-society meeting and Tulu's funeral and I didn't want to grind my way through the day with this dull ache.

"Meridy, you okay?"

My head snapped up and I forced a smile for Mother. "Fine, just fine."

"You had a little too much to drink last night?"

"What?" I half laughed.

"Ah, don't think I don't know the symptoms of a hangover."

"I've just had a few very, very long days. And today won't be any different."

Mother glanced sideways at me. "You didn't forget about the meeting this morning, did you?"

"Nope." I stood.

"Darling, could you sit down for a minute?"

I sat and rubbed my temples. "Yes?"

Mother lifted her chin and glanced off toward the window. "I wanted to let you know that last night after you went to bed, Sissy told me about your part in the fire."

I slumped back against the chair. "She was always a tattletale."

Mother's head turned in my direction, but I was smiling at her. She smiled back. "She wasn't tattling. She wanted to be the one to tell me so that I wouldn't—in her words—freak out on you when you told me. She knew my initial reaction would not be the proper one. And she was right."

"Oh?" I lifted my brows, and my headache seemed to ease.

She waved her hand dismissively. "I don't know why you never told me."

"You wouldn't have wanted to hear it. I tried to tell you, in the very beginning, but you wouldn't listen." Speaking the truth was getting easier and easier, as if the first truth released the others. "And, Mother, you sent me away—off to live at Mawmaw's."

"I did that to protect you."

"I know." I reached over and patted her leg. "After that, I just couldn't tell. The whole ordeal was buried too far down. At least until now."

"Is it why you came back with the idea of raising the money?"

"Yes. I guess I thought that if I did something to make up for what I did . . ."

"It was a very long time ago—an accident. You do not have anything to make up for."

"Well, I did when they were trying to make Tim donate half his life's work."

"Speaking of Tim, you've been spending an awful lot

273

of time with him. Is there . . . are you . . . ?"

"No, Mother. I love Beau. And always have. I'm not sure where we'll go from here, but—"

Mother grimaced. "Sissy and the girls are moving in with me."

"What?" I shook my head.

"She can't stay there . . . with Penn."

"I know . . . but I just never thought she'd leave him. Ever."

"Me neither. But she decided last night . . . Be sweet."

"I always am." I batted my eyelashes.

She laughed and the sound washed over me like a baptism. "Well, why don't you go get dressed now? We don't want to be late."

Mother and I arrived at the historical society building; she touched my arm lightly before we entered the room. A rectangular table dominated the room; dust motes danced in shafts of morning sunlight blurred in the bubbled-glass antique windows. Ten men and women who had approved my arts festival proposal sat around the table with notebooks and ice water in front of them.

I glanced around the table; Tim sat at the far end chewing on the end of a pen, staring down at some blueprints. Noticing us, he waved and winked.

I made my way to him. "What are you doing here?"

"I wanted to be in on this. I was looking over the blueprints with Mr. Cragg. I told him I'd do the work. Now go sit down."

Mr. Cragg stood up, coughed. "Okay, let's get started. I know a lot of you want to go to Tulu's funeral today, so we don't have much time. Would anyone like to ask any questions or make any comments before we proceed through this arts festival packet that Mrs. Manning has prepared?"

Charlotte Hamlon stood. "I have a couple of things to say. I know I was outvoted, but I have to tell you that I think this is an insane idea." She pointed at Tim. "I still think he needs to pay, and all this effort and work that Ms. Dresden has proposed is outrageous." She wrinkled her nose as if my name reeked of garbage.

I jumped up, held out my hands. "Okay, enough of all this 'Tim has to pay' nonsense. Tim might have given the party, but he did not start the fire that burned down the Keeper's Cottage. I started the fire with a firecracker. Now"—I turned to Mrs. Hamlon—"will you please drop the let's-make-Tim-pay mantra?"

Stifled laughter poured across the table, and Mrs. Hamlon gasped, tipped her chair as she stepped backward. "You what? I told you their family was crazy." She pointed at Mother and then me. "I saw her"—she shook her head in disgust—"skinny-dipping in the middle of the night yesterday. They're crazy."

Mother stood now and I shook my head, whispered, "No, Mother."

She pushed a stray hair off her face. "Charlotte, you may take your accusations elsewhere." She dropped her pink alligator purse on the table. "Can we move on to the arts festival now?"

"Yes, we can," Mr. Cragg said, and pounded his hand on the table.

We all sat as Mrs. Manning handed out packets about the arts festival to be held on the Fourth of July of the following year.

I glanced over at Tim. His face was placid—the way I'd once known it as a child. My heart tripped over itself—I had done the right thing. In all the confusion, how had I ever thought there would be any other way? God, I felt good.

Charlotte Hamlon stood again. "This is insane. You are all insane." She grabbed her purse and stomped to the door, bumping into Danny's parents as they walked into the room, blinking in the overhead lights. Several women jumped up and moved toward the Garretts.

"Hello." Chris Garrett nodded at the table. "I'm sorry we're late . . . bad traffic on 278. Meant to get here before you all started."

He turned and addressed Mr. Cragg. "Well, hello there, Dean, good to see you."

Bee elbowed him in the side and he continued, "Well, we're here to help with the arts festival. It has recently come to our attention that Danny's bravery was partly in response to his having started the fire. Although we don't have the money to give you, we'd love to help with this arts festival. If renovating the Keeper's Cottage is that important, we'll do what we can." Chris nodded and lifted his chin high.

We were all left staring at each other.

Mr. Cragg coughed. "Anybody have anything else they'd like to say?"

Voices overlapped.

"What can I do to help?"

"How many booths can we accommodate?"

"Can I be on the acquisitions committee?"

Mr. Cragg hollered, "Whoa, everyone, sit down. All we are here to do is divide up the committees. Mrs. Manning has spent hours figuring out how many people we need on each one. And we need you to rope in some of your friends. Can we let her speak now?"

Silence finally filled the room as Mrs. Manning stood with ten packets in her hand. "Okay, we're only in the very beginning stages, but I see how we can make it work."

I looked at Mother, mouthed, "Thank you."

"No need," she whispered back.

Oh, yes, I thought, *there was plenty of need.*

Cucumber sandwiches lay next to cheese straws on silver trays. On Mother's back porch, Bee and Chris Garrett sat next to Tim on the wicker couch plumped with overstuffed floral pillows. Squished between them, Tim looked like an overgrown boy. The Garretts laughed at some story Tim had just recounted about Danny beaching a Boston Whaler.

Sissy sat in a chair with a glass of iced tea—slightly spiked with a splash of Bushmills—surveying the crowd from behind her sunglasses, which hid her tear-swollen eyes. Her linen skirt was pressed in straight folds like a schoolgirl's uniform, and her white blouse looked like it had just been taken off the rack at the store. Her hair was pulled back in a severe ponytail.

I sat on the opposite couch across from Tim and the Garretts; Mother scurried around bringing more trays of food and drink.

"Mother," I called out to her. "Come." I patted the pillow next to my seat. "Sit."

She brushed back one piece of hair that had come loose from her bun.

"Relax—everyone's fine," I said, swished my hand toward the Garretts, Tim and Sissy.

Bee Garrett lifted her iced tea. "Here's to Meridy Dresden for the awesome arts festival idea."

"Aye, aye." Everyone lifted his or her glass.

"Absolutely not," I said. "This is not about me!"

"It's all about you," Sissy said, threw her head back and laughed. "It's always about you."

"Very funny." I lifted my glass.

Tim lifted his glass. "Oh, yeah—Sissy, I heard about your midnight swim. Here's to you too." He winked at her.

Sissy dropped her head. "Oh. My. God." Then she eyed me. "I'm going to kill you."

I held up my hands. "Wasn't me, big sis. Wasn't me."

Tim went over to Sissy and patted her shoulder. "Nope, my nosy neighbor told me. I don't think I'm the only one she told."

Sissy took a long swallow of her spiked tea. "Okay, I

278

lost my mind for a moment or two. You know hanging out with Meridy will do that to you."

I laughed. "Go ahead, blame me."

Sissy leaned forward, shook her head. "This is the oddest gathering I've seen on Mom's back porch in years."

Bee Garrett reached for her cardigan. "We really should get going. We didn't mean to intrude."

"Sissy McFadden." Mother used her maiden name and it seemed appropriate. "That was rude."

"Oh, oh," Sissy said. "I didn't mean it rude. This is great fun. . . . I mean it. So much more interesting than trying to figure out what fabric to cover the couch in or what flowers to cut for the garden parry. . . . This is like—I don't know—like real life."

I let out a holler and swooped across the porch to my sister; I grabbed her in a hug. "There you go . . . real life."

Sissy laid her head on my shoulder and stifled a cry. "Oh, God, I'm making a fool of myself. Forgive me. I've had a terrible few days and I haven't slept and Mom put a tad too much Bushmills in here and I'm going back to bed now." She stood, curtsied and turned toward the screen door.

"Stay," Tim said.

Sissy glanced over her shoulder. "Me?"

"Definitely you—you liven up the crowd."

Mother groaned. "Just what I need—two daughters livening up the crowd." She turned to Bee Garrett. "Please stay. I've ordered Puggy's Ribs for lunch and they're delivering them any minute."

Ah, Mother had used the hook of food. If the Garretts left now, it would be not only rude, but insulting. Food—the great Southern gathering force.

I seconded Mother's invitation. "It is so good to see you in this house, to hear your voices. I remember when you taught me how to divide the roots of the daylilies to give them room to bloom. And remember when you gave me that pot of peonies to plant in the side yard?"

"Yes." Bee nodded.

"I remember so much now." I looked at Chris. "Remember when Danny was at basketball camp in North Carolina? You said I looked so lonesome sitting there on my front porch that you took me fishing."

"We caught a bluefish and you reeled it in by yourself," Chris said, grinning.

I shook my head. "I don't know why I thought that forgetting was such a good thing. Too much good in there."

"Yes," Bee said, "too much good."

I glanced over at Mother; she sat back on the couch and I actually believed there was the hint of a smile on her lips. Then the doorbell rang with our delivered ribs and I'd never know for sure.

CHAPTER TWENTY

"Every back is fitted to the burden."
—GULLAH PROVERB

Mother was waiting for me in the downstairs hallway. In my bedroom the scraps of paper from the dolphin box skipped across my pink hand-painted dresser. I dropped my hand on the notes to keep them from falling to the floor. I had separated Danny's dreams from my own, but the wind mixed them again. I gathered the notes and placed them in the box with the two pictures. I felt I had to do something significant with these dreams—something besides stuff them back where they had started—but I didn't know what.

A bizarre tumult of emotions overwhelmed me. Through the years I had become accustomed to feeling one emotion at a time—frustration, fatigue, excitement. They came individually wrapped. But now joy and longing combined with loss and emptiness.

I returned to the closet, trying to decide what to wear to Tulu's funeral. I grabbed a pale green skirt and short-sleeved cotton top. It was at least 102 degrees outside. I scooped my hair up into a ponytail and glanced in the mirror. I had broken all my own rules about sunblock these past weeks, and my face and cheeks were brown and freckled; the face of the twelve-year-old child who'd once lived in this room stared back at me from underneath the years. I winked at her and walked out of the bedroom. I reached the top steps and for one moment I believed, again, that I could fly down them.

Mother squinted up at me. "That's what you're wearing today? This is a funeral, Meridy. . . . At least put on some lipstick."

"Mother, I couldn't care less."

Mother rolled her eyes. "Sissy," Mother called up the stairs, "you coming?"

Sissy appeared at the top landing, the twins coming up behind her. "Yes, we're coming, we're coming." She glanced at me. "Oh, look at you—you look like you're fifteen years old: no makeup, ponytail and cute outfit. I could get ready for hours and never look that cute. Go away."

"Me?" I said. "You look like you should be on the cover of a Lilly Pulitzer catalog."

"Please, let's go," Mother said.

And there we were: the McFadden women without their men, walking out the door together. I grasped both Sissy's and Mother's arms. I don't know if there had ever, in our entire lives, been a time when the three of us were together without either a husband or father to define us.

The naked sun pressed down on the beige tent over Tulu's grave site in the old Gullah graveyard she'd taken me to only a few days ago. I swallowed rising tears. Mother, Sissy and I paused near the rows of chairs lined up in front of the raw wound of earth that would take Tulu's casket. I touched Mother's shoulder, ran my hand across the top of Anyika's gravestone. "Did you know Tulu had a daughter who died when she was a few days old?"

Mother nodded. "Yes, it was terrible. You were a baby yourself, and I could barely imagine how horrible it must've been for her."

Sissy touched the stone, looked at Mother. "How come you never told us?"

"No need for young—"

"Children to know such things." I finished the sentence for my mother.

"Exactly," Mother said, and marched to a chair in the back row.

Sissy and I sat next to her and waited for the processional to arrive. Sissy's daughters, Annie and Amanda, loitered in the back, uncomfortable. A hearse pulled up to the decaying fence. Men, women and children lined up on either side of the car, rocking it back and forth, singing spirituals and crying out in many voices that combined as one in the small graveyard.

"What are they doing?" Sissy asked, her eyes wide.

Mother leaned toward her, whispered, "They are releasing Tulu's spirit."

Sissy raised her eyebrows. "Okay . . ."

"Wait till you see what they do with the youngest baby," Mother said.

I leaned in. "Yeah, Mom, I heard about Tulu's husband's funeral."

"Well, someone should have warned me. I'm prepared this time."

I realized I had just called her Mom instead of Mother. A smile spread across my face.

Someone took the seat next to me and I turned to Tim. "Hey," I whispered under the songs and voices.

"You doing all right?" he asked.

"Hanging in there. You?"

"Just great." He nodded toward the incoming crowd. "I haven't been in this graveyard since we used to dare each other to touch the graves at night."

"Tulu brought me out here a few days ago."

He nodded, and then leaned over to nod hello to Mother and Sissy.

Weatherly and Mitchell pulled up in their BMW on the far side of the graveyard. I smiled as Weatherly tried to pick her way across the soft ground in her three-inch heels. A sudden image of Betsy's, Penni's and Alexis's faces if they saw this funeral or this graveyard passed through my mind. No mints here, for God's sake.

"What're you smiling about?" Tim whispered in my ear. "It's a funeral—no need for that."

I turned to him, but he was smiling back at me. "I was picturing my friends from Atlanta coming here, seeing this."

Then the preacher stood at the front of the tent and began the service. Everyone mourned Tutu in their own way—with weeping, prayers and song. Men and women stood and regaled us with stories of the woman I had known in a limited way. Their speeches allowed me to see her from many angles, to discover aspects of her I would've never known even if I had visited her every day. There were family stories from her children, tales of how she delivered babies, cared for the sick and carried on the Gullah traditions even when others were ashamed.

When they passed the baby over the open grave, Tim leaned in. "What in the . . . ?"

"That's Tulu's youngest grandbaby. They do this to keep her spirit from coming back and bothering the child," I whispered. Tim raised his eyebrows at me.

When the funeral was over, a tall dark man stood on a chair. "We will be celebrating my mama's life this evening on the Seaboro public beach—all are invited."

I glanced out to the river; the sun was sinking behind the marsh in a glow of yellow and fuchsia. Deep in my heart I believed it was a show of nature from Tulu—a gift.

Seaboro's public beach was hushed, as if it too was mourning Tulu's death. As Tulu's friends and family arrived, Sissy appeared at my side. "You okay?" she asked.

"I've never been better." I rolled my eyes.

"You upset about Beau?" She tilted her head.

I nodded. "Yes. But I've done and said everything I can. I don't know what else to do—I'll figure it out tomorrow." I shrugged.

She laughed. "Who are you, Scarlett?"

"No, I just need to get through this before I can face that."

"You were always so much stronger than me."

"No, Sissy. That is not true."

Tim's voice hailed us from behind, and we turned. "Hello, McFadden girls. Looks like trouble over here."

"No trouble here," Sissy said.

Something that didn't belong flashed in the corner of my eye: a man in khakis and a pressed golf shirt.

Penn.

His back was to me and his head swiveled around. I leaned toward Sissy, whispered, "Penn."

"Damn," she said.

"Come with me," Tim said, pulled her hand.

"No," Sissy said, straightening her shoulders, tossed her hair. The twins stood by her side, chewing on their forefinger nails in identical motions. She turned to me. "How do you think he found us?"

I shrugged. "I have no idea."

"Amanda, Annie, I'll be right back. Stay here with Aunt Meridy. Please." She grimaced.

The girls nodded. Tim and I stood still, as if a hurricane were headed toward the beach and there was nothing we could do about it but watch.

Penn stalked toward Sissy and the twins. "What in the hell do you think you're doing?" he said, his lips barely moving over his clenched teeth.

Sissy's chin lifted. I couldn't remember the last time I'd seen her so strong, so determined. "Penn, lower your voice—this is part of a funeral." She turned to her girls, hugged them. "Why don't y'all go find Grandma while I talk to your dad. She's over there—under the tent."

As the girls ran off, Penn reached Sissy's side, grabbed her arm. "You cannot go into the bank accounts and empty them. Where the hell is our money? Where did you put it?"

"Hmmm," Sissy said, "I forget. I know I didn't buy a condo or a catalog's worth of lingerie. I'm not sure what I did with that money."

He pulled her toward him. "That is not funny."

"Get your hand off me." She yanked at his arm.

"No, not until you tell me where our money is."

Tim stepped up beside them. "I believe the lady asked you to take your hand off her arm." A dent in Sissy's arm was turning reddish purple where Penn's fingers dug into her flesh.

"Who the hell are you?" Penn said, but released Sissy's arm.

I stepped between Sissy and Penn. "Penn, this gathering is being held in Tulu's honor. Can you come spit your venom some other time, please?" I used my most syrup-sweet voice and batted my eyelashes at him.

"Do you know what your psycho sister did? She emptied the mutual bank accounts and canceled all the credit cards."

"Oh," Sissy said, "I didn't realize that reporting all our credit cards as stolen would cancel them. I'm so . . . sorry."

His eyes narrowed; his tongue curled out to settle in

the corner of his mouth. "You will not get away with this. You will not. You want to make this into a war, you can."

"I'm not making anything into a war, Penn. I'm protecting myself and my girls. Now, why don't you go back to your little condo and let us mourn an old friend? By the way, how did you find us?"

"This town is about as big as a damn postage stamp. Half the cars in the town are parked on the road, and there's your Jaguar—the car I bought you—parked in the sand. I don't know why you've been whining about moving back here since the day we got married. Now you've got your wish—you can stay." He turned on his heels and stomped through the sand, leaving us in silence.

Tim spoke first. "Wow. Seems like a nice enough guy. Sorry things aren't working out."

Sissy and I started to laugh, subdued giggles at first but growing until the joy rolled out in raucous laughter, tears rolling down our faces. Sissy punched the side of Tim's arm. Mother came up beside us with the twins. "What is going on here? What'd I miss?"

"Not much." I glanced at the twins and my heart ached for them. "Let's go get something to eat. It looks like the most awesome spread of food over there I've ever seen."

We were all walking toward the tent and tables when Tim grabbed my arm. "Who is that?" His head slanted toward the right.

I turned to find B.J. standing at the edge of the sand

and grass waving his arms.

I ran toward him and swept him into a hug. How good it felt to feel his skin next to mine, smell his hair as it brushed up against my face. I held him for a moment longer than he held me. I stepped back and looked at him. "This is such a nice surprise . . . so nice. How did you get here? How did you know . . . ?"

"I came home yesterday to surprise you and Dad for the weekend. Coach gave us Thursday and Friday off—an unheard-of four-day weekend—and Dad told me how a very dear friend of yours had died and . . . well, anyway we needed an excuse to go to the beach and . . ." He spread his hands wide. "Here we are."

"We?" I looked behind B.J., twisting in search of Beau, my heart lifting.

But B.J. motioned to a small blond girl coming up behind him. "This is Heather . . . my, well, my girl-friend, Heather."

Heather pinched the side of his arm. "Was that all that hard to say?" Her gold eyes narrowed and she pouted her lips out at him, then nodded at me. "Hi," she said, held out her hand. "I'm Heather Cook."

I shook her hand, nodded. "I'm Meridy, Beau's mom. Nice to meet you, Heather. I'm so glad y'all came."

"Oh," Heather said, elbowed B.J. "He just needed a driver because he lost his license."

"Thanks, appreciate that." B.J. wrapped his arm around her, squeezed.

"How did you find us?"

"Well, I went to Grandma's house and it was empty.

There was a gardener out front trimming the bushes. He wouldn't let me in the house, even when I told him who I was—but he did tell me where I could find you."

I cleared my throat, avoided B.J.'s eyes. "So, how's Dad doing?"

"Good, I guess. He said there was no way he could come with us—I guess the actual trial started today. But the new lawyer stopped by with some lasagna or something last night." He cocked his head. "So I guess he's getting fed."

Someone has to take care of poor Beau.

A rush of nausea rose, but I forced a laugh. "Yeah, I can see Harland bringing me dinner when Dad is out of town. We do spoil you men. Let's go say hello to Grandma and Aunt Sissy. Your cousins are here too."

He laughed. "An entire family reunion."

Except for your father.

B.J.'s hair was longer; stubble covered his chin in a goatee pattern. "Nice beard," I said.

He rubbed his hands across his face. "Like?" He lifted his chin.

"Come on." I pulled him toward Mother, Sissy, the girls and Tim, who all were waiting for us. After the hugs and kisses and introductions, we piled food on our plates and sat at a round table in the corner of the tent.

Heather spread her hands over the table, bangs falling across her eyes. "This doesn't look like a funeral. . . . It looks like a party."

"The funeral was this afternoon. This *is* a party—one that celebrates Tulu's life. All that food"—I pointed to the table—"is her favorite dishes and recipes."

Voices overlapped as we all tried to talk to B.J. at the same time.

Sissy grabbed his hand. "We've missed you so much. I'm thrilled you're here. I can't remember the last time the girls saw you."

"Two Thanksgivings ago," Amanda said.

"Well, I'm glad you're here. I do love you," I said.

"Me too," Mother said to my son.

B.J. looked at Heather. "They are so embarrassing."

"I think they're adorable." She pointed her plastic fork at him and grinned. "You should bring me around more often."

The evening passed in the warmth of my family until fatigue and too much food caused my eyelids to droop. Children fell asleep on blankets and curled on parents' shoulders. I stared into the darkness toward the place where the Keeper's Cottage once stood. My heart lurched with memories. What had happened there had once deadened my heart, but now the cottage shook my heart awake.

I closed my eyes and attempted to picture my home in Atlanta with Beau in it. But I couldn't find the house—only a watercolor version blurred at the edges, faded in the middle. I walked down to the shoreline, where the tidal currents flowed out. I whispered good-bye to Tulu and remembered some of my last words to her, how I'd promised to allow the river to reach my heart. "I promise," I said into the quiet night.

CHAPTER TWENTY-ONE

"When you are here, you are home."
—GULLAH PROVERB

I had slept deeply, dreamlessly, yet woke with Beau's absence like a physical emptiness in a full house. But I smiled at the thought that my son slept on the couch in the sunroom downstairs. The house was quiet in the still morning. I tiptoed down to the kitchen to find Mother drinking coffee. I kissed her cheek. "Good morning, Mother."

"Good morning, dear."

"We have a full house, don't we?" I sat at the table.

"Isn't it wonderful? There isn't an empty bed to be found," she said.

Sissy walked into the kitchen, rubbing her eyes. "Why are you two up so early?"

"We always are."

"We always do."

Mother's and my voices overlapped and we laughed.

Sissy poured coffee into a large mug. "Any plans for the day with all these people here?"

"I have a society breakfast meeting this morning, but that's about it," Mother said. "So—I'll just meet you all back here around lunchtime." She stood and walked out of the kitchen, her dressing gown whispering behind her as if it held a secret that followed her wherever she went.

Sissy sat next to me. "God, what a day yesterday. It was the never-ending day."

"I know. Have you talked to Penn this morning?"

"No, and I have no plans to." She leaned back in her chair. "Now, don't get me wrong when I tell you this . . . because this is all terrible and horrible and disgusting, but you know, I haven't loved Penn for a very long time. But I wouldn't have done what he did. I wouldn't have cheated on him or lied to him for all those years. I was trying to figure out how to love him again . . . how to feel something for him. And his affair has destroyed part of me: the part that might trust or love him again. But it has also freed me to find some joy in life."

"Wow," I said, leaned on the table. "A little deep for first thing in the morning, Sissy." But I grinned, then stood and hugged her.

"I was never able to admit to myself how I truly felt—but now I can."

"Sometimes it takes a little pain to make us face how we truly feel," I said to my sister, as much as to myself.

She put down her coffee mug. "Did you ask Beau to come here?"

"Yes, but his trial, the one he's been preparing two years for, started yesterday. So I need to go home . . . tomorrow. I'll spend some time with B.J. today and then head home."

"Well, I want you to stay here."

I lifted my eyebrows. "You do?"

"Yes, I do." Sissy stood, pulled a frying pan from under the sink. "You want scrambled or poached?"

"Scrambled would be great." I leaned back in my chair and smiled just as the phone rang. I grabbed it, leaned against the wall. Mr. Jenkins, the local school superintendent, was on the line. "Mrs. Dresden, we were wondering if you could please stop by the board-of-education office on Monday."

"Oh, I'd love to, but I'm headed home tomorrow." I knew it as I said it.

"Home?"

"Yes, back to Atlanta."

"Oh, I see. Well, is there any way you can stop by today, then?"

"Well, can you tell me what this is . . . about?"

"The culture class curriculum you wrote."

"Oh, you've read it. . . ." Mother had taken it to them. I must've written something wrong, accidentally insulted some group or made a mistake in dates or geography. "No problem."

"Thank you, Mrs. Dresden."

"Meridy, call me Meridy, Mr. Jenkins."

"Yes, Meridy. See you in a little while."

The four main buildings downtown were all constructed of tabby and brick, with slate roofs and pillars in front. Sunlight hid behind low, full clouds, but the heat was the same as if the sun glared down from a clear sky. I stood in the middle of the square, where a statue of a Confederate soldier presided in a chin-up position with a musket in hand. I rubbed the base as I walked across the street. On the front steps at the board-of-education building, pansies filled pots to overflowing. A child blew by me on a scooter, and a honey-colored butterfly landed on the steps. I wanted to take a snapshot of each detail, wanted to take it all in and use it to build strength to face what lay in wait at home.

I walked up the stairs and entered the dank building, eventually found Mr. Jenkins in his office at the far end of the hall. I knocked with the tips of my fingers. The door flew open and Mr. Jenkins motioned for me to come in. A desk almost the size of the room filled the small space.

"Sit, sit." He motioned to a chair crammed in the corner.

I sat and crossed my legs, smiled and waited for him to speak.

He sat on the corner of his desk and looked down at me over spectacles that appeared as though he'd bought them at an antique flea market. "Mrs. Dresden, I know you did not write this curriculum for our school system, but for a system in the Atlanta area. I also know that you are going back there tomorrow."

I nodded. "Yes, I am. But if you see something in the pages that isn't correct or you feel . . . misrepresents the area, I'm perfectly willing to change it. I tried very hard to accurately—"

He held up his hand, shaking his head. "Quite the contrary, this is one of the best pieces of work I've seen come through this office in ages. Work has become so slipshod—no one cares anymore. This is . . . a beautiful piece of work. So we have a proposal for you. Now, of course, the board hasn't approved this yet, but I wanted to talk to you before you went back to Atlanta. We want to hire you to teach this to the elementary schools in Seaboro County. We have nine elementary schools in the county, and that would require that you teach this curriculum at a school a month—one week a month—for nine months. We aren't a rich county, but we could pay you the same salary as we do all the specialty teachers. Now, now . . ." He held up his hand. "Please don't answer too quickly. Think about it. Please."

He was offering me a job? "I don't . . ." I rubbed my palms together, spread them apart. "I don't live here."

"Yes, I know that. I thought you might . . . recon-sider."

"Where I live?"

"Yes."

"I have a husband, a house. . . ."

He nodded. "I understand. Our other option is that you could train someone else to teach the class. Or you could travel here once a month for a week at a time." He tapped the papers on his desk. "I want this cur-riculum taught to our children in the Lowcountry. This is valuable."

"Thank you, Mr. Jenkins. I enjoyed writing that cur-riculum more than I've enjoyed anything in a long, long time."

"I can tell by reading it. I can tell."

I stood formally. "I don't think I'll be able to do this. But can I think about it, call you?"

"Fair enough." He held out his hand and I shook it.

I left the building feeling something unfinished floating on the horizon: The dreams, the papers, they needed a place to rest.

I stood in front of the Keeper's Cottage. Finally, I pushed aside the yellow CAUTION tape and stepped inside the structure. The floors creaked beneath my feet, making me jump. I slid along the perimeter of the rooms and walked to the back of the cottage.

Seeing the fireplace in the kitchen, I closed my eyes and tried to imagine Danny. The last time I had seen him had been in this place. I allowed the old and simultaneously young love to wash over me. He'd taught me what love was and made me safe inside his circle of complete belief in me. And I wasn't here to wish him back. Other people mold us by their love—mothers, sisters, lovers. They make us who we are. Danny Garrett had loved me well enough to make me the woman I'd once dreamed of being.

I reached down into my satchel, pulled out the scraps of paper with Danny's dreams written on them, bound by a rubber band. I pulled up a loose piece of pine floorboard that was attached at only one end with an iron nail head. I peered below to the foundation of the cottage, and then I stuffed the papers into the far corner of the hole and released the board, which snapped back into place with an echo of finality. I wanted Danny to have his dreams back—he'd died so that my dreams, and those of the others there that fatal night, could live.

Maybe there was a piece of my heart I had lost to Danny, a piece that he'd kept for himself in the sea, but I owned the rest of my heart and it was awake, fully awake. I touched my finger to the floorboard, tapping it home.

I slipped the dolphin box back into my satchel—I'd kept his picture and my own scraps of paper. I saved them, not because I wanted to bring him back, but because I needed to remember these past dreams, as they were the smaller hints of all I'd meant to be.

I left the cottage and made my way out the back door toward my car when I saw a silhouette against the front door of the cottage like an iron cutout of a man. Something familiar in his stance, the way he tilted his head: Beau. I gasped, turned too quickly and slipped, fell. I jumped up, called out to him.

He started toward me and I ran to my husband, life finally reaching my heart. Whatever turbulence waited there, I was rushing willingly toward it.

I stopped before him but didn't speak.

He reached out, touched my face just as he had under the portico all those years ago. My heart reached for him, but still I waited.

"I'm sorry," he said.

"Why?" I whispered.

"For taking so damn long to listen to what you were trying to say to me. I was stubborn and angry and my ego was bruised and I couldn't hear you. I couldn't hear you with all the noise in our life—until I was home alone and the loneliness around me let me hear what you were trying to say."

"What are you doing here? Are you okay? How did you know where I was?" I asked all in a jumble.

"Whoa." He laughed. "Slow down. Your mother told me where you were and I'm here because I love you."

I sank against Beau's chest, wound my arms around his middle. "I love you so much too. Please don't ever think I don't."

"Don't talk yet. I've been practicing in the car for hours and you have to listen to the whole thing. . . ." He smiled.

I nodded.

"It was all so empty at home. So damn empty. All there was to do was work and think about why you wanted to leave me."

"I didn't want—"

Beau held up his hand. "Then I realized what you'd told me—ten, twenty times—that you didn't want to leave me, and I realized that you weren't leaving me. I'm still hurt you never told me about your past, how you felt about it. I hate that you carried all that guilt around with you. But here's the deal, Meridy. . . . I love all of you—who you *were,* who you *are,* who you'll *be.* All of it."

"Am I allowed to cry if I don't talk?"

"Yes." He reached for me this time and held me.

I took a shaky, deep breath and inhaled the T-shirt and warm fragrance of my husband. "Why aren't you in court? Didn't the trial start yesterday?"

He nodded. "I needed to come to you."

I didn't want to laugh, but it bubbled up from a place of such relief I couldn't stop it. "You'll get in so much . . . trouble with Harland."

"What's he going to do? Ground me? Some things are just more important than a job." He laughed, scooped me into his arms. "I left the courtroom, drove here. The least I should get is a kiss."

I grabbed both sides of his face, kissed him. I stepped back. "You smell like your pillow," I said. "I've missed that . . . you. I'm sorry." I caught myself. "I've said that so much lately. I didn't want to put us through this—I just had to come, and I thought I could help Tim without involving . . . you without hurting you . . . us."

"I felt like I was fighting a ghost. I was up against a memory and I believed you cared more about a dead boyfriend than me. . . ."

"No. I was coming home. . . . I am coming home," I said. "I was so busy trying to be perfect for you all these years, earn your love, that I stopped listening to myself, so why wouldn't you stop listening too?"

He held up his hand. "I'm just trying to tell you what has kept me away. You should've seen your face when you told me about your childhood—about Timmy and Danny. I hadn't seen your face light up like that in a very long time. I thought the only way to get you to love me like that was to get you to come home. To *make* you come home and prove you loved me. Then . . . after you told me you were trying to bring yourself back, not

Danny, I finally understood. I really did. I know I can be slow . . . but I do love you. So"—he pulled me closer—"this is the cottage you're helping to save?"

I nodded, afraid that words would chase the longing to the far corners of my heart where it often hid. "And my curriculum came out so . . . well that Seaboro offered me a teaching job. Isn't that funny."

"Is that something you'd want to do?"

I tilted my head. "I don't know. . . . I was focused on getting home—to you."

"Well, if it's what you'd like to do . . . we can figure something out, don't you think?"

"By the way," I said, "what was Ashley's deal?"

"She annoyed the living hell out of me. She was bored and wanted to be involved in this case. Harland hired her. She went a little overboard . . . bringing meals, stopping by, trying to help."

"She wanted you."

"Oh, well." He smiled. "You can't always get what you want."

"No, you can't."

"I just want you, Meridy. Everything else is worthless if we're not okay."

I reached up and touched the side of his dear, familiar face. Our marriage would endure, like the cottage behind us—unfinished and awaiting restoration. The foundations of both were intact, offering the hope, and promise, of broken places mended, empty spaces filled.

Author Note

The fictional character of Tulu in this novel was inspired by the Gullah culture of South Carolina. Gullah, which is both a culture and a language of African slave descendants, is rich in tradition, spirituality and history, and still exists in the Lowcountry. The Gullah proverb "If you don't know where you are going, you should know where you came from" epitomizes Meridy's journey. In the Gullah culture, proverbs are used to teach and advise, offering wisdom and humor. I am not an expert in Gullah culture, merely an admirer. For further information on the Gullah culture, contact the resources below.

The Penn Center

Tucked in the heart of the South Carolina Sea Islands, this center is the site of one of the country's first schools for freed slaves.

Penn School National Historic Landmark District
P.O. Box 126
St. Helena Island, SC 29920
Phone: (843) 838-2432
Fax: (843) 838-8545
E-mail: *info@penncenter.com*

Gullah/Geechee Sea Islands Coalition-Homebase

P.O. Box 1207
St. Helena Island, SC 29920
Phone: (843) 838-1171
E-mail: *GullGeeCo@aol.com*

Center Point Publishing
600 Brooks Road • PO Box 1
Thorndike ME 04986-0001 USA

(207) 568-3717

US & Canada:
1 800 929-9108